Ann Granger has lived in cities in many parts of the world, since for many years she worked for the Foreign Office and received postings to British embassies as far apart as Munich and Lusaka. She is married, with two sons, and she and her husband, who also worked for the Foreign Office, are now permanently based near Oxford.

Watching Out

Ann Granger

headline

First published in 2003
by HEADLINE BOOK PUBLISHING

First published in paperback in 2003
by HEADLINE BOOK PUBLISHING

10 9 8 7 6 5 4 3 2 1

ISBN 0 7472 6802 9

Typeset in Plantin by Avon DataSet Ltd,
Bidford-on-Avon, Warwickshire

Printed and bound in Great Britain by
Clays Ltd, St Ives plc

Papers and cover board used by Headline are natural, recyclable
products made from wood grown in sustainable forests.
The manufacturing processes conform to the environmental
regulations of the country of origin.

HEADLINE BOOK PUBLISHING
A division of Hodder Headline
338 Euston Road
London NW1 3BH

www.headline.co.uk
www.hodderheadline.com

To Caroline Graham, in friendship
and with many thanks for her
encouragement and support

Chapter One

Six of us huddled together for warmth upstairs in The Rose pub. None of us said a word. Our attention was fixed on a large dusty wicker laundry basket. It had a faded label on one side reading: RETURN TO THE HOTEL ROYAL, YARMOUTH and on the opposite side, another label reading: PROPS. DO NOT REMOVE.

'Right,' said Marty at last with forced heartiness. 'Let's see what's inside!'

The Rose was an old-style London tavern. It had brown glazed tiles on the outside walls and smoke-stained anaglypta on the internal ones. The original saloon and public bars had long since been knocked together, making one big room at the far end of which was a small dais. On this, Freddy, the landlord, invited singers and comics to entertain his customers. Those desperate enough to break into show business accepted his offer, and stood up there as vulnerable as the coconuts at a fairground shy, while the customers whistled and shouted rude remarks.

Upstairs, where we found ourselves in suspicious contemplation of the laundry basket, there was a proper – if small – stage with curtains. This, besides being what Freddy called 'the functions room', was also his private theatre, where he put on bigger shows. Freddy was inordinately proud of his record as a theatrical entrepreneur. The shows didn't take place often but when they did, they were acknowledged locally as being unmissable and the seating a sell-out.

Not a man to throw money around, he put a modest amount into the production of the shows and always got it back at the door. He knew how to sweat the maximum effort out of a production while getting someone else to do all the work putting the show together. As an organiser, Freddy was unrivalled. But his natural stinginess showed in our surroundings. The functions room hadn't been redecorated in years and the faded velvet curtains on the stage looked about to collapse under the weight of their years and accumulated grime. There was a lingering background smell to the place to which every bit of the pub's one-hundred-and-twenty-year history had contributed.

The reason for our presence there was that on this upstairs stage, at Freddy's invitation, we were to perform a dramatic adaptation of Conan Doyle's novel *The Hound of the Baskervilles*. It was Freddy's latest shrewd idea for entertaining the masses and making a few quid at the same time. It had been adapted by our director, Marty. He was a playwright himself, and would dearly have loved to be putting on one of his own plays. But Freddy wanted traditional entertainment and what Freddy wanted, Freddy got.

'Perhaps,' Marty had said optimistically, 'if we do this really well, he'll let me put on one of my own plays next time.'

This was extremely unlikely, but creative artists and writers are fragile souls, and Marty needed all the encouragement he could get.

For those of you who don't know the plot of Conan Doyle's yarn: the Baskerville family is threatened by a supernatural hound because of some ancestor's crime. Sir Charles Baskerville has been found dead and near his body is the imprint of a hound's paw. His heir, Sir Henry, has just arrived in England from Canada to take up his inheritance. The family doctor goes to Holmes because he's afraid the hound will get Henry, too. So Holmes sends Watson off to Devon to guard Sir Henry, and himself hides out on the moor. Then there's a butterfly hunter called Stapleton and his sister (who's really his wife), and an escaped convict (related to Sir Henry's housekeeper), and it all gets a bit complicated. The climax, of course, is the appearance of the ghastly hound in pursuit of poor old Sir Henry, who is rescued by Holmes and Watson and the mystery revealed. There are a few other characters in the original story but Marty had cut them out. You'll understand why.

I was cast in the female lead, Miss Stapleton, the woman Sir Henry Baskerville falls for. Marty himself was playing Sir Henry. He couldn't play Holmes because he wasn't the right shape. Everyone who thinks Holmes thinks along the lines of Basil Rathbone in those wonderful black and white movies, or Jeremy Brett in the old television series. Marty was short and dumpy with a plump face, receding fair curly hair and spectacles. He bore a strong resemblance to a teddy bear. I wasn't sure myself that he was right for the role of Sir Henry Baskerville but perhaps I didn't look right for the part of an exotic beauty like Miss Stapleton, so I couldn't criticise. I am on the short side and my hair is clipped close to my head, except in front where it's longer and sticks up like a bushy tiara. I was persuaded to have this style by a trainee hairdresser with ambitions.

Marty had found someone called Nigel, who was tall and thin, to play Sherlock Holmes. My friend Ganesh was playing Dr Watson. I know Dr Watson in the stories isn't Indian, but I'd felt strongly that Gan would be good in the part. Ganesh had been difficult to persuade, never having had any particular interest in the stage, but we'd kept on at him because Marty had taken strongly to the idea of having Ganesh in the role. Even with two of us working on him he held out, but finally it was his Uncle Hari who settled it for us. Hari has a secret romantic streak which normally finds its outlet in watching endless videos of Bollywood films. He was convinced that to have Ganesh playing Watson at The Rose pub was the first step on the stairway to the stars. Hari's enthusiasm for the whole project of the play was alarming. He was even prepared to allow Ganesh to leave the shop early to get to rehearsals – provided he didn't do it too often.

We had been reading through the play over at my flat. This hadn't proved as straightforward as it sounds. Marty, who had printed it out, was mildly dyslexic and deciphering his script in the nature of an adventure. We had all become somewhat short-tempered by the time a chunky frizzy-haired girl asked about costumes.

As she was to play two roles (Sir Henry's housekeeper and Holmes's landlady, Mrs Hudson), she had a special interest. Marty told her he'd decided she was to pad herself out with foam rubber to be plump for Mrs Hudson and wear a mob cap to cover her hair. For Sir Henry's housekeeper, she'd be thin again and wear a pince-nez. Marty himself had made a pince-nez out of wire and the mob cap was actually a large shower cap he'd borrowed from his landlady. He produced both articles from a plastic bag with an air of modest triumph.

It didn't have quite the effect he'd hoped for. The frizzy-haired girl was particularly unimpressed. Had we to make all our own costumes, or could we run to hiring them from a proper theatrical costumier? she demanded with some asperity. No need, Marty assured us. Apart from the fact we didn't have any money, costumes were supplied by Freddy.

Encouraged by this, we'd progressed from the reading to the pub for a pint. After that, we went upstairs to inspect the costumes left over from other productions Freddy had put on, a Victorian music hall among them.

Marty opened the lid of the laundry basket, releasing a powerful musty smell.

Nigel said, 'Whew! It whiffs a bit, doesn't it? Are you sure someone didn't hide a body in there?'

Marty plunged in his hand and withdrew the first item. It was a dusty bowler hat. 'There we go!' he exclaimed, buffing it up with his sleeve and then holding it out to Ganesh.

'Forget it!' said Ganesh, rearing back. 'I am not wearing a bowler hat.'

'It's all right, mate,' said Nigel consolingly. 'I've got to wear a deerstalker. Freddy's borrowing one from some-body. There's no way anyone can look anything but a prat in a deerstalker.'

'That,' said Ganesh stiffly, 'is because you are Holmes. I am only Watson.'

So that was it. It wasn't the bowler at all. Despite his professed unwillingness to act in our play at all, Ganesh was secretly miffed at not playing the lead. We were into our first episode of artistic tantrums.

The cold was getting to us by now. Freddy didn't believe in switching on radiators which weren't going to earn their keep. If anyone was rash enough to hire the room, he'd switch on the heating. By then, of course, the room was like a morgue and the radiators had no chance. I could imagine our audience for the play, if we ever got to our first night, sitting there in overcoats. The really wise ones, who knew the venue, would bring hot-water bottles. We, on the stage, would shiver our way through. Only the frizzy girl, whose name was Carmel, would be warm as Mrs Hudson in her foam padding.

'Get on with it, Marty,' I begged. 'Before we all freeze solid.'

We all dived in, pulling things out, putting them on one side or tossing them back. We tossed more back than we put aside.

'Yuk,' said Carmel, 'it all stinks.'

'It just wants airing,' said Marty, in a vain attempt to head off our criticism.

'I'm not wearing any of it,' said Carmel. 'I reckon it's all got fleas.'

'Well, take it home and wash it, whatever you want to wear,' persisted Marty.

'I don't run a bloody laundry,' she snapped.

'You don't have to. Just take it down to the launderette

round the corner and bung it in one of the machines.'

'Marty,' I felt I had to say, 'I don't think many of these things would stand being churned around in a washing machine. They're all as old as the hills. They haven't been looked after and the sweat has rotted the cloth.'

'See!' screeched Carmel.

'It's Victorian period,' said Marty desperately. 'All you and Fran need are long skirts and blouses with sleeves. Can't the pair of you rustle up a couple of long skirts? Try Oxfam.'

'I thought we were supposed to make a bit of money out of this play, not spend our dosh on costumes,' she sulked. 'And I need two. I can't wear the same thing in both parts, especially if I'm fat in one role and thin in the other!'

I pulled out a striped skirt and matching jacket top with leg-of-mutton sleeves. 'I'll take this home and have a go at washing it by hand,' I said. I pushed it into a Tesco carrier bag.

Marty cheered up. 'That's the spirit. Come on, Carmel, the show must go on and all that.'

'This ain't the bleeding Palladium,' she retorted. 'I'll borrow some things from my mates – if I can.'

We left it at that. There's always one grumbler in any group tackling a joint project. We'd pretty well all got the measure of Carmel. She'd groused like mad about everything from the start and would go on grousing to the moment the curtain went up. But, in the end, she'd rally round and fix herself some sort of costume. She was just stroppy by nature.

Some people would tell you that I am, too. But I was trying to be supportive of Marty because I could see his nerves were getting frazzled. He was investing a lot of hope and personal commitment in the play; however even single-minded dedication turns blue with cold.

We reached an unanimous decision. If we lingered, we'd be carried out suffering from hypothermia. We pushed everything back in the basket except the things we were taking home. Ganesh reluctantly put the bowler in a bag. Then we all clattered downstairs into the bar to be greeted by a welcome blast of warm air.

Business was brisk down there, even though they didn't do food except peanuts and crisps. Freddy had a system with the crisps. He opened a carton, for example cheese and onion flavour, and everyone had to have that sort until the box was empty and then he opened another which, if you were lucky, might be barbecued beef or salt and vinegar – or it might just be cheese and onion again. Those were the only three flavours Freddy sold. He didn't sell them all at once because he reckoned there wasn't room behind the bar for effing packets of crisps lying around all over the place.

No one argued about this with him. Freddy was a formidable sight, not particularly tall but with meaty arms and a torso like a beer barrel on legs. The regulars of The Rose held him in hearty respect and, since he was backing us as regards the play, we had to be especially nice to him. He and a muscular, shaven-headed barman were working flat out that night. Even Denise, Freddy's wife, had been called in to help. I say 'even' because on principle Freddy didn't allow women behind his bar. Denise was the only one for whom an exception was made, and that only in emergencies. Denise was herself a well-built woman so that together with Freddy and the beefy barman, there wasn't much room behind the bar. The three of them kept getting in one another's way. Freddy, I could see, wasn't in the best of tempers. But you don't go to The Rose if it's old-world charm you're after.

The downstairs dais was empty tonight, yet despite the absence of live music and dying comics, the place was packed. The air was thick with smoke and the smell of spilled ale. No one, yet, had started a fight. To be fair, unruly patrons got quickly ejected from The Rose. That was one of Freddy's reasons for not having barmaids. Muscle, he reckoned, was what you needed behind a bar, not glamour.

'I've got to go home,' said Ganesh. 'I need to get up in the morning to take in the newspapers at six.'

Marty said he had to go home, too, and work on the script.

'Don't change anything!' we all begged him. We'd only just managed to decipher the lines he'd given us and start to commit them to memory.

He said it was a matter of working on the technical side of it. We let him go. Nigel and Carmel sloped off towards the bar, followed by Owen, who was playing the villain, and Mick, who was playing Sir Henry's butler and any other role not accounted for. I said I'd walk as far as the shop with Ganesh. However, as it turned out, before I'd reached the door I heard my name being bawled across the room in a female voice.

'Fran! Don't go! I've been waiting here for you for the best part of an hour!'

I turned and saw Susie Duke teetering towards me on

her four-inch heels. Daywear, for Susie, is jeans and trainers. But if she goes out anywhere she likes to dress up. She wore a very short skirt and a tight purple sweater with spangles on it. Her blond hair was scraped up and secured at the back of her head with one of those giant spring clips. From her ears dangled hoop earrings the size of bracelets.

'I'm off!' said Ganesh immediately and disappeared.

'I saw you come in with your mates,' said Susie, seizing my arm and hauling me back towards where she'd been sitting. 'I thought you were never coming downstairs. What were you all doing up there? That play, I suppose. Hurry up, or we'll lose the table.'

Actually, we were in no danger of losing the place she'd been keeping. It was a banquette in a window recess and, as soon as she'd got up to run after me, Freddy's dog had scrambled on there and stretched himself out. The dog was normally kept out back in the yard. It was a solid, muscular, bullet-headed mutt with yellow eyes and an unfriendly disposition. No one had tried to move it from the seat and its expression let us know we'd better not try.

Susie, however, wasn't put off. 'Go on, Digger, get down from there. You're not allowed!'

Digger rolled yellow eyes at her and growled.

'Shouldn't try it, darling,' advised a man at a nearby table. 'He'll have you.'

'Freddy!' yelled Susie towards the bar. 'Get your dog out of our place!'

Susie in top gear has a voice like a banshee. There was no ignoring it. Freddy whistled and Digger jumped down and strolled off.

'Right,' said Susie, banging the seat vigorously with the flat of her hand to remove dog hairs and succeeding in raising a cloud of ancient dust. 'Sit down, Fran, and I'll get you a drink. What d'ya want?'

'A half of lager,' I said. I knew I wasn't being offered this drink for nothing. Susie was struggling to keep afloat a leaky boat called the Duke Detective Agency and I had a feeling it was to do with this. I had a good idea what proposal she was going to come up with – and privately resolved to have nothing to do with it.

Susie tottered off to the bar to fetch our drinks. I settled down and watched her. I couldn't help remembering the first time I'd seen her. She'd been standing in the doorway of her flat, rather the worse for gin, grief and anger. She'd had good reason. She'd been in mourning. But remembering that brought to mind another image and an unpleasant one: that of her husband, Rennie, slumped in the driver's seat of his car, a length of twine wrapped tightly round his neck, cutting into the red, swollen flesh. I shook my head slightly to dispel the picture. I can't say my liking for Susie had been extended to the late Rennie, a seedy little PI who had not had a great talent for making friends. But my liking for his wife didn't mean I wanted to work for or with her, which is what I suspected she was going to suggest. She'd already mentioned it to me once before.

'Cheers!' said Susie when we were nicely settled under the watchful eye of the resentful Digger. She raised her glass in a toast. 'Here's to crime.'

'I can think of things I'd rather toast,' I said.

She shook her blond head and the hoop earrings swung. 'One man's meat is another man's poison. I mean, like, one person being dodgy makes legitimate work for me. Now, then, Fran.'

Here it came.

'Have you thought any more about what I said?'

'Yes, I have,' I told her. 'Don't take this wrong, Susie. But I don't think I'm cut out for your sort of work.'

'Don't give me that!' she snorted. 'You love poking your nose into any funny business that comes your way.'

I didn't see my own detective efforts in that light and was mildly insulted. 'Only if it involves me directly,' I said.

'Who are you trying to kid?' asked Susie. 'You can't resist it.' She leaned on the table between us and I inhaled a noseful of some strong cheap scent. 'I need you, Fran. I can't manage the business on my own.'

'Do you have to stay in the business?' I asked her, stupidly, I knew.

'I haven't got any other bloomin' business, have I?' she snapped. 'What other job would I be offered if I went down the Job Centre? I'm too old. You gotta be sixteen or they won't take you on anywhere.'

'You look great,' I assured her.

'For my age, yeah,' she mumbled. 'Which, if you're interested, is thirty-nine. On the open market, that's well past the sell-by date. You'd better remember that.'

I pointed out to her that I wasn't yet twenty-two.

She gave me a sardonic look. 'Time won't stand still, you know, Fran. The rules aren't different for you than for the rest of us. You want to get your act together. And I'm not talking about that play you and your mates are putting on.'

I had to defend the play and my own participation in it. 'You know I want to make acting my career,' I said crossly.

'The play may not be the best show ever put on stage, but we mean to make it as good as we can. Why don't you come and see it, instead of knocking it? You might be surprised.'

If I sounded annoyed with her, it was because she'd hit on a tender spot. We do all have dreams and I was hanging on to mine because I didn't have anything else. I certainly wasn't going to throw in the towel and go and work for her.

'Besides, I have a job!' I added loftily. 'At the new pizza place, the San Gennaro, and business is booming, I can tell you.'

She was unimpressed. 'Yeah, sure. How long is it going to last?'

It was something I'd been asking myself. 'Why?' I asked her sharply. 'Have you heard something?'

'No!' she retorted a shade too quickly. 'But I know a fly-by-night operation when I see one. You'll turn up for work one day and find the restaurant's closed and, more than likely, the place full of rozzers. Here today and gone tomorrow, that place.'

'Between you and me,' I confessed, 'I've been thinking along the same lines.'

'See?' She was triumphant. 'You're smart, Fran. You're a natural for the private detection business. You've got the nose for it.'

'But not the stomach. I know the kind of work Rennie took on. I'm not spying on wives or husbands who're playing away from home or snooping out people's credit-worthiness. I'm not shoving summonses in the hands of people I don't need to offend. I'm not slogging all over

London looking for witnesses who don't want to be found.'

'You'd be good at that,' she urged. 'You know people out there on the street. They'd talk to you.'

'Sure, they'd talk to me and tell me where to go. They know better than be witnesses to anything. It's called survival, Susie. See, hear and speak no evil. I know I've done some investigating in the past, but only because it's been forced on me. It's been because something's happened that I couldn't ignore. I've looked into things I've considered have mattered and I've done it in my own way. That's a whole world away from the sort of work you're talking about.'

Susie looked thoughtful. But she hadn't really listened to what I'd said. She was still fixed on persuading me and was about to change tactics. Out of the blue, she asked, 'You got a driving licence?'

I shook my head. 'Ganesh started to teach me when he had the greengrocer's van, back in the Rotherhithe days. But he hasn't got any transport now so that was that.'

'I'll teach you,' she offered.

'Why?' I demanded.

'I owe you,' she said. 'You found out who killed my Rennie. I owe you big. Let me teach you to drive. Get yourself a provisional licence and I'll get us some L-plates.'

I was attracted by the idea but there was a big drawback. 'What sort of car have you got?' I was really asking, did she still own the car in which Rennie had been found dead. Because I wasn't getting in that car, no way.

She understood me. 'I got rid of the Mazda,' she said. 'I got a nice little Citroën. I told you, Rennie had insurance. I found the certificate hidden in that china cat he gave me one Christmas. He was funny like that, Rennie, kept secrets.' She tugged at her purple sweater. 'The insurance company paid up, though, sweet as anything. See? I got new gear and everything.'

'I'll think about it,' I said. 'Right now I've got the rehearsals as well as my job—'

'No, don't think about it, do it.' She pushed herself away from the table and stood up. 'I gotta go. I'll be in touch, Fran.'

As I watched her teeter away I reflected that Susie was pretty smart herself. She'd caught me off guard with her offer of driving lessons. Whatever I'd been expecting, it hadn't been that. I hadn't refused her outright which meant, in her book, I'd accepted. It would now be difficult to wriggle out of it without seeming churlish. Besides, I fancied having my driving licence. But in between the three-point turns and the hill starts I suspected I'd be hearing a lot about the career opportunities offered by the Duke Detective Agency.

Chapter Two

I was feeling jittery around this time and problems arising from the play weren't the only reason. Have you ever felt you've made a big error of judgement? I'm sure you have. Don't feel bad about it. It's human. 'Make your mistakes and learn from them!' my grandma used to say to me. I didn't listen, of course. At least, not to the bit about learning from them. But though I've made lots of mistakes in my life, I've generally made them one at a time. That way, events have remained just about manageable. Now I was beginning to get an uncomfortable feeling I'd made two misjudgements at the same time. There was just the faintest hint in the air that things might spin out of control. I'd begun to wonder if I was losing my touch.

Don't get me wrong. Life was certainly not all bad news. Before I'd started worrying about making bad decisions, I'd been feeling pretty buoyant. For a start, I'd recently moved into a ground-floor flat belonging to a charitable housing association. Previously I'd spent a period dossing in someone's unused garage, so to have a decent roof over my head was bliss. Before the garage, I'd had a basement flat and been flooded out. Before that again, I'd lived in squats. So you can see, my accommodation history has been chequered.

My name is Francesca Varady, known as Fran. Permanence hasn't played a great role in my life. My mother walked out when I was seven and didn't walk back in again for fourteen years. I was brought up by my father and grandmother. I lost them both in the same year, the year I turned sixteen, and I've been on my own ever since. Dad died first and because Grandma was the tenant of the flat we lived in, when she died, the landlord was able to throw me out. Continuing with the drama course I was on hadn't been an option either.

I can't tell you how wonderful it was to have a proper roof of my own over my head at last. I was getting into the swing of normal existence quite well. I'd got used to not having all my possessions in a bin bag. My dog, Bonnie, liked my new place because there was a garden she could potter round. Everyone who visited the flat said how lucky I was. I knew it. The nomadic progress of my adult life seemed over at last. This was as permanent as it was likely to get. Even Ganesh approved. Provided I didn't mess things up, my life was all going to be upwards and onwards. Once you start thinking like that, it's asking for trouble.

Ganesh and I have been friends since I lived in a squat in Rotherhithe and he lived with his parents who ran a greengrocer's shop round the corner. Redevelopment had moved us all on. Ganesh's parents had gone to open a new shop in High Wycombe. Because there wasn't room for him, he'd gone to live with and work for his Uncle Hari, who ran a newsagent's in Camden. I had drifted up to

Camden, too, and the big plus was that we were not far from one another and still friends.

Just to prove how normal a person I was going to be from now on, I had also been offered and taken a new regular job. But that's where I was now beginning to suspect I'd made my first mistake.

As I'd reminded Susie, I was working as a waitress in a pizza place called the Pizzeria San Gennaro. Before that it had been the called the Hot Spud Café and run by one Reekie Jimmie. Then Jimmie had gone into partnership with an Italian who wanted to start a chain of pizza parlours. Jimmie had been kept on as manager and I'd been hired as one of the staff.

I didn't mind serving up pizzas. I didn't mind, not really, the naff uniform of peasanty-type skirt and a red waistcoat. I got on all right with my colleagues. But I was uneasy about Jimmie's role and the whole set-up behind the restaurant. Because something was going on, I felt it in my bones. That was why I'd reacted so sharply to Susie's hints. She was drawing on experience and so was I.

When you've lived on your wits for nearly eight years as I'd done, you develop a sense for these things. You need it. Every time I set foot in the restaurant, I had the feeling I was the audience in some kind of magic show, the sort where the magician shows you the girl in the cabinet. The cabinet looks solid, the magician walks round it tapping the sides and the floor. The girl is real enough. But then, hey presto, she's gone. Nothing is what it has seemed to be, and scratch your head though you might, you can't work out what's going on. That's how I felt about the San Gennaro.

The business was doing well, mind you. It was in Primrose Hill, beyond Camden High Street, going towards the Regent's Park Road. It's a pretty name for a nice area of early Victorian houses, forming an urban island, inhabited by well-heeled media and showbiz types and other top professionals. Jimmie's Hot Spud Café had always been an anomaly in the area and the pizzeria was much more in tune with local demand.

The San Gennaro wasn't just any old pizza place. The old café had been transformed by Silvio, who'd bought in as Jimmie's partner and was very much the controlling force. We had a gleaming new kitchen and the restaurant area was fantastic. The walls were covered with beautiful tiles imported from Naples. They formed murals showing an Italian garden landscape overlooking the Bay of Naples and complete with Vesuvius. Even the restaurant's toilets had been given the tile treatment and the customers washed their hands amid the ruins of Pompeii. The tiles were greatly admired by the customers and some asked where they could be obtained. This gave Silvio the chance to refer them to an import company which, I suspected, formed another of his business interests.

Our pizzas were good and needed to be, considering they cost a third more than a pizza anywhere else. We also kept a good selection of Italian wines, not just house plonk, because our clients were the sort who reckoned they knew their wines. Several customers had become regulars and we were instructed to welcome these with particular enthusiasm. It looked all very cosy. So, what was wrong?

For a start, Silvio was undoubtedly a shrewd businessman. Anyone could see that. But why should such a man risk putting someone like Jimmie in charge of an enterprise with such good prospects? Jimmie was a nice man, mind you, a friendly chain-smoker without, as far as anyone could see, any natural aptitude for cookery or the restaurant business. We all wondered how he ever got into it in the first place.

When he told me he was giving up the Hot Spud Café, I wasn't surprised. I knew he'd thought about a pizzeria, but I didn't really think he'd go in for it, not seriously. I expected him to go off and do something more suited to his abilities. Don't ask me what. He must have something he's good at. Everyone has something, be it ever so unlikely. But there was Jimmie, in the pizza business, just as he'd said he'd be and, from the cash-in-pocket point of view, doing very much better. He'd got himself a whole new set of flashy clothes and taken to wearing dark glasses, even in the winter. The outfit made him look like one of those spivs in fifties films. All he lacked was the snap-brim hat. He even tried, for a couple of days, using a cigarette holder. I think he must have seen pictures of Noël Coward. However, thank goodness, he couldn't get on with it and the cigarette holder disappeared. All the same, he looked like a man who was doing all right.

So why did it niggle at me? Why not just be happy the poor bloke was doing well for once? Yes, of course I was pleased he had his financial worries behind him. Wouldn't we all like that? But money has a way of blinding you to other concerns, some of them important. It's tempting to say, 'Hey, I'm doing all right so don't rock the boat.' Who needs bad news and awkward questions, especially when everything should be looking rosy? But if I took my eye off the money Jimmie was making, the landscape took on a very different and darker hue.

Ganesh said I was being a pessimist. He got quite cross about it. 'You've got to have more than your gut feeling about it,' he kept saying. 'Where's your evidence? Give me some facts.'

I pointed out to Ganesh that installing Jimmie as manager was in itself an odd fact. What was more, although he was called the manager, he didn't appear to have anything to manage. He didn't keep the accounts because someone came in and did that. The same accountant, a taciturn, middle-aged, toad-like type, giving the impression he was as broad as he was tall, handed out our pay packets at the end of the week. Mario, who was in charge of the kitchen, and Luigi, who was in charge of the bar, told Jimmie what to order by way of supplies and whom to order it from and Jimmie happily did it.

Pietro, the accordionist who supplied the music of an evening, and Bronia, Po-Ching and I, the waitresses, all got on well together in a low-key way, as I said. But there was something about the place which had got to us all. We never discussed anything to do with the pizzeria, not even a casual remark one workmate might make to another. We talked about the sort of stuff you do when you want to avoid committing yourself to the wrong opinion: pop music, what's been on the telly and Bronia's sure-fire Polish cure for colds which involved eating a lot of onions and drinking pints of camomile tea. It was rather like working under the old East German system, I suppose, when you never knew which of your workmates might grass you up to the Stasi. We didn't trust one another. We were all

21

keeping our heads down. We did our jobs. We never showed any interest in anything but taking and fetching orders and clearing tables. We got paid on time and on the surface everything was hunky-dory. But underneath it all we were each as jumpy as a cat who's strayed on to another cat's territory.

The other two girls appeared to accept it more calmly than I did. Probably they regretted the job wasn't more fun but that's as far as it went. As for me, who was more attuned to danger than Bronia or Po-Ching, I had a sinking feeling in the pit of my stomach as soon as I got near the place. I knew I shouldn't be there at all and that, at any moment, the resident tomcat would shoot out from behind a dustbin and duff me up.

Pietro, who'd done time and whose defensive instincts were also well honed, was equally uneasy. I knew it from his body language. But we never said anything. I waited tables and Pietro hunched over his accordion as if it stood between him and whatever bad thing was out there. When he wasn't playing his Neapolitan medleys he sat with the accordion on his knees and stroked it, caressing the stops, murmuring to it as if it had been a living creature.

If I'd only had all this to worry about it would have been enough. But I'd rashly committed myself to the play.

Although, as I explained, I was never able to finish my drama course, my determination to break into acting one day has never left me. So when Marty, an old friend from college days, showed up and said he was putting on a play at The Rose pub, of course I jumped at the chance to be in it. Not only was it an opportunity to act before a proper paying audience but I am a real Sherlock Holmes fan so when I heard it was to be *The Hound*, I was well and truly hooked.

Since then, my original enthusiasm had taken a few knocks. I'd begun to suspect that Marty was to the theatre what Reekie Jimmie had been to the baked potato. We'd get a production all right at the end of rehearsals, but goodness only knew what it was going to be like.

By the next morning I'd made a firm decision to take up Susie's offer of the driving lessons. It seemed foolish not to. I stopped off at the post office on my way to work and collected an application form for a provisional driving licence. I filled it in during my coffee break, trying not to be put off by the box which asked if I wished to donate any of my body organs in the event of my death. I didn't think lessons with Susie would be that dangerous.

Jimmie came in while I was doing it and took a great interest, telling me his entire motoring history, every car he'd ever been in since the age of six, or that's what it felt like. Then Luigi found out and I got his golden oldie memories of his first car, his second car . . . What is it with men and cars?

Jimmie asked me how much the licence was going to cost me. I told him, twenty-nine pounds. He asked if I had that much spare cash. I could just scrape it together, I explained, if I lived carefully. (When don't I?) He sucked his teeth, went away and came back with thirty quid from the petty cash.

'Call it a loyalty bonus, hen. You've worked hard here, and before this you and that boyfriend of yours were good customers of the old spud place.'

A wistful note touched his voice when he mentioned his former establishment. Perhaps the gloss of being manager was starting to wear off. I wished he hadn't used the word 'loyalty' when I'd been harbouring so many suspicions about the pizzeria. I also wished he hadn't called Ganesh my 'boyfriend' because he isn't, not in the way Jimmie and a lot of other people think. I could have told Jimmie Ganesh was 'just' a friend, but that's an expression I never use. It makes it sound as if friendship isn't important, but it outlasts lots of other relationships. Ganesh is the best friend I've ever had or am likely to have. I suppose we could let it turn into something else, but we both know that would be a mistake. Don't tinker with something that works. Besides, Ganesh's family probably have other plans for him, not including me. This is something Ganesh won't discuss.

I didn't get a chance to explain this to Jimmie because that's when Luigi turned up with his motoring reminiscences. I doubt Jimmie would have understood, anyway. Luigi certainly wouldn't and I wouldn't have made the mistake of letting Luigi know anything about my private life. Our barman was a youngish man with cold black eyes and always reminded me of those lean cats you see padding along the pavements close to the wall as night falls.

I took the money and my completed application form and got out of there.

You'll know the old joke about London buses: that you wait for one for ages and then three come along at once? Other events in life happen like that too. You jog along nicely for weeks, it seems, with nothing breaking the routine, then it's as if an unseen hand has thrown a switch somewhere and things begin happening.

I count the day I sent off my application for the provisional licence as the day things started to happen. The pot that had been simmering was coming to the boil, although I didn't realise it at first.

Perhaps in a sense the unseen hand belonged to Susie. Her intervention in my life, though apparently harmless enough, had set wheels in motion. Some people are like that. When they're around, things happen.

Chapter Three

As it turned out, it was the following week before the next incident occurred. The weekend had been pleasant, cold but clear and sunny. On Sunday afternoon Ganesh and I decided to take some exercise. We strolled along the canal from Camden Lock towards Regent's Park where it runs right through the zoo. We could hear the animals, the birds fluttering in their aviaries just on the other side of the boundary, and see the ibex wandering about their compound right above the canal on the farther side. There were families out walking. Little children in colourful jackets and woolly hats ran along jumping the puddles on the towpath. People walked their dogs. I thought how nice it was and how much better things look on a sunny day. Why was I worrying about the pizzeria and Jimmie? There was nothing wrong. It was only the short grey winter days which had brought on my suspicions. I decided I was suffering from a variety of Seasonal Affective Disorder, what they call SAD Syndrome, when lack of sunlight causes you to see everything in the darkest hues and being miserable is just a way of life.

But not today. Today everything was going right. Even Ganesh seemed to feel the effect of the false, forty-eight hour spring. He pulled a piece of paper from his pocket and said diffidently, 'I've written some new poetry.'

Ganesh is a good poet but it had been a long time since he'd read me any of his work.

I said, 'Great, I thought you'd given it up.'

'No, I just don't have the time. Hari never lets me stop. Serve that customer, watch those kids, open those boxes, stack those shelves, sort the newspapers, go to the whole-saler's . . .' Ganesh heaved a sigh. 'Now I'm in the play as well.'

Dismayed, I apologised. 'That's my fault, Gan. I'm sorry. I didn't realise—'

'No, no, it's not your fault, Fran. It's nice to have something different to think about. Although Hari's so keen on the play, he's beginning to get on my nerves with it. He keeps talking about it. You'd think it was a top West End show!'

'He's proud of you.'

'Hah!' said Ganesh. 'If he gave me some free time so I could learn my lines, it would be something. Do you want to hear my poetry?'

He read it out to me as we walked along. The water rippled in the canal and the houseboats rocked at their moorings. I thought, if every day was like this, life would be wonderful, just to be with a good friend, talking about things which really mattered to us, and pretending, almost, that we were in the country and not in a great city.

'Thank you for reading it to me,' I said when he stopped and tucked the paper away. 'I'm glad you've written some more. It's a gift and you ought to use it.'

I thought about Susie and wondered if now was the moment to tell Ganesh about the driving lessons she'd offered. I decided not to. Ganesh had reservations about Susie Duke and I suspected he might not be best pleased she was to teach me to drive. There was no point in spoiling this lovely day with a squabble. Besides, I hadn't yet received my provisional licence.

A distant voice from my early years echoed in my head. I identified it as belonging to Sister Mary Joseph and had a brief mental image of her, black baggy skirt, navy cardigan and veil. She wore round rimless spectacles of the John Lennon variety and, when the light caught them, you couldn't see her eyes at all, just two shiny discs. She suffered with bunions and her brown lace-up shoes were distorted into amazing bumps so that her feet looked like a couple of Jerusalem artichokes. She was a great one for not speaking unless you had something important to say.

'Let your speech be silver, but your silence golden!' she informed us.

We gazed at her, six-year-olds, totally unable to fathom what the words meant but entranced by them. I repeated them to myself all the way home and for years had an image of Sister Mary Joseph saying 'something important' and a shower of silver coins falling from her mouth.

Today I would let my silence be golden, and keep the news of my prospective driving lessons for another occasion.

On Monday, life returned to normal with a vengeance. You would think the sunny weekend had been a dream. I awoke in the early morning to hear raindrops pattering on the window. The temperature had plummeted. Bonnie huddled beside me on the bed. Well, it was February and what could we expect? But even so one's entitled to complain about it. Bonnie certainly thought so. I had to push her out into the cold wet dark garden. She came in again so quickly I wondered whether she'd managed to perform the necessary task she'd been sent out to do.

'All right,' I said. 'But I've got to go to work and you'll have to hang on till I get home.'

She gazed at me with reproachful brown eyes. I wrote a note to my neighbour across the hall, asking him to let Bonnie out when he got up. He had a key to my flat for that purpose. I slid it under his door and set off.

It must have rained all night because the uneven pavement was dotted with puddles. Bus queues huddled under the overhang of the shelters. The buses were crowded with soaked passengers and the interiors smelled like wet bread. I didn't even try to get on one. I walked to work with pedestrians who scurried along, hiding beneath umbrellas. I didn't have an umbrella. I turned up my collar, jumped flooded gutters and splashed through puddles, grateful for my strong boots. I carried my uniform in a plastic carrier along with my trainers, as Doc Martens with a peasant skirt weren't quite what the San Gennaro wanted. Trainers and a peasant skirt looked pretty weird, too, but so far I'd got away with it.

The rain let up for a bit during the morning and by mid-afternoon turned to a steady fine drizzle from a steel-grey sky. As it was February, darkness set in early. Today the weather conspired with the season to give us twilight at four. By five night had fallen. Inside the San Gennaro it was warm and cosy and looked bright and cheerful with all the lights switched on. The tiled picture of the Bay of Naples reminded us of a kinder, warmer climate. The air smelled enticingly of pepperoni and cheese. We'd done a roaring trade at lunchtime and it was just beginning to ease off. I cleared a couple of tables and took the dishes out to the kitchen.

As I walked in I was met with a blast of cold air from the open back door. Mario the cook stood there talking to someone who was outside. I couldn't see who the other person was and from what I could hear it was a pretty one-sided conversation. Mario was telling the other person to clear off in a series of expletive-dotted phrases. He might be named Mario but he was born and bred in south London.

Mario put in long hours at the San Gennaro, working both the busy periods, lunchtime and evening. Generally he took the quiet afternoon period off. At this time he was replaced for a couple of hours by an elderly Greek named George. When not required to cook anything, George studied the racing fixtures in the sports pages of his tabloid newspaper, carefully marking the horses which were to gallop off with his money. It was only because we'd unexpectedly been so busy that Mario had sacrificed his mid-afternoon break, and it hadn't improved his temper.

In the background George sliced mushrooms with dogged concentration. I set down my heavily laden tray with a clatter which took Mario's attention. He turned his head sharply. The expression on his face gave me a jolt. He looked angry and, more than that, vicious. Then the grimness seemed to melt away and he said cheerfully, 'Oh, it's you, Fran. Got another order?'

'Not at the moment,' I told him. 'I thought I'd stack the washer.'

Under the new regime the place had an automatic dishwasher. In the days of the Hot Spud Café all washing-up had been done by hand by casual labour. At one time Jimmie had hired an impecunious artist named Angus to do the job. Then Angus went off to try his luck selling paintings to tourists in the world's sunspots. Before he left he said to me, 'Whatever I earn in Europe, it can't be less than Reekie Jimmie pays me here and I'll be living in the sunshine which beats Camden as far as I'm concerned.'

A seldom-sober derelict had taken over the job at the café. I suspected Jimmie paid this human wreck even less than he'd paid Angus.

The same old wino now worked as the San Gennaro's sweeper-out and toilet-cleaner in the early morning. The only reason he still had a job was because, unexpectedly, Jimmie had insisted on it. It was, I think, the only thing he'd bargained with Silvio about and won.

'I told Silvio, he'd got to give the old sod a job,' Jimmie had confided in me. 'The poor wee fellow depends on it. It's like . . .' Jimmie sought for a way to explain it. 'It's all the old bugger's got, right? Working here. I told Silvio, you canna take it away from him.'

That's why I worried about Jimmie. He was a bad cook and bad businessman and the state of his fingernails had to be seen to be believed, but he had a core of decency. There's not a lot of that about in the world I inhabit.

I went over to the dustbin and began to scrape food off the plates before stacking them. I always did that and so did Po-Ching. But Bronia never bothered, just put everything in the machine, and we were for ever cleaning out the filter when it was her shift. From my position by the bin I could see past Mario into the yard.

A young kid stood there. He couldn't have been more than sixteen. His short dark hair was plastered to his scalp by rain. He had luminous dark eyes like you see in an old icon, huge in a narrow face with a pointed chin. His sweater was way too big for him and his jeans bagged over the ankles. His trainers were mud-caked. He looked like the proverbial drowned rat. For all his puny appearance and the fact he was shivering with cold, there was something resolute about him. He'd been getting an earful from Mario but he was standing his ground.

'I want to see Max,' he said. His accent was pretty heavy and I guessed his vocabulary didn't go much beyond the basic few words. The way he spoke suggested he'd repeated the same sentence many times, doggedly and without much hope.

'There's no bloody Max here!' Mario shouted. 'How many times do I have to tell you? Now – clear off!'

He stepped back and slammed the door in the kid's face. I wasn't quick enough looking down at my dirty plates and he caught my curious gaze.

'Kid wanting a job,' he said briefly.

'Oh,' I said and moved over to the dishwasher.

Po-Ching, who was on today's evening shift but had been called in early to help me out, saved the day by trotting in with an order for two napolitanas with side salads and a cannelloni and garlic bread. We didn't just do pizzas, we did a couple of other things as well.

Mario got cracking at his special pizza oven. George busied himself with the cannelloni. I went back to the restaurant and, because there wasn't anyone else wanting food, went behind the bar to give Luigi a hand stacking glasses and putting empty wine bottles in boxes. He'd just picked up a box and was going to carry it out to the backyard when one of the people who'd given Po-Ching's order came up and began to ask about wine. Luigi put the box of empties in my arms. I sidled out and backed through the swing doors into the kitchen.

Mario was fixing the salads. He took no notice of me and didn't bother how I was going to manage the back door. I perched my box of empties on a worktop, opened the door, held it with my foot, retrieved my box of bottles and managed to get through before the door slammed on me.

It was still raining. I went over to the shed in the corner of the yard where we stacked the empties ready for collection. The door was ajar, which wasn't unusual. It wasn't as though the place was kept locked. We only ever put junk like the bottles and rubbish awaiting collection in there. I put down my box again, pushed the door open inwards and had stooped to pick up my box when something shot out of the shed and cannoned into me. I yelped and sat down in the mud.

The person who'd tried to bolt past me tripped over my ankle and fell flat. He scrabbled to his hands and knees and stared at me, terrified. It was the thin kid.

I didn't know what was going on here but I knew instinctively I didn't want Mario to see it. Any second now he'd finish Po-Ching's order and be free to glance out of the window. I remembered his angry face and voice, and I knew if he saw the boy was still hanging around, the cook was likely to come out and clout him. I motioned towards the interior of the shed.

'Get in there! Go on, quick!' I ordered with a glance at the kitchen window.

Something in my voice made him do as I said. He got to his feet and, still crouched, scurried back inside. I collected my box of bottles and followed.

The light was poor in there. There was a tiny window but so grimy it was as good as useless. The only real light, such as it was, seeped in through the door, which was still ajar.

I could make out the kid on the far side of the shed, pressed against the wall. I put my box of bottles on top of some others and asked casually, 'What's your name?'

He didn't answer. I could smell the fear on him. I tapped my chest and said, 'I'm called Fran.' I pointed at him. 'You?'

He wetted his lips with the tip of his tongue. He'd understood. He wasn't sure he should tell me. Probably, if he gave me a name, it would be a false one. In the end, he plumped for acting dumb and shook his head.

'OK,' I said. I understood. 'I don't know what's up but I think you shouldn't hang around here.'

He stared at me silently, his body tense, ready to leap aside if I moved forward.

I tried again. 'Go home, right? Here is bad for you.'

At least he understood that. 'I want to see Max,' he said again in that dogged way.

'We don't have anyone working here called Max,' I assured him.

He twisted his hands together. 'Max comes here. I see him.'

'What does Max do here?' I asked.

He frowned and looked distressed. 'Max comes here,' he repeated.

'He's a customer?'

'No. Nothing buy. Max works here.'

'Look, I work in this place. I know there is no Max.'

He frowned and rubbed the toe of one trainer into the dirty floor. 'I have seen him.' He looked sullen now and I sensed that behind his obstinate manner lurked tears he was determined not to shed in my presence. I wondered how old he was. His small build might be misleading, but I didn't think he could be much more than sixteen or seventeen at the most.

His statement, that he'd seen Max at the pizzeria, flummoxed me. I ran through the names of the staff in my head. None of us was called Max or anything which might sound like Max or be abbreviated to Max. I didn't know what the old cleaner's name was but I couldn't believe the kid wanted to see him.

I said, 'I really think you're wrong about that.'

At this an unexpected anger entered his voice and face. 'No, you are wrong! You tell me lies. I know he is here. He works here. I have seen him! You are like the other one, the cook. You tell me lies.'

Now the tears were brimming in his eyes but his rage kept them back. Just for a split second I thought he might leap at me and strike out. This put me on the defensive both physically and mentally. I asked myself why I was bothering with this unknown trespasser anyway.

I opened my mouth to snap back, 'Go on, get out of here!' but mixed with his anger was a real desperation. Added to which his conviction that he could find Max here was compelling, even if I knew we didn't have anyone of that name.

Clearly we'd get nowhere arguing about it. If I didn't return soon, Mario would wonder what was keeping me. Not only would Mario not take it kindly if he saw the boy still lingering, but he'd be mad at me for talking to him when I should be working.

'Listen,' I said urgently, accompanying my words with a pantomime of gestures. 'I'm going back indoors, into the kitchen. I'll talk to the cook. While I'm talking to him, you go, go the way you came. How did you get in here?'

He pointed up at the shed roof. I deduced that meant he'd come over the back wall on to the roof and from there dropped to the ground.

'Can you get back that way?' I gestured at him and then upwards.

He nodded.

'Good. I'm going now. You wait until I'm in the kitchen, then you go, you understand me?'

He nodded again.

I could only hope. I made my way back to the kitchen. I was just in time. Po-Ching had collected her orders and Mario was wiping down a work surface right by the window.

'Look at this!' I said in a loud aggrieved voice. I tugged at my skirt, wet and smeared where I'd fallen under the kid's onslaught. 'I'm covered in muck! The rain's made it slippy out there. It's really dangerous. I was skidding all over the place.'

Mario inspected my muddy attire and chuckled. 'Come down on your backside, did you? Wish I'd seen it.'

'Ha-ha! I could've broken a wrist or something, you know.' I'd moved round so that now, in order to speak to me, he had his back to the window. I couldn't see past him to the shed. I just hoped the boy was on his way over the wall. 'I can't go back to waiting tables like this,' I went on. 'I'll have to change back into my jeans.'

'You can't serve tables in jeans,' said Mario. 'Company policy. You've got to wear your uniform. Silvio likes it that way.'

'Silvio wouldn't like me out there covered in mud. Neither would the customers.'

Mario considered the problem. 'Business is easing up. Po-Ching can probably manage on her own until Bronia comes in at six, provided she isn't bloody late again. You go on home.'

'I'm paid by the hour,' I said sulkily. *Go on, whoever you are, you must be over the wall by now.*

'It'll be all right,' said Mario. 'You had an accident on the premises. Luigi should've been doing that job, anyway. He's barman and the bottles are his business. You won't lose any money. I'll fix it.'

'I'd better go and tell Jimmie then,' I heard myself say, 'as he's manager.' I regretted the remark. I didn't want to give Mario any reason to think I found anything dodgy about the set-up here.

Mario looked surprised at the mention of Jimmie. 'Oh, him,' he said. 'Right, if you want to. Tell him I said we can manage.'

As I moved towards the door into the corridor which led to Jimmie's office, Mario added casually. 'You don't want to worry him about that kid asking for a job.'

'What kid?' I asked blankly.

Mario smiled. 'Good girl,' he said. 'I'll fix you a pizza to take home with you for your supper. What do you want on it?'

'Everything!' I said and he grinned.

'Cheeky little mare, aren't you? All right. I'll fix you the best pizza you ever saw.'

Jimmie was sitting behind his desk in a cloud of smoke, reading a tabloid newspaper. He'd acquired a little television set which sat in the corner flickering out the evening episode of *Neighbours*. That shows you how bored Jimmie was with nothing to do. Honestly, I'd known night-watchmen with more active duties. Manager, indeed!

'I fell over in the yard and I'm going home, Jimmie.'

'Sorry to hear that, hen. You hurt yourself?' He put down the tabloid and stared at me in concern.

'No. But I messed up my uniform. Mario says they can manage and I won't lose any pay. Bronia should be coming before long.'

'Right you are, hen,' agreed Jimmie and went back to the sports pages. 'Away to your home.'

He was another one who had an inbuilt instinct for the rules here.

I changed into my outdoor things and went back to the kitchen when Mario, still grinning, handed me my pizza in a box. If nothing else, my accident had cured his bad humour. I carried the pizza home and ate it in front of my gas fire. True to his word, he had put nearly everything on it: tomatoes, cheese, mushrooms, pepperoni, black olives, chopped ham and anchovies. It was all I could do to eat most of it, even with feeding Bonnie the pepperoni. I put a big slice remaining into the fridge for another time. I didn't feel like moving much after that.

I sat watching early-evening TV until I'd digested my supper enough to be able to wash out my skirt and hang it up to drip-dry in the tiny shower room.

Already in there was the costume I'd brought from The Rose. I'd examined it carefully when I'd got it home, as a precaution before I dunked it in the tub. It was beautifully made, once lined throughout with silk, now in tatters, and with real mother-of-pearl buttons at the wrists and down the front. It even had a worn label stitched in it, though not one I recognised: *Worth. Paris.*

I felt sure its origins weren't in the theatre. It was the real thing, a bit of fashion history. I had washed it with great care. It was being slow to dry. I fingered it now to test it. How did women manage the laundry years ago when they wore these cumbersome things? I had an idea they wore detachable collars and cuffs. In oil paintings both men and women always look so elegant in those beautiful clothes. However, if you ask me, our ancestors must have been a smelly lot.

Occasionally, throughout my evening activities, I wondered about the kid in the shed. Chiefly I speculated whether I'd see him again. Given his reception by Mario, there didn't seem much point in his coming back. In fact, it would be outright dangerous. But there had been something about that youngster, some kind of inbuilt obstinacy which I'd sensed and, possibly, even identified with. If there was something he wanted at the San Gennaro, one narrow squeak wouldn't put him off. Desperation, too, lends a sort of reckless courage. Even when a course of action is foolish, if you have no other, then you have no choice.

'Max . . .' I mumbled to myself. 'Who the heck is Max?'

For a week after that nothing very much happened, nothing out of the ordinary anyway. I went to work. Ganesh and I practised our lines on one another. The boy and his quest for 'Max' were pushed out of my mind. I hadn't told Ganesh about my encounter in the backyard of the pizzeria because I know he doesn't like me 'meddling', as he calls it. The boy had not come back, at least not while I'd been on duty. I was working mostly lunchtime shifts now, having swapped my evening shifts with Bronia so that I could go to rehearsals. Perhaps, after all, he'd realised it wasn't wise to risk running into Mario again. Or perhaps he'd found the mysterious Max. Or perhaps . . .

But at this point I firmly told myself to stop my imagination running riot. The boy and I had been ships that pass in the night. London is full of people who drift into sight, touch one another's lives briefly, part and vanish. Where do they come from and where do they go? Who knows? Does anyone care? Very few.

Up to now, we'd been rehearsing in my flat. However, we really needed to get to grips with the stage in the upstairs functions room at The Rose. We explained to Freddy we'd have to rehearse there from now on.

'Right you are,' he said. 'Help yourselves. No one's booked the function room for anything else. How's the play going?'

We assured him it was coming along splendidly.

'I've been selling tickets to my customers,' said Freddy with a steely look in his eye. 'They want their money's worth.'

Marty told him he had absolutely nothing to worry about. Privately, I thought Marty did have something to worry about. If, after all his brave words to Freddy, the play was an unmitigated disaster, he might experience the theatrical wish 'break a leg' in a whole different context.

However, even I was excited at the thought of actually being up there on the stage, rehearsing properly, and set off for The Rose for our first run-through there feeling that things were going right at last. The whole thing suddenly felt more professional. We were also due to meet up with a new member of the cast that evening, an essential one: the Hound of the title.

The animal in question belonged to Irish Davey, who was training it for the role. It was to make just one appearance, at the climax of the play, when it would bound from one side of the stage to the other. Irish Davey had promised there'd be absolutely no problem teaching it to do that.

My route took me via the newsagent's where I was to collect Ganesh and leave Bonnie, my dog, with Uncle Hari. Here and there, street-sleepers had already settled down in doorways. One form wrapped in a dirty blanket looked small and pathetic and it reminded me of the boy. I stopped and peered into the doorway. All I could see was a mop of dark hair. Was it him?

There was a scuff of a footstep and breathing behind me. I whirled round. A young man had appeared from somewhere, badly dressed, scruffy and unshaven, wearing a woolly hat pulled over his long, matted hair. He didn't look friendly.

'You want something?' he asked.

'No,' I said. 'I thought he might be someone I know.' I pointed down at the slight bundle.

'And?' He sounded even more unfriendly.

'Look,' I said. 'I'm not out to make any trouble. I met up with someone the other day, a young boy, and I've been worried about him.'

He gave me a crooked, mirthless smile. 'That's not a young boy.'

I glanced down at the huddled figure in the blanket. Was it, in fact, a girl? Fewer girls slept rough than boys.

Just then the shrouded figure moved, shook back the blanket and sat up. It was an elderly man, a small, shrivelled gnome-like figure. What had appeared dark hair was iron-grey, darkened with grease. He looked at me, terrified, and then past me to the woolly-hatted man, whom he seemed to recognise, fixing a hopeful gaze on him.

'It's all right, Billy,' said the woolly-hatted man, surprisingly gently. 'It's a mistake. The lady's looking for someone else.'

'I'm sorry,' I said to Billy, who looked back at me with the clouded gaze of someone whose mind is already half into the land of shadows. I turned back to the woolly-hatted man and repeated, 'I'm sorry.'

'It's all right,' he said. 'We all keep an eye out for him. If anyone takes an interest in him, we check it out.' His expression grew grim again. 'Some people, some of them drunk and some of them not, think it's a joke to mess around with him. His mind isn't too clear.'

'He ought not to be here,' I said. The man didn't reply. I hadn't expected he would.

I continued on my way. The encounter had rattled me. It also brought the unknown boy back into my mind. Was someone looking out for him, as the street-dwellers were looking out for Billy? Or was he alone in a dangerous and alien world? I decided to tell Ganesh about him after all.

'I've got something I'd like to talk to you about,' I said as we hurried towards the rehearsal. 'But we're running a bit late. There isn't time now. I'll tell you later.'

Ganesh put his foot in a puddle and growled, 'Whatever it is you've got in mind, don't do it.'

That night there was an awful racket in the bar downstairs and we could hear echoes of it upstairs in the function room. It was still freezing cold and we complained to Denise about the lack of heating up there. There would have been no point in complaining to Freddy. But Denise was more understanding and had unearthed a Calor gas heater which was doing its best in the middle of the stage. If you stood within a metre of it you were all right. Any further away and you still froze. I was standing in the wings by the curtains, trying not to breathe in too deeply. They smelled of dust, damp and mould.

'We ought to try these out,' I warned Marty. 'They mightn't work. Who's in charge of curtains, anyway?'

'Denise,' he said, harassed and shuffling bits of paper

43

furiously. 'Curtains and prompter. On the night, that is. We'll have to manage without her until then.'

'How can we? I mean, we need our prompter now and she needs to know when to work the curtains.'

'I'll prompt, OK? Denise will be here for the dress rehearsal. She's done the curtains for other productions. She won't screw up. All right, everyone! Now I've marked on the stage with chalk where the furniture is going to be when the curtain goes up. So, we'll run through Act One.'

'Where are we getting the furniture from?' asked Carmel immediately. 'Is it going to be as ropy as the costumes?'

'All we need are two chairs, a table and a fireplace.' Marty pointed at the relevant chalk marks as he spoke. 'It's all in hand. Freddy's got a mate making up a fake fireplace out of chipboard.'

'What about the scenes on the moor?' I asked.

'No problem,' said Marty airily. 'We can use the backdrop they used for the pantomime.'

'Marty!' I protested. 'The pantomime was *Babes in the Wood*. In *The Hound of the Baskervilles*, Sir Henry is pursued across the open moor. People keep meeting up with one another on the moor. The whole moorland setting is vital to the atmosphere of the entire story. You can't have a forest in the background.'

'It's dark and sinister,' argued Marty. 'And unless some of you are volunteering to paint another backdrop . . .'

'Nigel and I will,' offered Owen unexpectedly. 'Right, Nige?'

'Yeah, sure,' said Nigel. 'If old Freddy will give us the paint.'

'Moorland,' I insisted. 'Open heath and lots of rocks.'

They seemed happy they could do that. Marty looked cheerful for once, instead of harassed.

'So, this is Sherlock Holmes's study,' he began again. 'He and Watson are sitting in front of the fire when Mrs Hudson comes in and announces a visitor. She and the visitor enter left, over there. Watch out for the dodgy bit of flooring. Holmes and Watson, take your places.'

Nigel and Ganesh walked to their chalk marks. Mick, who was playing the country doctor who comes to see Holmes and tell him about the mysterious hound, straightened up, cleared his throat and generally got into acting mode.

'Fran?' whispered Carmel. 'Did you manage to wash that grungy costume?'

'Yes, it's drying. It's quite nice really,' I muttered.

She didn't look as if she believed me. 'I've got a mate who's going to lend me long black skirt. Catch me wearing anything from that box. You'll probably get some horrible skin disease.'

'Aren't you Mrs Hudson?' I hissed. 'They want you in this scene.'

'Carmel!' bellowed Marty. 'Where the hell are you?'

'Keep your hair on,' she said and scrambled up into the wings. 'Right.' She raised her voice. 'MR HOLMES! THERE IS A GENTLEMAN TO SEE YOU!' You could've heard her a mile away.

'Knock!' yelled Marty. 'She doesn't just barge in. She knocks on the door first.'

'There isn't a door. How can I bloody knock?'

'Knock on anything.'

'Stamp on the floor,' suggested Owen.

Carmel stamped. There was a snapping noise and she shrieked. 'I've put my ruddy foot through the floor.'

'I told you to mind that dodgy patch.'

'You didn't tell me where it was and Owen said to stamp my foot, so I did.'

'I didn't say stamp it like a blooming elephant,' said Owen.

After this things got worse.

'Right,' said the weary Marty. 'We'll move on to the first scene in Baskerville Hall. There will be a fireplace over there—'

'Is this the same fireplace as is in Holmes's study?' asked Carmel.

'Of course it is. How many ruddy fireplaces do you think Freddy's mate is going to make?' Marty had had about enough of Carmel.

'The audience will think it's the same room.'

'No, they won't.'

'If it's got the same furniture and the same fireplace, they will.'

Marty said through gritted teeth, 'They won't because there will be family portraits on the wall.'

'Family portraits?' we all chorused. 'Where are those coming from?'

'I'm painting them!' yelled Marty.

'His painting isn't like his spelling, is it?' muttered Ganesh. 'They won't all look as if they've been done by Picasso with a hangover?'

We struggled through the rest and all met together on stage for a free and frank discussion, that is, a blazing row.

Everyone felt rather better after that. If nothing else, it warmed us up.

We were distracted from our 'brainstorming session', as Marty liked to call it, by a commotion at the door of the functions room. A draught swept across the stage. A thin, wiry figure with a mop of red hair, gripping a can of lager, lurched in. In his wake came a large black creature, shoulders hunched, head down, placing its huge paws on the ground with uncanny silence, like a prowling panther.

Instinctively, we all drew back and huddled together like sheep.

'Is dis d'place where we're doing d'play?' The redhead waved the can at us and the sinister black beast collapsed with a thump on the ground and slobbered, chomping its huge jaws as if in anticipation of a tasty meal.

Irish Davey had arrived – and the Hound.

'Perhaps I ought to have told you,' said Ganesh to Marty. 'I don't get on with dogs.'

'Well, I don't!' said Ganesh crossly.

Rehearsals were over and he and I were walking back towards the shop.

'You know I don't like dogs and they don't like me. Even that tyke of yours doesn't like me.'

This was true. I don't know why it is, but dogs start acting up the minute they catch sight of Ganesh. Little dogs, big dogs, hairy dogs, dinky poodles with pink collars and bows in their hair, it makes no difference.

'It's because you're scared of them,' I said. 'They sense it.'

'I'm scared of them for a very good reason. They bite.'

'When were you last bitten?' I argued.

'That's not the point. I keep out of the way so I don't get bitten.'

I wanted to shout at him, why had he agreed to be in the play, then, knowing there was a dog in it? But if I did that, he'd very likely say he wouldn't play Watson and leave us in the lurch. So I said as confidently as I could, 'Irish's dog was all right. It did just as Irish said it would. I held it in the wings and let it go when he signalled. It ran straight across to him and you've got to admit, it did look the part.'

Ganesh snorted. 'Did you see the way it was staring at me? It was sizing me up. It's got nasty eyes and have you seen its teeth?'

I told him he was just being paranoid.

We abandoned the subject by mutual consent.

'What did you want to tell me?' Ganesh asked, after we'd progressed half a street's length in tetchy silence. 'You said, on the way to The Rose, you wanted to discuss something.'

I was surprised he'd remembered. I thought about the thin kid. Ganesh wasn't in a good mood. Irish's dog was still on his mind. It wasn't the moment to start talking about anything that had happened at the pizzeria.

'Susie Duke's going to teach me to drive,' I said. One advantage in holding back nuggets of information was that they could be useful at moments like this, when a diversion was required or Ganesh asked awkward questions. I'm not sure that's what Sister Mary Joseph had in mind but it worked.

'Where and in what?' he asked tersely.

'She's got a new car, a Citroën. I don't know where. I

suppose we could start round the flats where she lives.'

We'd reached the newsagent's. Ganesh stopped by the door which led from the street to the upstairs flat.

'Fran, learning to drive with Susie is one thing. If you want to do it, do it. But if she tries to get you to work for that agency of hers—'

'I know!' I interrupted. 'I've already told her. I've got a job at the pizzeria and I don't fancy the sort of work she does.'

'Good. Just remember that. Don't get talked into anything.'

I denied strongly that I was likely to do anything silly. I asked him to have a little confidence in me.

'Well, all right,' he said grudgingly, putting the key in the lock. 'It's just I know how you fancy yourself a detective. And don't tell Hari about the driving lessons. You know how he worries.'

Chapter Four

After I'd sat and had a cup of tea with Uncle Hari and answered all his questions about the rehearsal it was really late. I knew I should have left at least half an hour earlier but, as Ganesh had warned me, Hari was so enthusiastic about the prospect of a member of his family being in a real theatrical production that we just had to go along with it. As Ganesh muttered to me, Hari was keener on the whole thing than any of us were, apart from Marty. I said I didn't think Marty was as keen as he had been at the outset.

'Show business, isn't it?' raved Hari. 'The smell of the greasepaint, the lights, the audience.'

I didn't know when I'd seen him so animated and happy. He's usually animated and worried. The responsibilities of being a businessman weigh heavily on his shoulders. If it's not his suppliers, it's his customers who give him grief. Hari is convinced that suppliers are out to cheat him and customers need to be closely watched or they'll pinch things. He lives in a world of sharks. I'm not saying he's entirely wrong, mind you. Local kids are adept shoplifters. It's just that he has so much trouble coping with it all.

It was therefore amazing that Hari, who worried about

every single thing every single day, didn't appear to have any worries about the play. But then, he hadn't attended our rehearsals.

It had stopped raining so Bonnie and I set out to walk home. I had got as far as Camden High Street, which was fairly busy, even if it was late. In among all the other pedestrians were several shabby figures making their way towards the night shelter in Arlington Road, so it was lucky that I noticed one more skinny unkempt figure in a baggy sweater. He was hanging about outside a fast-food outlet and at first I thought it wasn't the boy in the shed, but just another one like him.

Now, Fran, I told myself, *he's been on your mind and you're starting to imagine him everywhere, just as you fancied the huddled form of Billy in the doorway might be him.*

But even as I thought it, he turned and the light shone on his face. There was no mistaking the pinched features and huge dark eyes. He looked miserable and hungry.

I stepped up to him before he saw me and said, 'Hi! Fran, remember?'

He literally jumped, hopped up in the air, and stared at me, terrified. Then he turned and bolted off down the street.

I knew I wasn't going to get another chance to find him so I set off in pursuit, Bonnie scampering behind me. Fleeing figures probably aren't unknown in Camden High Street and chasing someone down a busy pavement isn't easy. I thought I was going to lose him but unexpectedly an outsider took an interest. A clothes shop with late-night opening was finally calling it a day. A thickset man was outside, reaching up with a pole to unhook garments hanging from the façade. As the boy raced past, the man dropped the pole and grabbed him by the neck of his baggy pullover. The boy ran on a couple of steps, the knitted neck of the pullover stretching until it would stretch no more. He skidded to a halt, choking, and the man spun him round to face back the way he'd come, and me.

I panted up to them. The thickset man said simply, 'What did he nick?'

Obviously the man thought the boy was either a pilferer or had grabbed my purse.

'Nothing,' I assured him.

The man scowled. 'These kids are always hanging round. They're so damn quick you don't spot them. We've got a system, the traders. The ones we know, as soon as we see them, we phone the other shops and warn 'em to keep an eye open.'

'Do you know this one?' I asked.

The thickset man shook the boy casually like a large dog which had caught a rat. 'Might do. They all look much the same.'

'He's not a thief,' I said firmly.

'What do you want him for, then?' He turned his suspicious gaze on me.

'It's a – a domestic incident,' I said. 'He's – er – he's my cousin.'

I'd nearly said he was my brother but, if the boy spoke, it would be clear he knew little English, and the brother story wouldn't wash.

The man let go of his captive and pushed him forward at the same time so that the boy stumbled into my arms.

'You can have him, then,' he said. 'Just take him away from here, right?' He gathered up the items of clothing and the pole and carried the lot into the shop. Then he locked the door, turned the sign hanging in it to CLOSED, and stood behind it, looking out at us.

The boy was standing by me, panting, looking scared out of his wits, eyes rolling.

'It's all right!' I urged him. 'You don't have to run. I'm alone. Just me and my dog, OK?'

He glanced down at Bonnie, who wagged her stumpy tail at him. Bonnie is a good judge of character.

'I was just going to buy myself some supper,' I went on. 'Would you like a kebab?'

He eyed me. 'You come from Max?'

He was still fixated on the ruddy Max. I sighed.

'No, because I don't know any Max. But I'd like to talk to you about that.'

He began to edge away. 'Can't talk to people.'

'You can talk to me, right? I work at the pizzeria. If there's a Max there, I want to find him too. I've got my own reasons, right?'

His dark eyes were assessing me all the time we spoke and I could almost hear the cogs in his brain going round. His instinct was still to run, but I might be the only lead he'd get. We were both aware of the thickset man watching us from inside the shop. He decided to gamble.

'Is all right,' he said grudgingly.

I suggested we take the food back to my place and, after some hesitation, he agreed. It was a peculiar journey. Sometimes he'd walk beside me and sometimes he'd drop back. Each time he did this, I thought he had changed his mind and was going to slip away. Twice I turned, thinking he'd gone, but he was still there, watching me suspiciously. I knew he was still undecided about coming to my flat. Perhaps he expected some sort of trap. I saw his gaze take in alleys and low walls. He was planning an escape route, should he need one.

'Your place, who is there?' he asked.

'Only me. Other people live in the house but only me in the flat.'

He looked as if he thought this was an unlikely tale. One young woman living all on her own in an entire flat was doubtless outside his experience. Perhaps he thought that after I finished work at the pizzeria, I moonlighted as a prostitute.

'Your father, your mother?' he demanded rather hostilely.

'Both dead.'

This answer earned an unexpected sympathy. 'Is sad,' he said. 'I am sorry.'

'No husband?' he asked next, after a few minutes.

'No husband, no family, nobody,' I said. 'How about you?'

'I, too, have nobody,' he said promptly but I knew he was lying.

We reached the house. He stood outside, looking it over, particularly interested in the lighted windows of the other flats.

'Who lives here?'

'Just people like me.'

Perhaps he hadn't met many people like me, because that wasn't enough.

'Who lives in that one?' He pointed at the window of the other downstairs flat, which was in darkness.

'Someone called Erwin, a musician. He'll be at work now.'

He pointed one by one at all the other windows in the façade of the house, wanting to know who lived there. Frankly, I was vague myself about the tenants on the upper floors but I managed some sort of answer which seemed to satisfy him.

He was still nervous. I got him through the front door into the hall, but at the door of the flat he stopped, his eyes rolling. He gave a frightened look up the stairs as, somewhere above, a door slammed. A burst of rock music flooded the stairwell and a snatch of voices in conversation, to be cut off moments later by another slam of a door. My companion took a step back towards the front entrance. Fortunately, no one came down from the floor above. If anyone had, he would have fled and I wouldn't have been able to stop him.

'See?' I said. 'Just people, like me, spending an evening at home.'

I put my key in my door and went ahead, switching on all the lights. He edged inside and stood ready to dash out again while I went round demonstrating that there was no one hiding in the shower with the dripping wash or in the kitchenette. Eventually, he sat on the very edge of my sofa and appeared to relax a little. Bonnie jumped up beside him and when I came back with two mugs of coffee, she had settled down nicely with her head propped on his thigh.

'Now, this Max,' I began. 'Why do you think he works at the pizzeria?'

'I see him there.' His hands cupped round the mug, he looked at me over the top of it. The expression in his eyes defied me to deny the presence of a Max at the pizzeria. He was a curious mixture of terrified and aggressive, like an injured cornered dog, snapping at the hands of would-be rescuers.

Patiently, I said, 'It's a restaurant. People come in and out all the time.'

He shook his head. 'Not eating there. He go in the office.' He gave a tight little smile. 'I watch.'

I was flummoxed. Jimmie's office? It didn't make sense. Jimmie was so obviously out of the loop at the pizzeria, his office was the last place anyone would go on serious business.

Just to check, I asked, 'What does he look like, this Max? Has he got reddish hair?'

I rubbed my own short-cropped hair which is a sort of red-brown. 'Paler than mine? Ginger like . . .' I looked around and ended up pointing at the mug I held which was a muddy orange colour.

'No,' said the boy decidedly.

That let Jimmie out. Jimmie's once-red hair had faded and was streaked with grey but still generally sandy in hue.

'Grey? Silver?'

Again a shake of the head. That let Silvio out. 'What colour, then?'

The boy hunched his shoulders. 'A bit brown, a bit grey.'

That didn't help but it indicated a man who wasn't very young. Luigi was in his twenties, had black hair and fancied himself as a lady-killer. Pietro had lank fair hair.

I asked him if he could give me a better description of Max and he came up with the information that Max was a fat man.

'How fat?' I asked.

'Very fat,' said the kid firmly. 'Eat very much.' He spread out his hands to indicate a vast girth.

That let out everyone at the pizzeria, as far as I could see. Silvio was slim. Mario was chunky but by no means fat. Luigi had the figure of a whippet. Anyway, the boy had spoken to Mario and failed to identify him as Max. Likewise, he'd seen George. The toad-like accountant might, just, have been described as fat but really he was just squat and square. The more this went on, the more I became convinced that the boy had got it wrong and Max didn't have anything to do with the pizzeria. But I knew it was no use telling him so. He was too fixed in his own mind about it.

'Well, I can snoop around,' I said. 'You know, try and find out.'

His reaction was unexpected. The wariness dropped from him, and he became embarrassingly and effusively grateful. He leapt off the sofa, dislodging Bonnie, and shook me by the hand. It made me feel terrible because if I didn't find out anything, he'd be so disappointed. I shouldn't have offered. Oh Ganesh, you should have been there at this hour to stop me doing something silly.

'Why,' I asked when I'd managed to cut short his thanks, 'do you want to find Max?'

This, I knew, was the tricky question. It would mean he had to tell me something about himself. He might not be prepared to do that even though he should realise that my offer of help meant I was entitled to know something about his problem. Every investigator needs a few facts. Sensible investigators get the facts first and decide whether to take the job afterwards. Trust me to do it the wrong way round.

He settled down on the sofa once more and Bonnie put her head back on his leg, albeit with a suspicious look up at him, as if to ensure he wasn't going to leap up and disturb her again.

'I want to find my brother,' he said.

I didn't remind him that on our way to the flat, he'd told me he had nobody. 'Brother?' I prompted.

He leaned forward and said urgently, 'I must find him. I must find him very soon.'

Bit by bit, it came out. He had entered the country illegally. His father, in Romania, had paid a good deal of money, raised with difficulty, to a crooked organisation which smuggled would-be immigrants across Europe and into the UK. Earlier, he'd done the same for the boy's brother who'd successfully made it here. They knew this because they'd had a letter from the brother. The family decided to send Ion, as I now found his name to be, by the same route. They'd sold their few remaining valuables and in addition borrowed money from the very people organising the illegal run. Not a wise thing to do. This left the family in Romania out on a limb, dependent on the two boys making their fortunes in England and sending some of the cash home, something the family seemed confident their sons would do. Yet any money Ion or his brother could earn in England would go first and foremost to the shady traffickers who'd brought them here in repayment of the loan. For the foreseeable future, they'd be paying it off together with the inevitable interest. They'd have no choice in this nor any legal protection. The loan would be 'paid off' when the dodgy lenders declared it to be, at a time of their choosing.

Ion had arrived in the UK after a long, fraught journey during which time he'd been out of touch both with his family at home and with the brother in England. On arrival, the brother had failed to meet up with him as promised. In fact, the brother seemed to have disappeared, vanished off the face of the earth. Ion had tried asking everywhere he could. The family was writing anxious letters. He didn't say how this correspondence was delivered and I doubted it was by regular post. I suspected new arrivals brought it. Nor did Ion say where he himself was living or how he was earning enough money to stay alive. But I knew there was a black economy out there, paying cash for work, no insurance, no tax, no records, no protection against unhealthy and dangerous workplaces or machinery. The cleaning business was known often to use subcontracted labour supplied by shadowy middlemen. Whatever he was being paid, it was clearly barely enough to keep body and soul together.

He had made all the enquiries he could without attracting official interest – or the racketeers' displeasure. Fellow Romanians had been the obvious people to ask, but they had not been helpful. The general opinion seemed to be that the brother had moved on somewhere else.

'But he would not do that,' Ion told me earnestly, leaning forward and displacing Bonnie again. Cheesed off, she jumped to the floor and settled down in front of the gas fire. 'He knew I was coming. He would wait for me.

Also there is the money. He must help pay back the money. I cannot do it myself.'

That made sense. So far, so good. I understood why Ion was getting panicky. If you'd entered the country, as he had done, in the back of a lorry, you were in no position to make anything but the most discreet of enquiries. Above all, Ion hadn't wanted to draw attention either to himself or to his shady employers. He couldn't go to the police or social services. It was a measure of his desperation that he'd been obliged to break cover and go to the pizzeria.

'Because Max works there and perhaps he knows something.' His voice rang with the despair of someone who is playing the last possible throw of the dice.

'But who *is* Max, Ion?'

The trouble was, he couldn't tell me, at least not in any way that made any sense.

Ion explained he knew very little of the people who ran the shadowy operation ferrying human beings across Europe. They dealt through middlemen. But he did know they were dangerous. One didn't cross them. For that reason, he hadn't yet let his father know the brother was missing. His father would almost certainly go to the man who'd arranged the journey at their end and ask questions, make trouble. The traffickers would hear of it and they wouldn't like that. Ion had to find his brother first, or at least find out where he'd gone before his father's pathetic and frightened pleas to know what had happened to his children had to be met with the truth. Despite his fear of the traffickers, he'd tried to contact the one person he knew in this country who was connected with them: the elusive Max.

'But you still haven't told me who he is, or how you know about him, Ion!' I urged. 'You say you saw him go into the pizzeria, but you don't seem to have any more information. So, how do you know the man you saw was called Max?'

Here things got worse. Ion's story went off into the realms of chance, not something which made me feel any better about it. The illegal travellers had been released from their lorry in a country lane. It had been a long journey and, as Ion explained with some embarrassment, there hadn't been any arrangement for toilet facilities. On being let out in the lane, Ion had promptly scurried behind the nearest hedge. From that side of the hedge, in the darkness of night, he'd heard a car draw up. A door slammed. Someone got out and he and the lorry driver talked in low voices. The lorry driver had called the man 'Max'. Curious, Ion had crept along the hedge to a thin part and peered through. He was just in time to see the man, Max, get back in his car. When he opened the door the inside light came on, and that had been the only glimpse he'd got of Max, but it had been enough.

'I remember him,' he said grimly.

After this, another lorry had arrived and taken them into London itself.

'So,' I said. 'How did you trace Max to the pizzeria?'

'I saw him,' he said simply. 'I saw him in the street and followed him. He went to the restaurant and he went inside. He didn't sit at a table. He went to the office. Afterwards I watched the restaurant. I saw him go there again, also to the office. He must work there, yes?'

Ganesh had always warned me that if I persisted in sticking my nose into other people's business, as he called it, one day I'd find my head wedged in a real hornets' nest.

'There's little sorts of trouble and there's big trouble, Fran,' Ganesh had declared. 'You're quite good at handling little sorts. But you can't handle big trouble. Just remember that and watch out!'

Of course, Ganesh was right. He usually was. I felt a mixture of emotions. On the one hand, I wanted to tell Ganesh *I'd* been right about something shifty going on under cover of the pizzeria. On the other hand, if this had to do with those who traded in human desperation, it was trouble of the big sort. These shadowy figures were organised and ruthless. I didn't know what had happened to Ion's brother, but I had a bad feeling he wasn't going to see him again. Had he asked questions, failed to pay over the latest instalment of the money owed, made trouble? Was his weighted body at the bottom of the Thames? Concreted into the foundations of a building site somewhere? Under the latest motorway extension? Could I say any of this to Ion? Of course I couldn't.

He was watching me now with a sort of trustful hope. My heart sank. It was already too late to pull back.

'I'll see what I can find out,' I said. 'But I have to be careful, you understand that?'

He nodded vigorously. He understood that well enough.

'Also, it may take some time. Wait a while, a week or so, and then come and see me here again. I can't promise anything. I don't know this Max of yours. I'll just keep my eyes and ears open. If I find out anything, I'll tell you when you come next.'

He bounced off the sofa again and grabbed my hands, babbling more thanks.

I saw him out with a feeling of deep depression. Hadn't I got enough trouble? Did I need this? The kid was counting on me. I couldn't let him down. But what could I hope to find out?

'You've done it again, Fran!' I told myself aloud. 'This time you might really be putting your head on the block.'

By the next morning I felt better. I had decided I wouldn't tell Ganesh the whole story – that would be unwise – but I'd tell him part of it, because he might come up with an idea. I'd do as I'd promised. I'd keep my eyes open at the pizzeria. Frankly, I didn't have to do anything but ask a few tactful questions, if that. Ion would be disappointed but heck, what could he expect?

Bright and early, I made my way round to the news-agent's, where they were pleased to see me. Hari wanted to go out for an hour or two. Could I stay and help? Hari would be back well in time for me to get to the pizzeria for the lunchtime shift.

I put Bonnie in the storeroom and took up position behind the counter with Ganesh. For the first hour we were fairly busy but then trade fell off and I went to make the coffee. I came back with the two mugs, handed one to Ganesh, and made my pitch.

'Gan, there's a kid been at the kitchen door at work, asking for someone called Max. We haven't got a Max working there, but he insists we do.'

'So?' Ganesh unwrapped a KitKat and broke it in half. He handed me my piece.

I bit some off and went on indistinctly, 'I saw the kid again last night, on my way home. I, um, got talking to him.'

Ganesh had a beady eye fixed on me. 'Yes?' he said in the kind of voice which meant he knew what sort of thing was coming and that he wouldn't like it.

'The kid's here illegally. He's trying to trace his brother, also here illegally. This Max – he thinks this Max might know something.' I told Ganesh Ion's story of having seen the fat man, Max, in the light from a car's interior, on a dark morning in a country lane. It sounded even thinner, now, telling it to someone else.

I thought Ganesh might blow up, there and then. I wouldn't have blamed him. Instead he said quite calmly, 'Why does he think he'll find Max at the pizzeria if, as you say, he doesn't work there?'

'He's seen him go in, more than once. He says Max didn't sit at a table. He went in the office. But we don't have a Max.'

'All right,' said Ganesh, still with the sort of calm which was beginning to worry me. 'I'll give you three possible explanations. Take your pick but choose carefully because this could turn out to be one of those situations, Fran, in which you just don't want to be! Nor do I,' he added. 'And I generally seem to get dragged in too.'

'Three?' I asked, surprised and ignoring the bit about dragging him in.

'One,' said Ganesh, ticking it off on his index finger, 'the kid's mistaken in the identification. It wasn't Max he saw in the street and followed to the pizzeria. Don't tell me that at night, in that lay-by, he was able to see clearly enough to remember exactly what Max looked like. Ion or whatever he's called was peering through a hedge. When Max got in his car the light would be behind him and he'd be little more than a dark outline. The boy's probably right about the man being very fat, but beyond that he can't swear to anything.'

'What about moonlight? What about the lorry's parking lights? Ion insists—'

'Two.' Ganesh rolled over my protests and moved on to his middle finger. 'And the most likely one. Where is the office door?'

'In the corridor which runs off beside the bar, going towards the back of the building.'

'Quite so. And is it the only door in that corridor?'

'No,' I admitted. 'There's the customers' toilet – Gan!' I gazed at him in admiration and wonder.

'Your young friend is mistaken in believing Max went into the office. He was watching from outside the pizzeria, through the window. The furniture and other customers would mean he had an obscured view. He certainly couldn't see across the dining area and into a shadowy corridor. What is he? Superboy? Max, if Max it was, simply went in the loo. The kid couldn't see what kind of door it was from where he was hanging around, spying. He must have gone in the pizzeria afterwards and looked to see where the door led. He saw two doors, one of them with "office" printed on it. He thought that was the one Max went through. But he'd muddled them up.'

'Gosh, Ganesh, you're really brilliant sometimes, you know that?' I told him. 'I really don't know why I didn't think of that. It's obvious.' Hurriedly I added, 'I mean, obvious, but I didn't think of it, you did. When he comes back, I'll explain it all to him. He'll have to understand he's made a mistake.'

Ganesh looked suitably pleased with my adulation. I was chuffed that I'd decided to ask him. Then I remembered something.

'Gan? You said you had three possible explanations. You've only given me two.'

'Oh, that,' said Ganesh. 'The other explanation is that your young friend is right and that Max is there somewhere, but you know him under a different name.'

Oh, great. Trust Ganesh to find a fly in the ointment.

'I don't see how it can be. The only other person who works there is the old chap who cleans the loos. He's an alcoholic, as thin as a rake. Max is a fat man, remember?'

Ganesh shook his head. 'Forget it. My second idea's the one I'd put my money on. The most obvious explanation is usually the right one, Fran. It's only people like you, who go round looking for trouble, who start fancying mysteries.'

Someone came in the shop and Ganesh went to deal with him. I thought over what he'd said. Yeah, he was probably right. But then I thought of something else. I felt sure Mario knew who Max was, or why should he have lied to me and told me Ion had been asking about a job? Mario had made me a super pizza that night as he'd promised. He really had put everything on it, even the most expensive ingredients. I know when I'm being paid to keep stum.

I needed a lead. The best place to get one would be from someone who had noticed something I'd missed, ideally someone else who'd seen Max so that I knew he wasn't a figment of Ion's imagination. Despite some admitted inconsistencies in Ion's story, I did believe it was basically correct. After all, he had no reason to invent Max, if Max didn't exist. Still, as Ganesh kept insisting, I needed some third-party evidence to back it up. Only then could I hope to put an actual identity to Max.

So, I needed someone who could provide the necessary evidence. I counted out help from Bronia and Po-Ching. They were busy not noticing anything amiss at the pizzeria. Then who else might be around the restaurant, observing and yet not being caught doing it? I thought again of the old derelict who did the cleaning. A mere shadow of a man, someone no one took any notice of, who flitted about in the background. Like the others, I'd ignored him until now. I couldn't remember speaking to him. I didn't even know his name, something I'd have to find out if I was going to approach him.

'I've got to go now, Gan,' I said, sidling out of the door. 'Or I'll be late for work.'

Chapter Five

Things were quiet at the pizzeria. That much I could see from the street, through the window. But what else could I make out?

I stood outside for a moment, putting myself in Ion's shoes. What could *he* have seen from here? Some of the tables, not all. A glimpse of Luigi behind his bar. Just a shadowy gap at the back to the left of the bar, which was the entry to the corridor where Jimmie had his office and the customers had their toilets.

I sighed. It could only mean one thing. Ion must actually have been inside the restaurant. It was the only way he could have got into the corridor and seen that there were two doors. (There were separate male and female toilets, of course, but the two entrances lay behind the single corridor door.)

The thought that Ion might have been on the premises made me very uneasy. How had he managed it? I decided he must have waited until Luigi left the bar. Luigi missed nothing. He wouldn't fail to notice someone like Ion sneaking in and he'd run him out in a flash. No way did Ion look like one of our customers. But without a shadow of a doubt, from here in the street, Ion could have seen neither door in the corridor. Thus, he could not have seen which one Max went through. His conviction that Max had gone into the office was based on guesswork, nothing more. It was a decision made after the event. He saw Max go into the corridor. He *later* saw there were two doors in the corridor. He then fixed it in his own mind that Max had chosen the office door.

There was another thing I'd neglected to ask him about. He'd claimed he saw Max go into the office (something I now knew he could not have done). But he had made no claim he saw Max come *out* again. Why? Because his observation had been interrupted? He'd been obliged to leave, not only the restaurant, but even the pavement outside the restaurant?

Thinking it over, I decided he must have chosen a moment when Luigi took the empty bottles to the yard. He knew he hadn't long before the barman returned. He'd scuttled inside, into the corridor, seen the doors, made his decision and left before Luigi returned. On what, then, had he based his decision? Had he heard voices through the office door? Had it been ajar? Had he checked out the toilets and found them empty? I should have asked all these questions and I hadn't.

I felt a spurt of annoyance, both with myself and with Ion. The kid had spun me an unlikely tale from the beginning. He might have persuaded himself about what he'd seen. To have persuaded me just meant I was gullible. To think I'd promised him I'd try to find out about Max! Could I consider myself released from my promise? Reluctantly, I decided not. I pride myself on keeping my word.

I couldn't hang about out here any longer or I'd be the subject of Luigi's suspicious gaze. I pushed open the door and went in. Luigi was polishing his glasses and listening to the piped Italian music on a continuous discreet loop. It was only in the evenings that Pietro arrived to replace it with his accordion. Luigi greeted me casually. I wasn't his type of woman, thank goodness.

I made my way past the half-open door of Jimmie's office. I could hear the television babbling quietly and, not quite so quietly, Jimmie's rhythmic snores. It was certainly tough being manager of a thriving concern.

I carried on to the employees' cloakroom. The effort expended on the customer restrooms had not been extended to the staff facilities. Our restroom was little more than a large cupboard attached to a minuscule loo. It contained one decrepit armchair, a washbasin in a cheap vanity unit and a row of coat hooks. In there already I found my fellow-worker, Bronia. She was to work the lunchtime shift with me and was also due to return to work the evening one with Po-Ching. Because most of the work was over the lunchtime period and during the evening, the system was that two waitresses were needed at those times, but only one in mid-afternoon. This meant, in effect, we either worked two short shifts or one long double shift each day. As there were three of us, working out the rota was something of a nightmare.

Bronia had put in a lot of hours lately. I did a lightning calculation in my head, feeling a bit guilty. One reason she'd worked so many hours was because I'd been working fewer on account of rehearsal time. I consoled myself with the thought that she was probably glad of the opportunity to do some overtime. I guessed she was saving up money for something. Most of us are.

Bronia returned my greeting with an inarticulate snort, unwilling to be distracted from the job in hand. She was standing before the spotted mirror, putting on her mascara with slow, even strokes. I admire people who can apply make-up successfully. Perhaps I don't have a steady enough hand, but it never looks right on me. If I try to define my eyebrows they end up at different levels so that I look as if I'm permanently puzzled. As for mascara, forget it. Even the waterproof sort seems to roll off my eyelashes and make sinister black splodges under my eyes.

I tucked my blouse into my red skirt, peered past Bronia into the mirror, ran my fingers through my fringe and decided that was the best I could do; then I headed for the dining area. A couple had already come in and taken a corner table. I went to get their order and took it out into the kitchen.

'Hello, Fran,' said Mario. 'Got yourself cleaned up, I see.'

I ignored that. 'Two cannelloni and have we got any garlic bread?'

Mario pulled open the fridge. 'No. If it's quiet later, you'll have to nip out and get some from the supermarket. Ask what's-his-name for some money from the petty cash.'

What's-his-name? Jimmie, our manager, by any chance?

Just after two, I got a moment to take a comfort break and headed for the restroom. Bronia was already there, getting ready to knock off until six. She had hung up her uniform of red skirt and waistcoat very neatly on a hanger. Admittedly it wasn't the sort of thing you wore out in the street, but I brought mine and took it away with me in a carrier bag. She never seemed to take either garment home. I wondered if she ever washed them. Perhaps she was ultra clean and tidy about her work and never got a splash of wine or a smear of grease on them. I noticed she was dressed rather smartly for going off shift, not in her usual jeans. She wore a charcoal-grey business suit and had twisted her hair into a knot on top of her head.

'You're going for another job somewhere, aren't you?' I whispered. I didn't have to be a detective to work that one out. 'You've got an interview. Do they know about it here?'

'I don't care if they know or not,' she said shortly. But she also kept her voice down. 'Yes, I've got an interview. Office receptionist. I really want the job, Fran. I don't like it here.'

It was the first time she'd ever said this openly. I asked her why, wondering if she'd received the same impression that I'd had, that something was going on.

She glanced sideways at me. 'The smell of the pizzas sticks to my clothes, my hair, everything, OK? Luigi pesters me to go out with him, and Mario, he pinches my bum.'

'He's never pinched mine,' I said.

She glanced at my nether regions and grinned. All right, I don't have the greatest figure in the world.

'Tell him you'll sue for sexual harassment,' I said.

She snorted again. 'First I get the new job. Then I ditch this one and tell both those men where they can go.'

She seemed more chatty than usual, probably because she was planning to leave. Even so, I hesitated to use the tenuous camaraderie to ask her any questions outright. I certainly didn't want to give her any information she didn't already have. If she didn't get the new job, she'd be staying on here and she might, in an unguarded moment, let slip to either Luigi or Mario that I was taking an interest in things which didn't have anything to do with me directly. But I can be devious.

'Bronia,' I said. 'Someone gave me a message to give to Max. Do you know where I can find him?' I hoped I sounded vague enough to make my query instantly forgettable.

'Who is he?' asked Bronia as best she could without moving her mouth. She was applying lipstick now.

'Um, I think he comes here sometimes.'

She shrugged. 'I don't know him. Ask Mario or Luigi. They know everyone who comes here often.'

'I don't think he comes often. I'd rather not bother Mario or Luigi. It's sort of a personal thing.'

'It's not a good idea to take messages between lovers!' declared Bronia, getting hold of the wrong end of the stick and turning very dramatic and Slav. I wasn't going to correct her.

'You're probably right,' I agreed.

Bronia dropped her lipstick into her bag and slung it over her shoulder.

'You look good,' I told her. 'Break a leg.'

'What is that?' she frowned.

'It's a theatrical saying. It's bad luck to wish good luck, you know? With the interview.'

'Sure. See you, Fran.'

She strode out briskly. Perhaps, I thought, I ought to take a leaf from her book and go hunting for a different job. Why didn't I, for goodness' sake? It was as if the San

Gennaro held me fast by a magic spell. I knew what it was. I don't like mysteries, right? I don't like to walk away from one before I've solved it. Whatever was going on at the San Gennaro, it wasn't going to beat me.

Trade, as usual, dropped off after two, and was slow enough to give me time to pop out for the garlic bread. I told Luigi he'd have to mind tables for twenty minutes or so while I went.

'I'm barman,' he said sulkily. 'Tell Mario, if he wants bread, he can mind the tables.'

'I don't think I will,' I said. 'George hasn't turned up and Mario's going to have to stay here until this evening. He's a bit annoyed.'

'You want to see annoyed?' demanded Luigi. 'Watch me!'

'I'll ask Jimmie to come out front,' I offered hastily. 'I've got to ask him for the money. Jimmie might be glad of something to do.'

'Send him out for the bread,' said Luigi. 'I don't want him blundering around out here, and he's not coming behind my bar.' He looked quite fierce.

'All right, all right,' I soothed him. 'I'll ask him to nip out and get the bread, but if he refuses, you'll have to mind the tables whether you like it or not. What's to do, anyway? There's not a soul in here.' For good measure, I added, 'And Jimmie's the manager, it's up to him what he does.'

Luigi gave me what could only be described as a very dirty look. 'That Bronia gone?' he demanded.

'Ages ago.'

'They need to hire another girl. I'm going to tell Silvio so. It's stupid, only having one waitress on in the afternoon.'

I left him to his sulks. If he didn't like it, that was his problem.

Jimmie was sitting behind the desk, still asleep with his head on his chest. The portable TV was showing an old black and white cops and gangsters movie. Jimmie looked older in repose. I wondered just how old he was. I'd always assumed him to be in his forties. Looking at him now, I was inclined to add ten years. If he was getting towards the end of his working life, I couldn't blame him for taking the opportunity to earn some good money for once, and not ask questions.

I bent over him and gently shook his arm. 'Jimmie?'

He started and sat up, blinking at me in alarm. Then he relaxed. 'Oh, it's you, hen.'

'Sorry to wake you.' I explained about the bread and that he'd have to cover for me waiting tables while I went for it. 'Unless you want to go for it yourself,' I added.

'Better you go, hen. I'll get the wrong thing. I can take table orders. I've been in this business a few years. I'm used to dealing with customers.' He had cheered up at the prospect. 'How much?' He'd taken out the tin of petty cash.

I told him and decided to take the opportunity to ask one of my discreet questions. I'd worked out what to say.

'Jimmie, do we need anyone else for the early-morning cleaning? Only someone's asked me if there's a cleaning job going here.'

He shook his head. 'No, old Wally can manage it. It's his job. I couldn't take on anyone else. Sorry.'

'That's all right.' I took the money. So the cleaner's name was Wally. Not Max. I hadn't thought it would be. That skinny old fellow could never appear to anyone as fat. But the idea I'd had when talking to Ganesh had been a good one. Cleaners get to hear and see a lot. No one takes any notice of a cleaner. Someone might have talked freely when he shouldn't and Wally could have picked up a word or two. Or perhaps heard a fragment of telephone conversation through a half-open door. As Ganesh had pointed out, the toilets Wally cleaned were right next door to the office.

I'd try and get a word with him tomorrow. That meant I'd have to come in early. I hoped Ion would at least appreciate the trouble I was going to.

Carmel worked in the supermarket (while waiting, like me, for that big acting break). Fortunately they were busy so, although I took her my garlic bread, she had no time to hold me up with chat. She just greeted me and put the bread past the scanner. She looked crosser than usual and her hair was so frizzy it seemed to have exploded.

'Hi, how are you?' she snarled at the customer behind me, as I moved away. The woman looked understandably alarmed. The supermarket might have a policy of greeting customers cheerily, but it needs a cheery personality to make it work.

There wasn't a lot of cheeriness back at the pizzeria. I hadn't been gone long, but even so, by the time I returned, things were falling apart in a big way. Against the pattern, three lots of customers had come in. They must have been waiting round the corner and watched me leave. One couple stared in a bewildered way at the plates of food they'd just been given. A woman was saying in a strong Australian accent, 'This doesn't look like it does back home!' and a fussy-looking man at another table was saying indignantly to his companion, 'It always happens when one's in a hurry!'

In the kitchen some heated argument was going on between Mario and Jimmie. You could hear them from the restaurant. Luigi rolled his eyes at me. 'I told you I didn't want him messing up everything out here.' He jabbed a finger at me to underline that fact that it was all my fault, whatever it was.

'What's to mess up?' I asked. 'He only had to take orders.' I'd only been gone less than half an hour, for goodness' sake.

'He doesn't know his veneziana from his margherita, that's what,' said Luigi. 'Mario's sent out two wrong orders in the time you've been out. That guy is a berk.'

I opened my mouth to ask why, then, Silvio kept him on as manager? But I managed to shut it in time.

In the kitchen, the atmosphere was heavy with culinary tantrums and resentment. Jimmie was red-faced and obstinate; Mario red and furious. Both looked relieved to see me.

'Thank Gawd,' said Mario. 'OK, Jimmie, you can get back to your office.'

Jimmie, our manager, remember, ambled out, muttering to himself. At the door he paused to look back and declare, 'I've been in this business thirty years!' before taking himself off.

'Thirty years? Thirty years selling hot dogs and burnt-up potatoes. He hasn't got a clue. He doesn't even seem to understand what kind of food we do here. Guess what, he's only got some barmy idea we should put his disgusting baked spuds on the menu here,' said Mario to me with a grimace.

'This used to be a baked spud café. It's what he knows,' I explained.

'It ain't a baked spud café now, right? It's gone upmarket.'

That wasn't the impression the unfortunate customers at present in the restaurant would have received.

'Where's that bread?' demanded Mario.

I handed it over and said I was just going to give the change to Jimmie to put back in the cash tin. Mario raised his eyebrows and gave a faint grin.

'Honest, ain't ya?'

'Yes, for what it's worth!' I snapped.

He nodded. 'You're a good girl,' he said suddenly, sounding, I bet, just like his own grandfather. 'You want to find yourself a nice boy, get married, settle down. Raise babies.'

'Thanks,' I said.

'You're a Catholic girl, right, Francesca?'

I explained I was a cradle Catholic, no longer practising. 'I've sort of dropped out,' I said.

He nodded, thoughtful. 'Doesn't matter. Once a Catholic, always a Catholic. It's, like, traditional, ain't it? I mean, you'd raise a Catholic family?'

I was pretty thoughtful, too, as I went to give Jimmie the small change. The last thing, the very last thing I needed, was Mario setting up a date for me with some acne-covered relative of his who couldn't find a girl for himself.

I'd been through all that kind of thing before. Grandma Varady had also been keen on finding suitable boys to match me with. Young as I was at the time, about fourteen or fifteen, it was already clear to me that what Grandma saw as possible life-companion material did not appear to me in that light at all. As soon as Grandma saw a boy with a pale, spotty complexion, spectacles and polished shoes, her face would light up. Usually these youths would harbour ambitions to study hard, please their parents and Get On. They wanted to be doctors, dentists, financial advisers or, in one case, a research chemist. Meantime, I fantasised about rock guitarists and actors.

'Musicians and actors will never be reliable,' declared Grandma. 'Marry one and you will always be poor.'

I wondered sometimes if my mother had thought my father would turn out to be a reliable husband, conscientious breadwinner, and general all-round good guy. Poor Dad, he had been the last of these, the good guy, but he'd failed miserably in the other two respects. He'd start business enterprises with people who invariably let him down. He'd take jobs for which he was unsuited and after a week or two he'd get the sack. He was a charming, kind man, and good-looking. I suppose he had other women friends after my mother left. He never brought them home and let me see them.

He may even have had them before she left, I don't know. But I doubt it. My father's other good quality was that he was loyal. Usually he was loyal to the wrong people, the ones who let him down. When my mother left, she let him down, whatever her reasons, and he was devastated. He'd always felt he could depend on her if on no one else.

So that left Dad, me and Grandma. She was Dad's mother and I used to wonder how he fitted into her idea of suitable. Dad and Grandma did their very best for me. They scrimped the money together to send me to a private school. When I was eventually expelled, I, in my own way, let Dad down. He never said so. Neither of them uttered a word of reproach. I reproached myself and shall do so to my dying day. But that's how it is when you do something to hurt people you love. You can regret it all your life but you rarely get the chance to put it right. I didn't. I hope they know, wherever they are, how much I still love and miss them.

Grandma Varady would have the satisfaction of being right about one thing. I have always been poor.

In the early evening, Bronia came back to begin the late shift. I was now finishing and knocking off. At our changeover in the restroom, I asked her how the interview had gone. She was cautiously optimistic.

'You won't tell anyone here?' she asked. We were conducting the conversation in hushed tones. 'Not that I care. But you know, I might not get the job and then, well, Luigi, he'd keep talking about it, reminding me. He's spiteful.'

'Not a word. Bronia, can we work the same shift pattern tomorrow? I know I'm down for the evening, but I've got a rehearsal.'

She sighed crossly. 'All right, this time only! You've got to do some evening shifts soon, Fran. I know you're in a play. But Po-Ching and me, we got lives, too.'

'I'll do all the evenings we're not rehearsing,' I promised. 'Look, I'm the one losing money by doing so few hours. You and Po-Ching are getting masses of overtime.'

'Money is not everything,' Bronia informed me. 'I like to go clubbing. I like to have boyfriend. How can I have boyfriend if every evening I work, work, work?'

I understood why she was so uptight. It was the tension after the interview, wondering what kind of impression she'd made, if she'd get the job. I managed to calm her down. 'Not much longer, Bronia. Then you'll have your new job and I'll be the one working here non-stop, trying to make up my lost pay.'

We retreated to the schedule pinned up in the kitchen and filled in the agreed shifts.

Mario, watching us, said, 'You girls keep changing the shifts round, I never know who to expect. The only one I can count on is Po-Ching. She never wants time off.'

'We don't have to work all the time like you,' said Bronia, getting stroppy with the prospect of another job in view. 'Just because you never take any time off, except a couple of hours in the afternoon, doesn't mean we don't have things to do.'

'I'm not even going to take my afternoons for a while,' snapped Mario. 'Because George's wife's rung up to say he's in hospital with his diverticulitis. But if you're running a business, that's what happens. I take Sundays, like everyone else.' We were closed on Sundays. 'You got things to do, you should do them Sundays.'

'Fran's in a play,' said Bronia. 'She's got to rehearse.'

'I heard,' he said. 'Over at The Rose. Now, I might take time off for that, go and see it!' He chuckled.

Mario in the audience. Now there was something to look forward to.

One way and another, I was out of sorts when I left the pizzeria, what with everyone getting at me and, apparently, my always being the one in the wrong. I stomped along the pavement homewards, telling myself that the only sensible thing to do was to put the pizzeria and everything (and everyone) connected with it right out of my mind for the rest of the day. Concentrate on the play, that was the thing.

I took out my front-door key as I got to the house and stepped into the gloom of the porch. I was unprepared for the dark shape which had been hunkered down in there and now rose up to give me the fright of my life. I screeched and leapt back.

'Is me, Ion!' the shape said urgently. 'Please, do not shout.'

'Oh, for crying out loud. What had I let myself in for? Ganesh would tell me it was my own fault. Was the kid now going to dog my footsteps?

'You scared me!' I said crossly. My heart was thumping like a drum. 'What are you doing here?'

He was apologetic. 'I wait for you.'

That made me even more cross. I wanted to tell him to clear off, but I suspected he'd hang around. It seemed to be his way. Either he didn't want to talk to you at all, or he decided he did, and dumped all his problems in your lap. I put the key in the lock and let us in. I didn't want other people who had flats in the house finding us talking together. I had an instinct about that.

Ion had lost all his wariness of the house. He shot through the door after me, straight to my own flat door, and hopped about impatiently as I turned the key in the lock. He didn't wait to be asked in. He was in before I was.

I glared at him as I shut the door behind us. This was my home, damn it! He was an intruder. He was a pest. And he was looking at me as if I'd just come down from the sky above in a golden chariot. My displeasure was making no impact on him whatsoever.

'You have news for me?' he asked brightly. 'You find Max?' He stared at me with shining eyes and gave a trustful smile.

'No, I haven't!' I snarled. 'I told you to give me a week. I'm not a miracle-worker. I've got other things to do, as well. Tonight I've got to go through my lines. I'm in a play.'

He frowned. 'But you have been to work today? At that restaurant?'

'Yes, I've been to work but no, I haven't found Max. But I am asking about him. I'll go on asking, but it isn't easy. You must understand, I have to be very careful, Ion.'

Anticipation had seeped out of him. He sighed and perched on my sofa like an abandoned puppy, all soulful eyes and bedraggled hair.

I wanted to repeat to him Ganesh's explanation, and my own sneaking suspicion, that the man he'd seen at the pizzeria hadn't been the man he saw by the lorry. That it was into the toilets and not into the office that his quarry had gone. That he was barking up the wrong tree. I hadn't the heart, cross as I was with him. All he had was hope and, right now, it was invested in me.

I did ask, 'Ion, did you go inside the restaurant? You said you looked through the window. But from outside in the street, you can't see into the corridor. I know, I tried today.'

His gaze shifted. 'Max was there.'

'But you said you saw him go into one of the doors in the corridor. You can't see the doors from outside the restaurant. Were you inside?'

'I saw Max. He went into the office. I do not understand what you ask.'

It occurred to me that Ion's understanding grew less when he didn't want to answer directly.

'If you went into the restaurant, that was foolish,' I said. 'You know the cook has a bad temper. Luigi, the barman, has an even worse one.'

'I saw Max,' he repeated for the umpteenth time. To my horror, his eyes filled with tears. 'You must believe me. You, Fran, you must believe me! Only you believe me about this. Only you help me.'

'I believe you!' I said hastily. 'I just want to be clear in my mind about what you saw.'

He still seemed to expect something more of me there and then. He was sitting on my sofa looking like the orphan of the storm. Perhaps he equated women with mothers and thought I, too, had maternal instincts and would look after him. I don't.

Nevertheless, I made us both beans on toast. It was the best I could do. He ate them with gusto. I wondered again where he lived and what he got to eat normally. But I didn't ask him. It would have been a waste of time.

Instead, I lectured him about not bothering me for at

least a week, and pushed him out into the street. I was a little sharper with him than strictly necessary but I was well aware this was a situation that could get out of hand.

I was beginning to think it had got out of hand already.

Chapter Six

The following morning the front doorbell rang at nine, just as I was crawling out of bed. Bonnie jumped off the duvet and bounced around happily at the thought of a visitor.

When I was sleeping rough in Hari's garage she was very protective of our sleeping place. Now we've got a proper home, she seems to think we have to receive all callers graciously. I know that ideally dogs don't sleep on their owners' beds but Bonnie's first owner had been sleeping rough and she was used to being curled up close beside a human. I did buy a dog basket, cushion and all, and tried to persuade her that it was her very own place. She sat in the middle of it with drooping ears, her little black nose pushed down and her brown button eyes rolled up, the picture of misery and reproach. I tried hardening my heart and insisting that we retired to separate sleeping places at night. She whined softly but insistently in the darkness and, when she thought I was asleep, crept out across the floor and got on the bed with me, positioning herself at the very end where she thought I might not notice her. In the end, I had to give way. Bonnie has found a use for her basket. She takes anything she wants to hide there and stuffs it under the cushion.

I padded to the bay window in the baggy Snoopy T-shirt which served me as a nightgown and peered through the curtains. Bonnie stood on her hind legs and tried to see over the windowsill as well but she was too small. She gave a short frustrated bark. I picked her up and she stared out intently.

A small silver car was parked outside with L-plates tied to the bumpers. As Bonnie and I watched, Susie Duke emerged from the recessed front porch and stared straight at the crack in the curtains. Bonnie whined and wriggled in my arms. Susie waved.

'Let me in, Fran!' she bawled.

I put down Bonnie, dragged on my jeans, and headed barefoot and muttering to the front door, Bonnie pattering excitedly along. I had to let Susie in before she started ringing again or yelling. She would wake up Erwin the drummer. Erwin has the flat across the hall. He plays gigs in the clubs until the early hours of the morning, then staggers home and sleeps till two in the afternoon.

As I mentioned before, the house belongs to a charity. It owns another one further up the road as well. Both are double-fronted Victorian villas, red brick with bay windows at ground and upper floors. Both have basements and recessed porches. They have small tiled areas in front of them and low brick walls. Ours also has a straggly privet hedge. I'm no gardener, but because the privet hedge is in front of my window I went out there and cut it back as soon as I moved in. I thought I did a neat job, but since then I think it's died altogether. There may once have been gates; if so, they've long since disappeared. There are seven flats to each house and the charity allots them at moderate rents to people who have little chance of renting a decent place but who, the charity reckons, are deserving of a fresh start. I got mine because my previous place was flooded out, leaving me to camp in a garage, and my mother died in a hospice run by a sister charity to the housing one.

Erwin says he doesn't know why he got his and puts it down to a brief stint as an altar boy in extreme youth. I gather his career in the church came to an end after some accident with a thurible involving a visiting dignitary.

Because Erwin and I have the two ground-floor flats, we have a sort of passing acquaintance. There are two more flats on the floor above and one in the attic conversion. However, I know little about the tenants. I recognise them as they run down the stairs and through the hall on their way out but that's about it. Occasionally I arrive home and find one of them on the payphone in the hall. We exchange nods. A couple of times I've answered the phone and it's been for one of the upper-floor tenants and I've toiled up there to knock on the door and yell, 'It's for you!' When this happens it's extremely irritating. Because Erwin and I are next to the phone, they seem to think we should automatically be the ones to go and answer it. I grumbled about this to Erwin who advised me to let it ring.

'They get it into their heads you won't answer it, they'll come downstairs.'

'But there's always a chance it might be for me,' I said.

'Get yourself a mobile,' advised Erwin.

The tenants of the two basement flats I hardly ever see. Occasionally I hear feet running down the steps beneath my window and glance out in time to glimpse the top of a head. They are hermetically sealed off down there away from the rest of us. I've lived in a basement flat and I know what it's like.

This may sound unfriendly. But all of us in the house had at one time been homeless. Some tenants, like me, had lived in squats. Some, probably, on the street. If you live like that you learn to respect one another's privacy. Goodness only knows, you don't have anything else. So this wasn't like a student let, all merry japes in term time and parties till dawn. Most of us were in the first proper home we'd had since childhood. For Erwin, who'd spent a large part of his childhood in council care, shuffled between children's homes and various foster parents, it was even more than that. We each guarded our individual pieces of turf jealously.

So when Susie bounced in and headed uninvited for my living room, it niggled. I stood in the doorway and gave her a frosty look. It was a waste of time.

'Hello, Fran,' she chirped. 'You look like you've been dragged through a hedge backwards. Been up all night?'

'No,' I told her. 'But it's a lot, holding down the job and rehearsing for the play, plus doing the odd hour at the newsagent's and everything else.'

'You've got to burn the candle at both ends when you're young,' observed Susie in philosophical mood. ' 'Cos when you get older, you find the flame's gone out and getting it lit again is bloody hard work. Ready for a driving lesson?'

I said quickly that my provisional licence hadn't arrived.

'Yes, it has.' She held up an envelope. 'The postman just gave it to me.'

'He's not supposed to do that!' I said, really cross. 'He's supposed to put in through the door.'

'Yeah, well, I told him I lived here, didn't I? Come on, Fran. Get moving. Strike while the iron's hot.'

What was it with her today? Had she been reading a book of sayings?

'I've got to be at work at eleven thirty,' I said, determined to regain control.

'What are you going to do until then? There's plenty of time. If you don't come driving with me, you'll crawl back into the sack and sleep until the last minute.'

This, of course, was right.

'I'll make us a cup of tea,' she went on, meaning well but once again treading on my domestic sensibilities, 'while you shower and wake yourself up. You'll need your wits about you behind the wheel.'

I was beginning to suspect that having Susie for a friend might be rather tiring. Working with her was looking less and less of an option. Ganesh, I thought, needn't worry on that account. I didn't see myself as an operative of the Duke Detective Agency.

Susie had made for the kitchenette and on her way there glanced through the open door of the shower room. 'Blimey!' She sounded awestruck. 'When are you going to wear that, Fran?'

She meant the Worth costume which was still hanging up in there.

'In the play,' I told her. I reached past her to unhook it and carry it out into the living room. It was dry. I should have ironed it when it was still damp. Now I'd have to dampen it down again. It hadn't washed badly, considering.

Susie was fingering the material wonderingly. 'This is a proper bit of quality schmutter, Fran. Or it was a hundred or more years ago.'

'You think it's the real thing?' I was interested. 'I thought it might be. It came out of the costume box at the pub.'

She was shaking her head. 'This is definitely the real thing. Look, it's got a label.'

I confessed I'd seen the label but didn't know the name.

'Well, I do,' said Susie. 'Charles Worth was really famous in his day and later on his son followed him into the business. Both of them, Charles specially, were top-notch dressmakers in Paris in Victorian times. They clothed the crowned heads of Europe.'

'Only their heads?' I was unable to resist the childish joke.

She did me a favour and ignored it. 'Just think, Fran, this might've been worn by a duchess.'

'Now it's got to be worn by me when I've ironed it,' I told her.

She was horrified. 'You iron it? Not likely. I'll take it home and press it properly for you. You'll ruin it. I used to work in the rag trade. I know what I'm doing.' She fingered the bodice. 'Pity someone took the whalebones out. See, these little channels in the cloth, that's where they went.' She moved on to the leg-of-mutton sleeves. 'You've got to stuff these with tissue paper before you put an iron on them.'

I was glad she was offering to do it and not sorry the whalebones had disappeared. She was still examining it when I came out of the shower.

'Look at the cut of the skirt, Fran. Each panel is cut on

the bias and each one is perfect. It's a lovely bit of tailoring. Look at the seams, all hand-finished.'

'Susie,' I begged. 'If we're going to have this driving lesson, let's do it. You can give the dressmaking class to someone else.'

It was only when I got in the car I remembered I had intended to go over to the pizzeria early to talk to Wally. Now it would have to be another day. It wasn't Susie's fault. I'd forgotten anyway. I don't usually forget my plans. I decided this was psychological – I was blocking out Ion and his hunt for Max. I really didn't want anything to do with it. Susie's arrival gave me a convenient excuse to put off my enquiries.

Susie pressed a small green book in my hand. 'This is the *Highway Code*. You've got to learn it.'

I riffled through it. 'What, all of it?'

'All of it. You don't know what the examiner will ask you.'

'I've got to learn lines for the play. I can't learn both,' I protested.

'Of course you can,' she said serenely.

Susie drove us back to the block of flats where she lives. It was quiet there in the mornings, she explained. It certainly wasn't a spot encouraging anyone to linger. The wind blew sharply around corners and along balconies, rustling the litter heaps. Weak sun glinted on abandoned needles. The local villains and other nightbirds were sleeping in late. Those who had legit jobs to go to had gone to them. The elderly were barricaded behind reinforced doors staring blankly at their television sets. Any other inhabitants were already banging on the counters at the local DSS office, arguing the toss about the inadequacy of their benefit giros. An average morning, in fact.

In case you're wondering, people don't choose to live on these so-called sink estates. They get dumped there. Some try to make things better, but generally after a while the struggle gets too much. They give up and do like everyone else.

I, with Susie beside me, drove round and round the block, troubling no one and with no one troubling me. The problems began when I stopped crawling along the roads and began to practise three-point turns on the weed- and lager-can-strewn patch of crumbling tarmac in the front of the garages. There weren't many lock-ups, nowhere near enough for demand, and Susie was lucky to have one. All the doors were sprayed with graffiti and heavily chained and padlocked. Susie was probably the only resident who kept a car in hers.

In no time at all, a gang of mean-looking kids materialised from goodness knows where. They gathered in a formidable mini-mob to watch me critically and shout a mix of advice and abuse.

The youngest was barely eleven and the oldest perhaps fifteen. I didn't doubt they were all expert at hot-wiring stolen cars and joy-driving them at furious speeds around the neighbourhood. My slow, cautious manoeuvres were contrary to everything they believed motoring should be.

'Go on, darling, put your foot down, you're not driving a hearse!' and 'Oy, granny, where'd you leave yer invalid car?' These were among the kinder comments.

'Darren Murphy, you mind your mouth!' yelled Susie at one of them. To me, she advised, 'Ignore them.'

'Oughtn't they to be at school or somewhere?' I asked.

'Kids round here don't go to school much.'

'Doesn't the school come looking for them?' I wondered naively.

'Would you, if you had had to teach them?' was Susie's reply.

I took the point.

The crowd was getting restless. They'd run out of verbal weapons and had begun to resort to the physical aggro natural to them. They danced in front of the car, making obscene gestures through the windscreen. They ran alongside and banged on the windows. They tried to open the doors but we'd locked them. So they pelted us with the empty lager cans so conveniently to hand.

'I've had this,' I told Susie. 'In a minute I'm going to run over one of them. Not on purpose, much as I'd like to, but accidentally. If I do, I'll get the blame.'

She conceded I was probably right. 'OK, I don't want the car damaged. We've done enough for one day. I'll put the car away and we can go over to the flat and have a coffee.'

I glanced at my watch and saw to my dismay that I had to be at work in three-quarters of an hour. Time flies when you're having fun. I explained this to Susie, who drove me home to pick up my uniform and then on to the pizzeria.

'You did really well,' she said as we parted. 'But I'll find us somewhere else for you to practise, Fran, somewhere really quiet. Oh, I'll press the costume and get it back to you.'

'Who's that?' asked Luigi with interest when I walked in. He'd been watching through the window, attracted by the unusual sight of me getting out of a car. 'She's a bit of all right.'

I told him, just a friend.

'I didn't know you had any friends who didn't go in for big boots and body-piercing,' he quipped. 'Has she got a husband or boyfriend or anything?'

'Her husband died and I don't know about boyfriends.' I toyed with the idea of telling him about the Duke Detective Agency but decided that might be unwise. I hoped he didn't find out.

We were busy and I worked through until six thirty. Nobody had time for any conversation. Mario sweated over his pizzas and snapped at anyone who put a head in his kitchen. Luigi was dashing up and down the cellar steps with wine bottles as if on speed. I wondered if he was on commission from Silvio when he sold the more expensive wines. He was certainly putting himself out persuading customers to buy them. I didn't get a chance to ask Bronia if she'd heard about the job.

That evening we had a rehearsal. It went as well as could be expected. I was tired, what with getting up early, the driving lesson and working flat out at the San Gennaro. I was sure I had bags under my eyes and it was an effort to summon up energy to give my part any zip. Ganesh also looked as if he'd rather sneak off backstage and have forty winks. Another member of our troupe, Mick, was in an even worse state. He had come down with a heavy cold.

Between blowing his nose and sneezing, he explained to us in detail about his chronic sinus problems, information we were none of us very keen to have. We were only interested in one thing, voiced by Marty, our director.

'But you can still act, right?'

'Of course I cad,' declared Mick, showing a confidence none of us felt about his abilities.

Mick wasn't the most subtle actor at best, relying on enthusiasm rather than stagecraft. In his role as the country doctor who brings news of dark doings at Baskerville Hall to Holmes at the beginning of the play, he strode downstage and uttered probably the most famous line in detective fiction.

'Mr Hobes! Dey were de fodprids of a gigaddig howd!'

Owen gave a muffled snort, Nigel uttered a single very rude word. Ganesh folded his arms and glowered.

'Mick,' whispered Marty, 'do you think you could try that again?'

Mick obliged. This time Carmel giggled nervously.

'Mr Holmes, they were the footprints of a gigantic hound!' enunciated Marty clearly by way of demonstration.

'Thad's wad I said,' returned Mick.

Marty passed a hand over his brow. 'Er, how long do these colds of yours generally last?'

'Nod log,' said Mick confidently. 'I god sub catarrh pastilles.'

'Swallow the lot,' advised Carmel. 'And don't breathe over me!'

We were all for that. Whenever Mick, in any of his various supporting roles, appeared on stage, the rest of the cast left a kind of firebreak of empty space round him.

On the plus side, Freddy had agreed to provide paint for the new backdrop so Nigel and Owen could start work. We would all have to pitch in as scene-shifters when required. Also, Marty had got hold of a tape recording of Irish Davey's dog howling. It sounded really good and creepy, echoing off stage and played at full force. It would make the audience sit up. It even caught the ear of Digger out in the yard. He began barking furiously until Freddy shouted, 'Shaddup!'

'I suppose,' said Ganesh tentatively on the way home, 'there's no way I can get out of this? Only, you know, Hari's expecting so much. Usha and Jay are going to be at the play, too, and Mum and Dad are coming from High Wycombe. Two of my aunts talk about nothing else. My mate, Dilip, is bringing his wife and kids—'

'We're all in the same boat, Gan!' I interrupted. I was too tired to be bothered with his problems. I had my own. 'The rest of us will just have to be so good no one pays any attention to Mick and his wretched blocked sinuses. The howling dog will be great. Marty's finished all the family portraits for Baskerville Hall. He's working so hard, Gan. We can't let him down.'

'I shouldn't let you talk me into things,' moaned Ganesh, adding fiercely, 'I had my hair cut for this!'

So it was my fault, as usual. I sympathised about his hair, which had been long and I'd thought looked very nice. For the sake of historical accuracy he'd had it chopped off short. It made him look different.

'You don't want to have sacrificed your hair for nothing,' I told him. 'You've got to stick with the play. It's called suffering for your art,' I added for good measure.

'No, I'm not!' he snarled. 'I'm suffering for yours!'

Far from our dramatic effort building *esprit de corps*, it seemed likely to turn us all into mortal enemies. Even my friendship with Ganesh was under strain.

'Cheer up, Gan,' I urged as we parted.

He muttered darkly and indistinguishably and strode off homewards, his hands in his blouson pockets and his shoulders hunched.

As happens when I'm very tired, I found, on going to bed, that I'd somehow gone past the moment when I could fall easily and dreamlessly asleep. My body was weary but my brain was wound up like a clock spring. After tossing and turning in vain, I got up, made some tea and switched on my telly. The temperature in the flat had dropped. I went back to the bedroom, dragged the duvet from the bed, dislodging an aggrieved Bonnie, and took it back to the sofa where I rolled myself in it and, mug of tea in hand, settled down for an hour's viewing.

The television is a good set, much better than the one I used to have. That one had an ongoing problem with the horizontal hold, guaranteed to drive you out of your skull. This new one (new to me, anyway) was a present from Ganesh's sister, Usha, and her husband Jay. Jay's an accountant and doing well. 'Upwards and onwards' seems to be their motto. The better they do, the more depressed Ganesh gets. Jay and Usha have bought themselves a twenty-first-century wide-screen telly like something designed by NASA. They've signed up to satellite television. Their excuse is that now Usha's pregnant, she's going to be watching more telly. I didn't quite follow the argument, but as they generously gave me their old telly, I went along with it. It was up to them if they wanted to turn into a couple of couch potatoes.

That night I watched an old, luridly coloured sci-fi film. It didn't take my mind off my problems. Dealing with aliens seemed relatively straightforward compared with dealing with missing illegal immigrants, dodgy restaurant owners, learning to drive surrounded by a mob of delinquents and appearing in a jinxed dramatic production. Bonnie had followed me into the living room, scrambled on to the sofa and reclaimed a part of the duvet. She snored beside me, lying on her back with four paws in the air. No problems for her.

After the sci-fi film they showed a football match taking place in some far-flung corner of the world. That sent even me off to sleep.

With all this on my mind, it was a wonder I remembered about Wally. In the morning, stiff in every joint from my night on the sofa, I got to the pizzeria early enough to catch the old chap after he'd finished his cleaning stint. I found him down in the cellar where he kept his brooms and pails.

The cellar was accessed through a hole in the floor at the far end of the corridor where the office and customer toilets were located. Once, I suppose, there had been a trapdoor, but it had been removed. The resultant opening was protected on three sides by a railing so you didn't pitch down there and break your neck. On the fourth side it was open, allowing you to descend the uneven, ill-lit stairs and risk life and limb that way.

I negotiated my way downwards. The cellar was quite big and very gloomy. Light was supplied by a single bulb dangling amid cobwebs from the ceiling and what little daylight filtered in through a grille at pavement level. The furthest corners were dark mysterious places into which I'd no intention of venturing. I didn't know what lived down there. The Giant Rat of Sumatra for all I knew.

Supplies which didn't require refrigeration were stored there, near the staircase: tottering towers of tinned tomato purée, jars of olives, green and black, anchovies, cans of olive oil. In addition, this was Luigi's wine cellar. Besides stacked cases, along one wall bottle racks had been installed. As I reached the foot of the stairs something moved a few feet away from me, just by the wine racks. I jumped, heart in mouth, before I distinguished a shapeless form and made it out to be that of Wally. He was just slipping a nicked bottle of red into his dirty old raincoat. It looked like one of our more expensive ones. He stared aggressively at me, wondering if I'd noticed.

'Hello, Wally,' I began, nice and polite. 'I just came down here for—' I looked round quickly. 'For some anchovies.'

'I hate them things,' said Wally.

'They're traditional on the pizzas,' I explained.

'I hate them things and all,' he mumbled. 'I don't know why Jimmie took up with this lot.'

'The customers like them.'

'Plonkers,' said Wally.

I persevered. 'The pizzas are selling really well and you know Jimmie wasn't doing brilliantly with the baked spud business.'

'You know where you are with a baked spud,' maintained Wally.

We had exhausted the topic of gourmet cooking. Wally sucked his yellow teeth and continued to stare at me. I took a pound coin from my pocket and held it out.

'It was a tip from a customer,' I explained. 'Share and share alike.'

Wally's purple-veined hand snaked out and the coin disappeared into his pocket where it chinked against the bottle of red. Wally began drifting away towards the far side of the cellar where he kept the tools of his trade. I followed him.

'Jimmie's been a good friend to you, Wally,' I reminded him. 'It's only because of him you've still got a job here. Like me, I've got a job here because of Jimmie. We both owe him. I don't want to see him get into any trouble. I'm sure you don't, either.'

Wally rasped a discoloured thumbnail across the stubble on his chin. He said nothing but he was listening.

I plunged on. 'Wally, have you ever heard anyone here call anyone else here "Max"? Has anyone called Max ever been here to your knowledge?'

'I don't know nothing,' said Wally. 'I don't know nothing about any Max. I clean the lavatories and the floors in the restaurant and kitchen. That Mario watches me like a perishing hawk when I'm in his kitchen. Like he thinks I'm going to nick something.'

I didn't mention the bottle of red weighing down his pocket.

'Cooks are fussy about their kitchens,' I said. 'I know Mario likes to clean his own work surfaces.'

Wally scowled. 'He says I ain't hygienic. Cheek. I was hygienic enough when it was a baked spud caff. I used to do the washing-up then. Jimmie always gave me a hot spud to take home for my supper.' Then, presumably in case I'd seen him take the wine and to make it clear to me that he wasn't doing the business any great harm by his pilfering, he went on fiercely, 'I can't stand their poncey wine, either. I've drunk better stuff outa them cheap plastic bottles.'

He picked up a wet mop and pressed it against a kind of sieve fixed across half the galvanised pail it had been resting in. Water trickled out and rattled on the bottom. Wally turned the mophead upwards and propped it against the wall. I wondered vaguely where his home might be. At best a hostel. More likely under a railway arch. I racked my brains for another line of questioning.

'Have you ever seen a young kid hanging round here? About sixteen, black hair, large eyes, pointed chin. He's foreign, doesn't speak much English.'

It was a shot in the dark but to my surprise, Wally nodded. 'Oh, 'im, yus, I seen 'im. I found 'im down here in the cellar one time.'

That really rocked me. I had worked out that Ion must have sneaked into the premises, but I'd never in my wildest imaginings thought he'd had the nerve to come down to the cellar. The possibility of being trapped underground should have kept him away. What had he thought he'd find here? Perhaps, I reasoned, he'd nearly been caught upstairs, been unable to get to the street entrance, and bolted down the stairs to hide. Wally might be able to supply the answer to that.

'What was he doing down here, Wally? Did he tell you?'

'Snooping,' said Wally, confirming my worst fears. 'He didn't have to tell me, I could see what he was doing. He wasn't pinching anything, just poking about in the corners. I told him to clear off.' He fixed his bleary gaze on me. 'Has he come back? If he has, he's stupid.'

Since Wally had met Ion, I felt that giving him a little more information wouldn't hurt and might encourage the cleaner to keep his eyes and ears open.

'He's worried, Wally. He's looking for his brother. If you see him here again, tell me. But don't tell anyone else. If you hear the name "Max" tell me about that, too.'

'I'm going home now,' said Wally, shuffling past me. He paused and looked back. 'You don't want nothing to do with that young boy,' he said. 'He's got trouble written all over 'im. People what go looking for things generally find more than they bargained for. 'Ow old did you reckon that kid is?'

I told him, I thought about sixteen.

'He won't see seventeen,' said Wally. 'Not the way he's going on.'

With that, he lurched across the cellar and climbed the rickety stairs. I watched him disappear as he reached the top, first his head, then his raincoat and finally his dirty trainers.

I stood there, rooted to the spot by his words. He wasn't the Delphic oracle, but his prophecy had a chilling conviction to it. I shook myself and told myself to buck up, it was being down in the grim cellar which made me feel this way and gave me a chill along my spine. I set off towards the stairs but before I reached them, footsteps clattered on them and Luigi came running down.

He stopped a few feet from me, looking angry, and asked, 'What are you doing down here?'

I held up my tin of anchovies. I didn't like his tone and I didn't see why I owed him an explanation.

'I saw you come down here,' he said. 'How long does it take you to find one tin?'

'Not long,' I told him. 'I was just having a chat with Wally about the old days when this was the Hot Spud Café.'

Luigi snorted. 'That old soak. Was he pinching bottles of wine again?'

'Does he?' I asked innocently.

'Yes, he bloody does.' Luigi's eyes glittered at me. 'I keep telling Jimmie to give him the sack.'

'That's up to Jimmie!' I snapped. I'd had enough. 'Wally does his job. Why don't you do yours?'

He moved a step forward but I stood my ground. 'Meaning?' he asked nastily.

'Meaning, it's no business of yours why I'm down here. You're the barman. I'm a waitress. I do my job. You do yours.'

'Yeah, well, I suggest you go upstairs and do your job, then. Customers are starting to come in. What are they supposed to do? Take their own orders to the kitchen?'

'Look,' I said. 'I don't know what's given you a sore head, but don't take it out on me, right?'

He gave a snort and moved away towards the racks of more expensive wines against the far wall. He stood in front of them, running his eye along them. He found a gap and pointed accusingly.

'The old bugger has had a bottle, see! There wasn't a space there. I restocked the racks last night.'

'I didn't see him take one!' I retorted. It was true, as far as it went. I hadn't seen Wally take the bottle. I'd seen him slip it in his pocket, but I know how to split hairs when accusations are flying around.

Luigi swung round and stared thoughtfully at me.

'I haven't got your rotten wine!' I told him. 'Where would I put it in this uniform?'

An unpleasant smile tugged at the corner of his mouth. He was a good-looking bloke and he knew it. I waited for him to make some remark about my outfit and me in it. Instead, he said, 'We don't sell rotten wine, right?'

He spoke quietly. There was something in his tone which really made me tense up and measure the distance between me and the stairs.

'If you say so,' I said. 'I don't know anything about wine.'

'We keep a good cellar for a small restaurant.'

I thought we kept it *in* a cellar, which wasn't quite the same thing, but I wasn't going to say so.

He swung back to the racks against the wall and pulled out a bottle. 'See this?' He jabbed a finger at the label, which I couldn't see properly anyway. 'This is the same as you get in the very best restaurants!'

'All right, all right!' I said. 'Who's arguing? Now, if you don't mind, Mario will be waiting for the anchovies.'

I walked past him to the stairs. As I reached the foot of them, I heard his voice behind me.

'I'll catch that old rogue pinching a bottle one of these days, see if I don't. You tell him, the next time you fancy coming down here and having a little chat with him, that I'm on to him.'

'Tell him yourself!' I flung back at him and scuttled up the stairs before he could reply.

He was right and there were customers in the restaurant. I put the tin of anchovies in my pocket and went to take their orders. But my mind wasn't on that. Why had it worried Luigi that I'd lingered down in the cellar? What was down there that he didn't want me to see?

Chapter Seven

Ion occupied my mind so much during the rest of my working day that Mario noticed my lack of concentration and bawled me out about it.

'Buck up, Fran! I know you've been rehearsing that masterpiece you're appearing in, but this isn't the perishing green room. Get a move on and keep your mind on what you're doing.'

I apologised humbly and said I'd been running through my lines in my head.

'Run the customers' orders through your head,' snapped Mario. 'And while you're about it, take this along to the office.'

He handed me a tray. It was very nicely set out with two cups of coffee, sugar and a little plate of Amaretti biscuits. Two cups? Jimmie had company.

My hands shook and the coffee cups rattled in their saucers. Could it be that Jimmie's visitor was the elusive Max?

I scurried along to the office. The door was closed but I could hear the soft murmur of voices from behind it. I tapped and Jimmie called for me to come in.

The company was Silvio, Jimmie's so-called partner in

the business and the driving force behind it. I might have guessed. It had been an irrational hope that Max would just walk in and let me see him, settling the question of his identity once and for all. Things are never that easy. Still, I felt a pang of disappointment. It was followed by curiosity and a faint apprehension. Silvio didn't drop in all that often but, when he did, everyone got edgy, even Mario.

'That's right, hen,' said Jimmie to me. Perhaps he was wondering why I was standing there, tray in hands, gawping at Silvio. 'Just put it down on the desk.'

I hastened to do so. Pull yourself together, Fran! I admonished myself. Jimmie winked at me as I set the coffee on the desk, just to let me know he was only putting on the grand manner while Silvio was there.

'Ah, Francesca,' said Silvio, leaning back in his chair and steepling his soft white fingers with their manicured nails. 'I hear from Jimmie here that you are to appear in a play.'

'Yes, sir,' I said meekly, like the parlourmaid in an Agatha Christie novel. Jimmie wasn't the only one to put on a false manner when Silvio was around. From the corner of my eye I saw my old pal's eyebrows twitch.

But it went down well with Silvio who nodded approvingly. 'Excellent, excellent,' he said. 'I am very pleased to hear about it. Jimmie tells me the landlord of The Rose, who is supporting your drama company, has suggested to him that we here at the San Gennaro sponsor the programme for the evening.'

'He did ask,' said Jimmie apologetically. 'And I said we would. It won't cost much, will it?'

Silvio gestured away the idea of the cost. 'I think we can do that. If you will let Jimmie have a list of the cast, he can print off some programmes with a small advertisement for the pizzeria.'

Jimmie, though cheering up at being told he'd not done the wrong thing in giving Freddy an assurance about the programmes, cast a hunted look at the computer. It sat in one corner of the room on its own little table. I fancied it had that air of superiority about it which machines adopt in the presence of mere bumbling humans.

Clearly, it affected Jimmie the same way. He turned a look of anguish on me. Poor guy, he had no more idea how to operate the computer than he'd have had of flying a jumbo jet.

It was the first I'd heard of Freddy arranging sponsorship for the programmes. To be honest, I'd given no thought to the programmes at all. But Freddy, an old hand at putting on these theatrical evenings, had naturally got all that organised. True to type, Freddy was getting someone else to do the job.

But not me! I returned Jimmie's agonised look with one nearly as panicky. They weren't hoping I was going to run off these programmes, were they? I'd only the vaguest knowledge of how to use a computer, hardly better off than Jimmie in that respect. I could call up the Internet and that was it.

Silvio intercepted our expressions of despair and added kindly, 'Luigi, the barman, he understands computers. He'll do it for you.'

'Right you are,' said Jimmie, hugely relieved. 'Aye, great idea.'

I was relieved too, but the feeling didn't last long.

Silvio had turned his look of gracious beneficence on me. 'And I, Francesca, shall attend the performance, naturally.'

'I'll be there too,' chimed in Jimmie, not to be outdone in staff support now that he knew he hadn't to touch the computer.

Oh cripes. Was there anyone who wasn't coming? Freddy's functions room would be crammed with eager punters.

'I have been keeping an eye on you, Francesca,' Silvio went on. 'Mario says you are a good worker. I am going to open another pizzeria, a larger one. There will be a vacancy for an assistant manageress. I think you would be very suitable.'

He beamed at me. Probably this was a cue for me to kiss his hand and thank him profusely. But my knees were like jelly. Here I was regretting I'd taken the job at the San Gennaro and there sat Silvio, dapper, suave and steely-eyed, proposing a career in catering for me. I suspected it was an offer I couldn't refuse. But I tried.

'I haven't got enough experience.'

Silvio's forehead puckered briefly before he made another elegant gesture. 'You're a smart girl. You'll learn.'

I was dismissed. I went, wondering exactly what he meant by his last words.

Friday was pay day. The squat, inscrutable accountant showed up and handed out our pay packets. 'Sign here!' was all he ever said. Getting paid at the end of every week was still a novelty for me and although I had my doubts about the job, getting that little brown envelope of cash was nice.

I had a new sense of determination today. Whatever I felt about Ion's story – and I still fluctuated between believing him and finding his story incredible – I had to do something about Ion himself. Above all, I had somehow to get it into his head that he must give up hanging round the pizzeria in his quest for his brother. Under no circumstances should he enter the premises again and even waiting outside in the hope of seeing Max was a bad idea.

I was aware this would be no easy thing to do. Ion was obsessed with the mysterious Max and the connection he claimed the man had with the San Gennaro. He was clinging to it as the only lead he'd got. In arguing against it, I would be like someone prising a drowning man's fingers from the edge of a liferaft. But the thought of Ion creeping down to the cellar, where he could so easily have been trapped and met someone more dangerous than Wally, had made up my mind. Besides which, I'd failed to find any trace of 'Max' and for the moment, anyway, really didn't see what else I could do.

The feeling of unease I'd had from the beginning about the pizzeria itself, however, persisted. The cellar, in particular, haunted my mind. I couldn't forget how angry Luigi had been at my staying down there for more than a few minutes. That he'd been angry with Wally I could understand. He suspected, accurately, that Wally was stealing. But I was sure he didn't think I was. So what could his objection to my looking around down there possibly be? There was only one way to find out. I knew I had to get down there again, and search undisturbed, but how and when? The answer came to me as my fingers closed on my pay packet. There was a way. But it would have to wait.

There was no rehearsal that evening. We were all supposed to be making sure we knew our lines. We had a week to go until curtain up. Between now and then, there was still a lot of work to do before the dress rehearsal and, after that, opening night! (One and only night, actually.)

I was getting a buzz of excitement at the thought of being up there on the stage. I was reasonably sure of my part. Ganesh was pretty good. Carmel was apt to forget the exact wording of hers and improvise, which threw everyone out, especially Nigel. If he wasn't fed the line he was expecting, he could dry up completely and stare reproachfully at the offender. As he was playing Holmes and so much depended on him, this could be tricky. Irish Davey hadn't brought his dog over to see us again so far. It had demonstrated it could do the one thing required of it, run from one set of wings to the other on cue, and that was good enough. Marty seemed happy and Ganesh was overjoyed at dogless gatherings. The dog would, Irish promised, be there for the dress rehearsal. Meantime, he'd keep it practising.

This gave me an evening to devote to tracking down Ion. The task wouldn't be easy. I didn't know where he lived or where he worked. Finding people in London is akin to searching for needles in haystacks if you've no precise location at which you know they'll turn up. I could wait for him to come to my place, as arranged, to learn how I'd got on with my enquiries. But I'd stressed to him he wasn't to contact me for a week and this time he'd seemed to understand.

In the meantime, anything could happen. Ion might get impatient. He could start snooping round again on his own account and get himself in real trouble at the pizzeria. Luigi didn't miss much. If Ion turned up again, hanging about outside, Luigi would probably notice he'd been there before. And if Ion, heaven forbid, ventured into the cellar again . . . My blood ran cold at the very idea.

Then I remembered the time I'd found Ion by the fast-food outlet in Camden High Street. I decided wherever it was he lived had to be in that area. We all tend to be creatures of habit and to mark out a familiar territory. If I went to the same place at the same time, I might just bump into him.

It was drizzling with rain when I reached the spot that evening after leaving work, and getting late. I like Camden High Street. It has an endearingly crazy quality about it and is full of eccentric little businesses selling everything imaginable. Do you want any kind of garment made in leather? You'll find it on sale there. Tattoo parlours flourish along its length. There's a touch of the fairground about it with its garish displays and the motley crowd which passes up and down it and frequents its packed and busy street markets. Now, in late evening, long after dark, there was only emptiness where earlier the markets buzzed with life. The shops were closed, but somehow this made their curious upper-floor adornments more obvious. In a way which is almost medieval many business have, fixed to the street frontage, monster representations of the goods they sell or the world they represent. You wander along beneath a giant pair of jeans or a figure of Elvis as if caught up in a wild carnival. Tonight, though there were fewer people around, the pubs and eateries were doing good business. The fast-food outlet, where I'd once found Ion, smelled of hot grease and onions. It was presided over by a ferret-faced bloke who looked as if he'd been steeped in his own cooking oil.

I bought the least greasy thing available, a hot dog, and said nonchalantly, 'I arranged to meet a friend here. His name is Ion. You haven't seen him, have you? He's a thin kid with big eyes, about sixteen.'

Ferret-face just stared at me; he didn't even try to give me an answer, not even 'no'. I wasn't really surprised. I hadn't expected anything but it had been worth trying.

I wandered off up the street eating the hot dog. It wasn't too bad, even if the bread was doughy. I kept my eyes peeled and scanned the damp pavements for Ion. I checked the pubs on my way, just in case, but as I anticipated he wasn't in any of them. I doubted he had the money to spend on a night out and he was rather obviously under-age to buy alcohol.

I walked right up to the Chalk Farm Road at one end of the High Street and then turned round and began to stroll back. By the Roundhouse I saw a familiar figure but not the one I was seeking. It was Marty, standing by the old engine-shed-turned-theatre gazing up at it wistfully.

'Hi, Marty,' I greeted him. 'Who knows, you'll have a play running there one day.'

'They're going to do Shakespeare here, did you know that?' he returned. 'Think of all the great playwrights of the past and then think of the demand for their work and the number of theatres and touring companies. It must have been great when the theatre was the common man's entertainment. Anyone who wrote a half-decent play was in with a chance.'

'There's television,' I said. 'They always want scripts.'

'I keep sending them in,' he said mournfully. He turned his bespectacled gaze on me and added in a minatory fashion, 'Do you know your lines?'

'I know my lines, Marty. I might dry on the night, but I know them now.'

He didn't take this as a joke. However, as I set off again, he fell into step beside me. 'What are you doing out here, Fran? Going somewhere?'

'No,' I told him. 'Looking for someone.' I hesitated. 'It's a kid I've met a couple of times. He hangs around this part of the world sometimes. He's about sixteen, thin, wears clothes too big for him. He's got large dark eyes and looks like something the cat dragged in.'

'Lots of kids in London look like that,' said Marty.

'Yes, you're right. I'm wasting my time.'

I had finished the hot dog and was getting wet. What was I doing, hanging about here on a fool's errand? I turned up the collar of my denim jacket. Trickles of water still found their way inside.

Marty seemed content to trail along beside me. Perhaps he was at a loose end or perhaps nerves about the play had overtaken him and he felt the need to be out and walking. We were nearing Camden Town Tube station when I decided to call it a day and go home. I still had to walk Bonnie before turning in for the night. Erwin might have taken her out in the afternoon. He had my key so he could let her out if I wasn't there. He sometimes took her down to the corner shop with him though she objected loudly to being tied up outside.

At that moment, as I was thinking of all this, I saw Ion. He was going into the Tube station. I exclaimed, 'Sorry, Marty, got to dash! There he is! See you,' and I was off in pursuit.

The Tube station is situated where Kentish Town Road and Camden High Street meet in a V-shape. The station is right at the point of the V. It can be entered from either side and, as a result, pedestrians wanting to go from one street to the other simply cut through.

This, I realised, when I dashed into the station after Ion, complicated things. I didn't know whether he intended taking the Tube, or was just on his way to Kentish Town Road. I ran out of the exit into the other road and scanned the street in vain. I dodged back inside again. The few seconds I'd taken might have been enough to result in my losing Ion altogether.

But there's another thing about the Tube station at Camden Town. It's one of the few which doesn't use automatic barriers. You still have to show your ticket to a uniformed figure sitting in a wooden hut. This slows things up when there's a crowd and, as it happened, things were busy. A train must just have come in because people were pouring off the escalators and making for the exit. Those wanting to go in the other direction struggled against the flow and among them I glimpsed Ion again. He was pushing his way past the checker, holding up his ticket.

He was definitely going to take the escalator down to the trains. But I hadn't a ticket and couldn't follow! I whirled round looking for somewhere to buy one. As I did, a man came hurrying in from the Kentish Town Road entry. He pushed past me, a big bloke wearing a shower-proof jacket with a hood pulled up against the rain. As I dodged back out of the way I caught a faint whiff of some odour on his clothing, and then he was gone, past the transport employee in his wooden hut and down the escalator to the trains.

I scurried over to the ticket-office window and bought the cheapest ticket. But by the time I stepped on to the escalator at the top, Ion was no longer travelling on it. I just saw the tall man in the hooded jacket jump off at the bottom. Of Ion there was no sign.

I ran down it and leapt off but Ion had long disappeared and I didn't know in which direction he was travelling. At Camden Town he had a choice. Four branches of the Northern line meet there. Headed north, one goes to Edgware and the other towards Finchley Central and beyond. Headed south, the lines both go to Morden but one goes via Charing Cross and the other meanders round via Moorgate. Ion could already be on a train and making for almost anywhere. The delay while I bought my ticket was enough to have allowed a train to pass through and carry him away. I decided to try the southbound line as it was most likely he was heading into central London. The platform for the line via Charing Cross was crowded. No train had gone through there for a while and one must be due at any minute. If I was lucky, Ion was somewhere in the crowd waiting along the platform.

I'm not one of those people who finds the underground system claustrophobic. But the stale air and the press of bodies beneath the blue-and-cream-tiled vault made me feel uneasy. The quicker I found Ion and got us both out of here, the better.

Starting at one end I began to work my way through the waiting throng of passengers. It was difficult. New people were joining those already there all the time. Perhaps there had been a delay because it seemed to me there were more people than there should have been at this hour of the day. I slipped and wriggled between the packed bodies, apologising when I got dirty looks. I'd nearly reached the end of the platform without sighting my quarry when a blast of warm air from the dark mouth of the rail tunnel struck my face. A train was coming. I had seconds to find Ion, if he was here. My eyes searched desperately among the remaining passengers.

There he was! Right at the far end. I called out his name and wanted to run towards him but the crowd knew the train was coming. It surged forward, blocking my path. Ion was lost to my sight again behind a jumbled press of bodies.

Everything happened at once, so fast I was unable to sort it out in my mind afterwards, try as I might. The train burst from the tunnel and, at the same moment, a figure with flailing arms, like a human spider, was precipitated from the platform into its path. I caught a glimpse of the driver's face, fixed in horror. Brakes squealed and women screamed. Men were shouting. The passengers already on the train, who'd crowded near the doors to get off, clung to anything or anyone they could reach. People on the platform were turning to one another in panic, those who hadn't seen demanding to know what had happened.

Those, like me, who had seen, were unable to speak and tell them. A corner of my brain was obstinately telling me this couldn't happen. It couldn't! But the rest of my brain told me it had. Ion's search for his brother was over for ever.

Instincts for self-preservation began to override the initial numbness during which I stood there, bodies jostling me. This was no time to panic and no time to hang around. At any minute, authority would be arriving and seeking witnesses. I didn't want to be a witness. I wasn't sure what I'd seen. The only images stamped on my memory were of that stick-thin figure falling and the stricken features of the driver. I hadn't seen exactly what happened. Ion might have jumped or fallen. But I knew in my heart he'd been pushed. He'd been looking for his brother and until that search was over he'd have kept going. Someone had realised that and taken action to stop him.

I kept thinking that, if I'd found him even a minute or two earlier on that platform, I could have prevented this. Then self-preservation took over again and a sort of logic. It was unlikely I could have prevented it, not if someone else was set on it. If I'd intervened I, too, would probably have been propelled over the edge. If I'd even been seen talking to Ion, I'd have been marked down as the next victim. Whoever had done this wouldn't leave witnesses walking around.

I pushed my way through the crowd towards the stairs. Uniforms, underground staff and police were already running down them. One made as if to stop me.

I said loudly, 'I'm going to throw up!' and he backed off.

I was telling the truth. My stomach heaved as waves of nausea rose up, choking me. I managed to get out of there before they closed the whole place off and bolted for home and safety.

Chapter Eight

I stumbled along the pavements on my homeward route, my feet taking me automatically in the right direction. Several times I almost collided with other pedestrians. Some spoke to me sharply. A couple of them swore at me. One woman asked if I was all right, but her boyfriend pulled her away from me, saying that I was probably drugged or drunk. I suppose I looked strange, stressed out, my movements uncoordinated. If a cruising police car had seen me, I'd have been picked up. It was a wonder I wasn't knocked down crossing the streets. I was oblivious of the traffic.

At the top of the road where I lived a narrow alley ran down the side of the first property, between it and the back of the property in the street at right angles to it. My head was slightly clearer and I was beginning to pull my wits together. Just as I reached the alley, my ear caught the sound of a movement somewhere in the darkness in there. I jumped back, because it might have been a mugger, although he'd have had poor pickings from me. As I moved, a car swept past and its headlights briefly illuminated the entrance to the alley. I saw that the noise I'd heard had been made by a kid of about thirteen or fourteen.

He was crouched in the alley, propped against the brick wall of the garden to the left. I saw his face briefly illuminated, white, thin, with large eyes and untidy dark hair. I could see his clothes were baggy. He was so like Ion in every way that it gave me a real shock, as if I needed any more that night. I pulled myself together and told myself I hadn't imagined him and it wasn't a ghost. But the impact made by the sight of him was so powerful, I couldn't walk on and leave him there. I had to speak to him, hear his voice, reassure myself.

I stepped into the alley and croaked, 'Who are you?'

The reply, predictably, was that I should f- off.

Ghosts don't swear at you, at least none I'd ever heard about. I felt a spasm of relief. But my eyes were adjusting to the poor light and now I could see more than just an outline and the pale smudge of his face. He moved again, something rustled in his hand, and I distinguished a paper bag.

All my fears, all my shock, were replaced in a flash by burning anger. I leapt towards him, grabbed the bag and wrenched it from his hand.

'Oy!' he yelled. 'What do you think you're doing?'

'Don't be stupid!' I shouted at him. 'What do you think *you're* doing? I shook the bag and its contents in his face. 'You're scrambling your brain and you'll end up killing yourself, more than likely!'

'It's none of your bloody business!' he yelled back. 'Give me that!'

I snatched the bag out of his reach. He scrambled to his feet and came at me, but I just stood there, shouting at him. I'm not sure what I said; I know I repeated that he was stupid, that glue-sniffers were pathetic misfits, that one morning someone would find him dead in this alley or one like it. I carried on yelling other things but I don't know what they were.

I must have looked so weird, and sounded so wild, that he got scared of me. He cowered back further down the alley and whined, 'What's your problem?'

'You!' I shouted. But I didn't mean him, of course. I meant Ion.

My anger fizzled out. I turned and walked off. I think he ran a few steps after me, but then decided I was a raving lunatic and it would be better to leave me alone.

I arrived back at the house, my heart thumping and my chest aching with the deep ragged breaths I was drawing. Erwin was leaving for the nightly gig, wherever that might be. Two other members of the band were there, busy loading Erwin's drum kit into the back of their battered van. The drummer himself ambled out of the front door, all six feet two of him, dressed in black leather and gold chains, wrapround shades perched on top of his skull.

'Hey, pretty lady!' he greeted me. Then, seeing my face, added, 'You got trouble?'

'Not me, someone else,' I told him.

But Ion didn't have trouble any more. Ion was dead. Whether he was at peace I didn't know. I knew I wasn't. Was he now going to haunt me, reminding me that I'd promised I'd help – and that I'd done nothing? Did a promise become null and void when the person it was made to had died? Or did it become even more of a responsibility? I remembered reading somewhere that a wish expressed by someone who knows himself to be dying is binding, and a deathbed statement is admissible as evidence. Ion hadn't known he was going to die when he ran down the escalator on to the Tube platform. But he had known he was living in a dangerous, twilight world – a world in which his own brother had already disappeared. In that sense, he'd known he lived with death at his shoulder. He had passed his quest on to me like an unwished legacy. It was binding on me just as much as it would have been in the circumstances of a deathbed. I had no choice in the matter. I had to find Max and do it in such a way that I didn't become a victim myself.

But had I already, in my unsuccessful enquiries, committed some fatal blunder? All the way home I'd been checking my recent movements, asking myself if there was anything I'd done which might attract the attention of those who'd killed Ion. The riskiest might well turn out to be having talked to Wally and specifically asked about the kid, even told Wally Ion had been looking for his brother. But I didn't think Wally would tell anyone else. As far as I knew, he didn't talk to anyone except Jimmie. Besides, by the time Wally had drunk that bottle of red wine he'd pinched, he'd have forgotten all about my presence in the cellar.

I was still holding the solvent-abuser's paper bag with the tube of whatever substance he was using in it. I saw Erwin give it a curious look.

I held it up. 'Not mine,' I said. 'I've just taken it off a kid in the alley.'

'Kids are always sniffing in there,' said Erwin. 'You want to be careful. He might have had some mates with him, further back in the dark.'

'I know. It just made me mad.' I managed to force some sort of naturalness into my voice. 'Nice outfit, Erwin.'

Erwin, pleased, removed the shades which had been perched on top of his head and put them on. 'The man's got to have style,' he informed me. 'Hey, I took that pooch of yours to the park and kicked a football around. She likes to chase it.'

I thanked him and waved him and the rest of the band goodbye as they rattled away.

I went indoors and threw the paper bag and its contents into my kitchen bin. Then I made it to the bathroom just in time to throw up.

I spent a wretched, sleepless night. Bonnie, knowing something was badly wrong, stuck to me like a burr, watching me with anxious brown eyes. I knew there was no way I could go into work the following day. I wouldn't be able to disguise the way I felt. I was shaky inside and out, my hands trembling, my stomach turning.

Early on Saturday morning I walked over to the news-agent's, knowing I looked like death warmed up. Ganesh took one look at me and said to Hari, 'I'm taking a ten-minute break.'

Hari, occupied as usual with trying to keep an eye on every single customer besides serving the one at the counter, yelped, 'What, now? Now you are going?'

Ganesh snapped back in Gujerati, grabbed my arm and towed me after him to the upstairs flat.

I collapsed on to the worn red velvet sofa. 'Gan, do me a favour? Ring the pizzeria and tell them I'm sick and can't come in today.'

Without a word, Ganesh picked up the phone. I listened to his terse explanation. 'She's caught a cold, right? One of the guys in the play was full of it at the last rehearsal and now she's got it, sniffing and coughing all over the place. You don't want her round the customers or the food, do you? You'll have the environmental health round.'

He put a hand over the mouthpiece and asked, 'Jimmie says, do you want a pizza sent round for your lunch?'

I shook my head.

Ganesh relayed my refusal. 'She says thanks, but she's not eating, just keeping to the hot lemon drinks and the aspirin.'

He put the phone down and joined me on the sofa. 'Well?'

I told him all about it. His new short hairstyle made him look a more serious person anyway, and by the time I'd finished my tale he looked like an undertaker.

He heaved a sigh. 'I'm not going to say I told you so, but I knew this was going to turn out badly. You've got a kind heart, Fran, and it gets you into scrapes. You couldn't help that kid. You were wrong to promise him you would. Offering to help is all very well if you *can* help. Otherwise, it just messes things up, makes matters worse.'

'You think my interference may have led to what happened to Ion?' I asked miserably.

'No! What happened to him was most probably going to happen anyway! He'd got himself into a heck of a fix. There wasn't any way out. He'd made enemies. Perhaps they caught up with him last night. Perhaps, after all, it was an accident.'

I said, 'It wasn't an accident. He was pushed.'

'You didn't see it.'

'I didn't need to see any more than I saw.'

There was a silence and then Ganesh asked, 'What are you going to do now?'

'What do you think I should do?'

He smiled wryly. 'You know the answer to that. I think you should do nothing at all. He's beyond your help and you don't want to attract the wrong kind of attention.' He sighed. 'I'm wasting my breath. What are you thinking of doing?'

'Carrying on looking for Max.'

'Why? What purpose would it serve? What can be done now?'

'I can help Ion get a sort of justice,' I said.

He rubbed his hands over his short-cropped black hair. 'You still think it's got something to do with the pizzeria?'

'I have to think it, Gan. I'd almost made up my mind Ion was mistaken about seeing this Max person there. I can't find anyone who knows about a Max. But I don't know. I've got a bad feeling about it all. Listen, the whole chain of pizzerias could be a laundering operation for money made smuggling people into the country. It would explain why they put Jimmie in as manager. You know how hopeless he is. He's just so happy to sit in that office and sign anything they put in front of him, he doesn't think to ask why he's there. I know why. He's there to be the fall guy if things go wrong. Then, if the police turn up, all the others will deny knowing anything and point at Jimmie, saying, "Ask him, he's the manager!" I can't do anything about it, that's the awful thing. I've got no evidence. I can't go to Jimmie and warn him. He wouldn't believe me.

The others might find out. I can't trust anyone there. Well, I trust Bronia and Po-Ching up to a point, but Bronia's going for another job and Po-Ching's a nice kid who doesn't need trouble.'

'Perhaps,' Ganesh said seriously, 'it would be better if you just didn't go back to work there ever, Fran. We're busy in the shop. We could use another pair of hands. I'll ask Hari if we can take you on, at least part-time. Then I'll go over to that pizzeria and tell them you've got another job.'

'Don't you think that's what I'd like? But it would look suspicious. Silvio has just offered me a better job as assistant manageress at a new branch he's opening. He won't like it if I just take off. Silvio isn't the sort of person you upset. Bless you, Gan, for wanting to help me out. You always do. You're a sort of rock, someone I can run to in trouble. It means a lot to me.'

He smiled. 'Oh, yes? I'm someone to run to, but not someone whose advice you can take.'

'I told you,' I reminded him. 'I feel I owe it to Ion.'

Ganesh looked even grimmer, if possible. 'Owe it to him to do what? Get yourself bumped off as he was?'

'No, to stick around and see if anything turns up.'

He uttered a hiss of annoyance. 'You can't ask around any more about Max. The police will be looking into Ion's accident. That's what they'll probably put it down as, a tragic accident. Who knows, they may have witnesses already and have got statements. You can't do anything, Fran. You know nothing about the kid except what he told you and you can't rely on that. My opinion, for what it's worth, is that he was wrong about Max. You don't know

what else he was into which might have got him into
trouble. Just forget about him and anything he said to
you.'

I said I knew he was right. 'But I've still got to go back
to work. If anyone there was involved in shoving Ion off
that platform, well, he might have spotted me at the Tube
station. There's nothing odd about that in itself, but if I do
a runner now, it will look like I saw something that I link to
the pizzeria. I've got to carry on just as normal.'

'I'm not sure I follow all that,' grumbled Ganesh. 'But I
suppose nothing I say will make any difference. It's all very
well saying you know I'm right. You'll still do whatever you
want. At least stay away from the place for a couple of
days. Anyway, you're supposed to have a cold, so you've
got to.'

After that, he went downstairs and came back with a
cross-section of the day's newspapers. We scanned them
to see if Ion's death had made the news. It hadn't. Either
the story had come in after the papers had been put to
bed or, more likely, it wasn't newsworthy enough. Notices
appear at underground stations not infrequently
informing passengers that no trains are running on such
and such a line 'due to an incident at X'. All too often,
that means another suicide. Ion's death wasn't unusual
enough even to be a filler, a couple of lines tucked in at
the bottom of the page.

'The weekend press is always full of magazine and
supplement stuff. Perhaps it will be in Monday,' said
Ganesh.

I doubted it. By Monday the world would have moved
on. Ion's death would be old news.

* * *

I set off back to my flat along pavements crowded with Saturday shoppers. I saw none of them, my mind clouded with depressing thoughts and an ever-increasing sense of guilt. I knew it was unfounded, but I couldn't shift it.

'It's normal to feel guilty when someone you know dies,' Ganesh had insisted before I left. 'Everyone does. You're not to blame for anything.'

My self-absorption meant that I failed to see someone trying to attract my attention, and didn't even realise he was calling my name, until he jumped in front of me and forced me to take notice of him.

'What's up, Fran? You deaf or something?'

All I needed. Sergeant Wayne Parry, the local CID's finest. He who, according to Ganesh, cherished hopes of being the man in my life. Not in a million years. He hadn't changed since I'd last seen him. Ginger hair, straggling moustache, manky jacket.

'Go away,' I said. Parry isn't subtle and it's no use wasting polite hints on him.

'Yeah, nice to see you, too, Fran,' he retorted. 'How are you doing?'

'Rotten,' I told him. 'I've got a cold and I'm on my way home.'

He looked concerned. 'You do look a bit washed out. Now, what's all this I hear about you being in a play?'

Spare me. Surely he wasn't proposing to be there too?

'I really,' I said, 'don't feel very well.' That was true enough. 'I can't stay and chat.' I moved off determinedly.

'That's a pity,' said Parry, falling into step beside me. I told you he wasn't subtle or sensitive. 'Because your name was mentioned just this morning and we were wondering, if you'd got a moment, if you'd stop by and have a word with the inspector. Inspector Morgan, that is.'

Janice Morgan was the best copper I'd ever come across, but that didn't make me a fan and I didn't want to run down to the nick and have a chat with her. But that she should want to see me just now set an alarm bell ringing.

'I don't know what you're on about, but unless you arrest me for something, I'm not going anywhere near any cop shop,' I told him. 'As far as I know I haven't committed an arrestable offence, so get lost.'

'There's no need to be unfriendly,' he said reproachfully. 'Where are you living now?'

I told him, because if they knew where to find me, they really didn't have grounds to take me in.

'I'll tell the inspector,' said Parry. 'You want to watch that cold, Fran, it's making you bad-tempered.'

He bared his yellow teeth at me and, thank goodness, made off down the pavement. People stepped aside to let him proceed unimpeded. This is not because Parry looks dangerous but because he looks like a copper.

I carried on back to the flat, wondering what I was going to do for the next forty-eight hours while I was fighting 'my cold'.

To have a place of my own had made me feel good. Now, however, it was more than pleasant, it was comforting and reassuring, probably something to do with wanting to return to the womb. It was a place to run to, a refuge, a den. I was inside and they were all outside, Mario and the crew at the pizzeria, Parry and the other minions of the law, the elusive and sinister Max and the unknown owner of the hand that had pushed Ion from the platform.

I made a cup of tea and switched on the telly. Bonnie was outside in the back garden. Calling it a garden was stretching a point. It was an area of untrimmed grass with, at the bottom of it, the remains of a wartime Anderson shelter. Erwin assured me that, in the summer, it was a good place for a barbecue and party. In winter, only Bonnie wanted to be out there. I was about to find out that I needn't have worried about being lonely. I was also wrong about being able to shut myself away from the hassle of life.

Around four o'clock my bell rang. I half expected it to be Susie. Another driving lesson was the last thing I wanted and I prepared a firm refusal. But when I peeped round the curtain, my heart sank. Inspector Morgan herself stood on my doorstep. I had to let her in. I'd no idea what she wanted but I should have realised, from my brief conversation with Parry, that this visit was on the cards. It had been foolish of me to think I could avoid Janice Morgan simply by refusing the invitation to go to the station for a cup of tea and a friendly chat.

'I'm sorry to hear about your cold, Fran,' she began when she got her foot over my threshold. She held up a bag. 'I brought you some lemons.'

I thanked her. She scrutinised my appearance and said, 'You do look rough.'

'I feel rough.'

'Just the cold, is it?' she asked. She was a lot smarter than Parry. I suppose that's how she made inspector.

When I say she's smarter I'm not referring to her dress sense, by the way. You might ask, with some justification, who am I to criticise? Most of my clothes come from Oxfam or those shops where the garments all have the labels cut out. But Morgan has the money to buy decent gear and what does she buy? Regular, Home Counties stuff; boring jackets, gored skirts, sensible shoes. I reckon she's in her middle thirties but the way she dresses, you'd think she was twenty years older. Today she had on a dreary grey wool suit and a white blouse. She looked like the sort of nanny upmarket families hire to look after their kids. I know why she does this. She wants to be taken seriously. She wants to avoid the sort of sexual harassment still around in a canteen culture like that of the police. But surely, by now, she must feel secure enough to push the boat out just a little?

'I hear you're appearing in a play,' she said, settling down on my sofa as if she meant to stay. She was another one who, apparently, considered my home to be Liberty Hall.

I mumbled that I was and had picked up my cold at rehearsals.

'How are they going?' Her voice was all bland innocence. It didn't cut any ice with me. She was here on business, not visiting the poor and needy.

'All right,' I said warily.

'You're putting the show on in the functions room at The Rose? Is that right?'

I nodded. She'd clearly done her homework and probably knew as much about the play as I did. But she wanted to make conversation and I did my best to oblige her. 'Freddy – the landlord – he's stage-struck. He's not charging us for the hire of the room or anything. It was his idea we do it. He's got a carpenter pal building some props for us. He puts something on every year. This is the latest Freddy production.'

She didn't, thank goodness, say she meant to come to the performance. By now, I reckoned every seat in the house must be spoken for, anyway.

Instead she said, 'It's nice to think the landlord is doing something for the local community.'

'Oh, Freddy's into all that kind of thing,' I said casually. 'Putting on charity boxing events and getting someone to raise money for a good cause by sitting in a bath of baked beans all day. Freddy never provides any of the action himself. He just organises others. I reckon local businessmen must duck and run when they see Freddy coming with another bright idea.'

'And now he's organised you and your friends into putting on a play.' She smiled.

'That's it. We're all working like mad at it. Marty, the director and the play's author – well, he adapted it from Conan Doyle – he's wearing himself to a frazzle.'

'What about the hound?' she asked. 'It is *The Hound of the Baskervilles*, isn't it?'

Oh, my, yes. She certainly *had* done her homework. I told her we had a dog. It had been taught what it had to do and we'd tried it out. I waited for her to introduce the next subject of conversation. She was interested in the play but it wasn't what had brought her to see me, I was sure. I wondered when she was going to get down to the real nitty-gritty.

'You've obviously been very busy,' she said. 'Pity about your cold. You're still working at that pizzeria, I suppose?'

Hairs prickled on the nape of my neck. 'That's right. I can't go breathing germs over the food so I've taken a sickie.' I remembered to fake a pretty good sneeze at that point, just to prove I wasn't skiving off. I don't think Morgan really fell for it but she was prepared to go along with it.

'Bless you!' she said politely. 'Sergeant Parry told you I wanted a chat?'

I mumbled agreement but told her Parry hadn't said what it was about.

'You weren't curious to find out?'

'No,' I said. 'I just wanted to get home and take some aspirin.'

She tapped her fingers on the arm of the sofa, her pale blue eyes studying me. 'Your family was Hungarian, right?'

I nodded. 'My grandparents came here in 1956, after the Hungarian uprising, with my dad who was just a baby. But I never knew my grandfather. He died just about the time I was born. He was a doctor.'

I knew I sounded wary and I was wary. She had just placed her first card on the table.

'A place of safety. That's a phrase which gets used a lot. Young people in trouble can be taken to a place of safety, witnesses who might be threatened . . . If you're a refugee, like your grandparents, fleeing an occupying army, a phrase like "place of safety" would have real meaning.'

I didn't bother to reply. She'd go on, anyway. I had a vague idea where this was leading and I didn't feel very comfortable about it.

'But your grandparents,' Morgan was saying, 'came here through the right channels. They didn't have to hide once they got here. They didn't have to invent fake identities. They didn't have to run whenever they saw a police officer. They weren't at the mercy of organised gangs nor did they owe money to people who'd use any means to collect. There are a lot of people living in London and other big cities around the country who've entered illegally. You know that, of course. It's always on the news.' She nodded towards my television set.

'Yes,' I said.

'Those people, they have no protection, nowhere to turn for help if things get bad. Smuggling these people into the country is big business and the gangs who run it are efficient and very unpleasant. They are also dangerous.' She stopped speaking and sat looking at me.

Obviously I was expected to make some comment. I said, 'What's all this got to do with me?'

'Nothing that I know of.' She smiled at me. 'Has it?'

'Got anything to do with me? Of course it hasn't! How could it?' I snapped back. I was getting fed up with this cat and mouse exchange. Morgan was good at it and could keep it up as long as she liked. She knew that sooner or later I was likely to get annoyed enough to say something I'd afterwards wish I hadn't. This time, I meant to make sure that didn't happen. 'What do you want? Why are you here? I'm sick and you're harassing me.'

She looked pained. 'Oh, come on, Fran. As if I'd do anything like that. This is a social call. Of course, you do have an ear on the street. You hear things, see things. I can tell you that we think one of these murky outfits which traffics in human beings operates from around here somewhere.'

'Look,' I said. 'I'm not a paid or unpaid informer. I haven't got anything to tell you anyway.'

I had a whole lot of suspicions but I was keeping those to myself. Morgan didn't like my investigating things. But so long as I didn't tell her what I'd been doing – and meant to go on doing – she couldn't tell me to stop doing it.

As for her warning, I didn't need Morgan to tell me the gangs who smuggled in illegal aliens were dangerous. I'd seen what they could do. That falling stick-like figure was burned into my memory for all time.

As if she could read my mind, Morgan said, 'Yesterday evening a young illegal alien, a Romanian boy, fell in front of a Tube train at Camden Town. We're not sure how the accident happened.'

I nearly asked, 'Accident?' but managed to stop myself. It had shaken me to hear her speak of Ion's death when it was so much in my mind. Ganesh had been right. The police were looking into it. Why did she think I could help? Because I worked at the pizzeria, I thought miserably. Well, if she was hoping I'd be her spy in that camp, she'd be disappointed, no matter what amount of gentle pressure she put on me. I particularly disliked the appeal to my conscience, pointing out I was the child of an immigrant family, as if I owed her cooperation. It was underhand.

'It may turn out to be suicide,' she was saying. 'He could have become quite desperate. It's a tragic affair, however you look at it.'

'Lousy,' I agreed.

'We think he probably came into the country in the back of a lorry. Despite the best efforts of the immigration authorities at the ports, it does still happen. The people who come in that way often find, if they do succeed in getting here, that they've jumped from the frying pan into the fire. In comparison, your grandparents were fortunate.'

I muttered, 'Oh yes, really fortunate, driven out of their home in the clothes they stood up in, my grandmother with her baby in her arms.'

'But,' said Morgan gently, 'they found a place of safety. Rather as you have here, Fran. This flat, it's very nice. I'm glad you've got a roof over your head at last. It's certainly better than sleeping in a garage as you were doing the last time we met. We're not sure where the youngster who fell in front of the train was living, but it would have been shared bed-space in some back room. No wonder they lose hope and decide to end it all. He wasn't the first, of course. I dare say there will be others like him.'

She had spoken of an accident and now she was speaking of suicide. The one thing she hadn't mentioned was murder. Was she waiting for me to do that? And to tell her why I thought it?

'We're investigating the incident, of course.'

'Good,' I said.

'We need witnesses.'

I didn't say anything. She gave a thin smile. 'You weren't anywhere near Camden Tube station last night, were you?'

I opened my mouth to deny it but managed to bite back the words. Why should she ask me such a thing? I searched my memory frantically. Had someone seen me there? Someone who knew me? I could lie. But if she knew I was lying, anything I said afterwards would sound like more lies.

I swallowed and made a decision. 'Yes, as it happens. Why do you ask?'

'We were looking at the security camera film this morning, Sergeant Parry and I, the one by the ticket office. We both recognised you.'

I felt a moment's relief that I had decided to own up to being there. It didn't last long. It was sheer bad luck that in such a crowded place the security camera had focused on me. It must have been difficult to pick out anyone in the crush but there I was, apparently, Fran Varady, for all my acquaintances in the Met to see and recognise. What was I? Jinxed? My mind buzzed. If the camera had picked me up at the ticket office, had it picked me up later, running away from the Tube station? A couple of seconds isn't long to concoct an explanation to cover all eventualities. I did my best.

'I was going to go up west,' I said. 'For the evening, change of scene. But when I got down to the platform I couldn't breathe. Because of my cold, you know? It was very stuffy there. So I turned round and came back up again.'

'So you weren't aware of any commotion?'

'Yeah,' I said uneasily. 'Something was going on but I didn't wait to see what it was.' I paused. 'Was that the kid falling in front of the train?'

There was a silence. When I didn't say anything more, Morgan spoke. 'It's natural to want to keep out of trouble. But if you saw anything at all, Fran, you should tell me what it was.'

'I didn't see what happened to that boy,' I said. 'Hundreds of people pass through that Tube station every evening. Ask any of them. Why pick on me?'

She stood up. 'You know my door is open, Fran, don't you? But my patience isn't limitless. I really hope you're not holding out on me.' Her voice was pure steel. But then, in a sudden change of manner, she turned friendly and added, 'I also hope the cold clears up and you can get back to your rehearsals and your job.'

I sat in the darkening room and tried to pretend she hadn't got me worried. Perhaps I should go and see her, tell her about Ion, the pizzeria, everything? Belatedly I remembered Bonnie. I found her sitting outside the back door, looking cold and reproachful. I spooned out extra dinner for her by way of compensation.

By now I had a splitting headache. I made a hot drink with one of Morgan's lemons and took an aspirin. I wondered if I was going down with a cold.

Chapter Nine

I wasn't to be given time to brood over what had happened. On Sunday morning Susie Duke turned up. I recalled too late she'd said something about another driving lesson that morning. I wished I'd remembered earlier. I could have rung and put her off. Now she was here and I really couldn't refuse to go out with her.

I could see the car, parked outside the house. My heart sank. I definitely didn't think I could face those kids again. Antisocial behaviour on a small scale I can cope with. At times I've been accused of it myself. But on a bigger scale, armed with stones, and surrounding me, well, that's something any sensible person would avoid. If Susie insisted on taking me out, I hoped she would remember to head for some quieter more upmarket area, despite the fact that the presence of the middle classes always makes me nervous and the feeling seems to be mutual. There would always be the possibility that some Neighbourhood Watch enthusiast, spotting us slowly touring the area from behind his lace curtains, would be on the phone to report suspicious behaviour on the part of two women, one punk and one hooker. After all, if we were in the burglary business and wanted to case the properties, sticking an Lplate on the bumper of the car would be perfect cover. But that was a risk I'd have to take.

I don't particularly aim for the punk look, by the way, but my hair is very short, I've got a diamond stud in one nostril and my clothes are suitable for the sort of life I lead. It might seem unkind to say Susie looked like a hooker, but honestly . . . She was dressed in tight jeans and a pink sweater and had done something to her blond hair which had turned it into tangled curls. I suspected she was aiming for the Barbie Doll look.

She had brought with her my costume for the play and produced it with a flourish from a holdall. It was beautifully pressed and looked quite different now from the bed-raggled rag I'd pulled from the box of props at The Rose.

'Gosh, thanks, Susie,' I said in gratitude and admiration.

She urged me to try it on to see if it needed any adjustment to skirt length and made me walk up and down the room in it.

'Because you've got to walk different, Fran, see? You can't go marching along like you do in jeans and trainers or boots. Have you got proper shoes?'

'I can't wear high heels,' I told her promptly. 'I fall off them. I've only got my trainers and boots.'

'I thought so,' she said smugly. She delved into the holdall. Her hand emerged with a pair of flat soft leather pumps – pink, naturally. 'I brought these, just in case. They're slippers really, but they'll do. They're about your size. Go on, try them on.'

I put on the pumps and walked round the room again. My feet looked like pink flippers on a cartoon animal.

'Better,' said Susie approvingly. 'Just practise wearing

them about and don't slap your feet down like that! You're not a ruddy penguin.'

'You know,' I told her in all seriousness, 'you'd make a really great wardrobe mistress.'

'I'm a good private detective,' she retorted. 'And I still need a partner. Have you given it any more thought, Fran?'

I told her I was in a bit of a fix as Silvio had offered me the job of assistant manageress at the new pizzeria. 'Turning him down isn't going to be easy. I suppose it's a compliment to be offered it. I'd get more money.'

She sniffed. 'If that's what you want. Spending the rest of your life worrying about other people's food. Not to mention all the rest of the hassle a manager gets. You're in the middle as manager. The customers get at you, the suppliers let you down, the owners give you grief because you're not meeting the profit targets.'

'I don't suppose Jimmie worries about any of those things,' I muttered.

Susie pursed her lips. 'If he doesn't, someone else does. What's he doing managing that pizza place? Especially if, as you say, he does nothing.'

'He's a partner in the business,' I offered feebly.

Rightly, she wasn't impressed. 'There's something fishy about that place and I don't mean the anchovies. Something's not right. Don't tell me it isn't.'

I wasn't going to deny it, was I? If I'd had any doubts, having Janice Morgan come round and angle for information in her clunking police way would have disposed of them.

I couldn't talk over my worries about the San Gennaro with Morgan and Ganesh was tired of my bending his ear about it all. I knew his views on what I should, or shouldn't, do now Ion was dead. On the other hand, talking to Susie was a different matter. Suddenly I found myself telling her everything. I suppose I'd been repressing the urge to share what I'd seen. The dreadful image of that falling, flailing figure was haunting me. All the previous night, every time I closed my eyes, I saw it again. We're always advised to 'talk' when we have something worrying us. Susie was someone new, someone sharp and she was accustomed, in a professional way, to hearing people's suspicions. Outlandish tales were nothing new to her.

She sat quietly until I'd poured it all out. 'You should have told me before,' she said then. 'I might have been able to help.'

'I couldn't drag you in. It was my problem and still is. Ganesh says it isn't, that I can't do any more. I've got to leave it to the police. The cops are investigating Ion's death. I know that because Morgan's been here. That's Inspector Janice Morgan. I've met up with her before.'

'I know her, too.' Susie was nodding. 'I know all the local coppers. Why did she come to you about it?'

'They recognised me on film from one of the security cameras at the station,' I said gloomily. 'But by the ticket office, not down on the platform, so I said I saw nothing. Why didn't the camera pick up what happened to Ion? No, it ignores the one part of the station where there's something going on and fixes on me buying a ticket.'

'That's security cameras for you,' said Susie. 'When they first came in Rennie and I worried they'd be bad for the private investigation business but half the time they're switched off or they've got no film in or are so fuzzy you can't make anyone out.'

'Well, apparently it shows me jumping around like a hopeful at a film shoot,' I growled. 'Add to that I work at the pizzeria.'

She looked puzzled so I explained my theory about the restaurant being a front for a money-laundering operation, probably based on the people-trafficking racket, and Jimmie being set up as patsy.

'We've got no proof.' She shook the blond curls. I noticed that, despite my words, she was associating herself with the problem. 'Let's look at the story the kid told you,' she went on. 'Starting with the missing brother. Well, anything might have happened to him. I don't mean he's dead. He could've found work somewhere in another part of the country. He could be in gaol, come to that. Or in a detention centre.

'The other bit of the story concerns this fellow, Max. You're taking it on trust Ion was right about recognising Max in the street. We know he saw someone he thought he recognised, someone who might have information about his brother. We know he followed that person to the San Gennaro and saw him go inside. The man went into the corridor where the office is but, also, the customer toilets. So if he was Max, he might just have gone in there because he was caught short in the street. On the other hand, if he wasn't Max, it doesn't matter whether he went into the toilets or into the office – Ion had got the wrong man.'

Susie placed the pointed shell-pink tips of her forefinger nails together and directed the resultant V-shape at me.

'I'm with Ganesh in thinking this Max business doesn't sound right. Ion saw the outline of a fat man talking to the lorry driver. He heard, he says, the driver call the fat man "Max". But the kid's English wasn't brilliant, you say. He probably spoke less when he dropped off that lorry than he did by the time he met you. He almost certainly understood even less. He thought he heard the name "Max". What he actually heard was a foreign word he didn't know and it sounded a bit like a name he did know.'

There was a horrible logic to all of this. Susie was right. The police deal in facts and I didn't have facts, not the sort they'd recognise. I had a wild story about a kid who'd spoken little English and had seen a man on a dark night, briefly illuminated in the open door of a car, a man he'd then claimed to have recognised again. I could imagine Morgan picking holes in that. But listening to reason has never been my strong point. I wasn't buying it this time either.

'If Ion had got it so wrong,' I said, 'why did someone shove him off that platform?'

'Did you see him pushed? Maybe he stumbled and fell. It was an accident. They happen.'

'It stinks,' I said briefly.

There was a silence. Susie watched my face. At last she said, 'Right, then. We have to find Max. Because without Max, we've got no lead at all.'

I shook my head emphatically, 'No, not you, Susie. Thanks for offering to help and all that. But I don't need another acquaintance falling under a Tube train.'

'They wouldn't do that twice,' she said with the calm assurance of one who knew the sorts of tricks gangsters get up to. 'Not just after doing it once – if that's what happened. It would be too obvious. The next person they'll take out some other way.'

She didn't say the next person might be me. She didn't have to. I shivered.

She produced a packet of gum and offered me a stick. I refused. I can't get on with chewing gum. I'm all right at first but after a dozen chews the flavour has seeped out and I find myself pushing an unpleasant wad round my mouth, disliking it more every second.

'I'm trying to give up the cigarettes.' Susie popped a stick into her mouth. 'Cut back, anyway. I allow myself five a day. I started smoking thirty a day after Rennie died. You know what I was like then. I went to pieces for a bit. But I'm fine now.'

'That's good,' I murmured.

We sat in more silence, Susie chewing, me sunk in gloom.

Eventually she said, 'You can't rule out suicide, Fran. You've got to face it. The kid was desperate. He hadn't found his brother. Or perhaps he had found out something bad about him, that he was dead. He owed money and he couldn't pay. He didn't have anyone to turn to for help, except you, and you were almost a total stranger. You hadn't found Max. He may have suspected you didn't really believe his story. At any rate, you wouldn't want him bothering you for ever.'

'I was pretty sharp with him when I last saw him,' I confessed. 'I told him not to come near me for at least a week.'

'Of course you did. Who wouldn't? But from the kid's point of view, life in a new country hadn't turned out the way he'd imagined it would. He either decided to end it all and went down the Tube with that in his head. Or it was a spur-of-the-moment thing. Either way, he jumped.'

'Anna Karenina,' I said moodily. 'She chucked herself under a train.'

'Right. People do, Fran.'

'Ion didn't,' I argued.

'You don't *know* that.'

'I do know it. I just can't tell you why. Yes, I can. It was the way he fell. He didn't launch himself off like a jumper. He fell awkwardly, making useless grasping movements with his hands. That's why I've got to keep on looking for Max. It's like you said just now. Max is my only lead. If I find him, I'll know Ion told me a true story. I'll know why someone wanted to shut his mouth permanently. I'll *know* he was murdered.'

'And then?' She stopped chewing and stared straight at me. 'What will you do then?'

'I don't know. Perhaps even tell Morgan about it.'

She made a tsk-tsk noise. 'You'll have to think it over, Fran, before you go to Morgan and change your story. You told her you saw nothing. You're going to have to admit you lied. You know how the police take things. If you change your story, they'll reckon you know more and are still holding out. But, like we've just been discussing, you don't really know more, not as fact. The police are obsessed with facts, what they can use as evidence. This Max story, I'm not saying it's not possible, Fran, believe me. But can you imagine yourself telling Morgan or Parry? You've got to wait until you've got something more. Then you can go to the cops. In fact, you'll pretty well have no choice.'

'All the same,' I said, 'perhaps I should have admitted to Morgan I saw Ion at the station. Like you say, it's not a good idea to tell unnecessary lies.'

'You can't tell her now without telling her how you knew him. And if you're right, it won't be only Morgan interested in what you might or might not have seen. Isn't that what you're worried about? Isn't that why you denied to Morgan that you'd seen anything? Once it gets out you were there and recognised the kid, well, that's going to set a few alarms buzzing. No point in making a target of yourself.'

'I do know that, thanks!' I was sorry to sound irritable but I couldn't help it. That's what happens when you pour out your troubles to someone. You always end up wishing you hadn't. I wished now I hadn't even told Ganesh. A trouble shared is a trouble doubled.

'What you need,' said Susie, 'is to take your mind off it for an hour or two. You need another driving lesson.'

I told her I wasn't in the mood to face those kids again.

She shook her head. 'I told you I'd find somewhere better. I've got the perfect place. You know the old cinema, the one they closed down? Round the back of that is a big open area, used to be a car park. We can go there. It's absolutely private. No one to see you.'

'It's also blocked off,' I pointed out. 'I walked past there the other day. To get to the back of the place, you've got to go down the side entrance and there's a chain-link gate across it. It's padlocked, if I remember rightly.'

She grinned, pulled a key from her jeans pocket and held it up.

'Where did you get that?' I gasped.

'Easy. It was in Rennie's stuff.'

I blinked at this second mention of her late husband. 'Where did he get it?'

'He did a job for the developer, the bloke who bought the site. The developer had a partner and suspected he was ripping him off. The partner was going there on the quiet and moving out all the valuable stuff like the lead pipes, bits of gilded carving, anything he could sell. So the developer put Rennie on to it.'

'And was Rennie successful?'

She nodded. 'Oh yes, Rennie was good. He got the evidence. The partner got his legs broken. The developer got financial trouble and the development was put on hold. Rennie never gave the key back. Forgot, I expect.'

She might believe that. I didn't. Probably Rennie wanted to take over where the bloke with his legs in plaster had left off, only not on such a big, obvious scale. Just pinching the odd thing.

'Susie,' I protested as I followed her out to her car. 'We can't go there, it would be trespassing.'

'Trespass in itself is a civil offence, not a criminal one. Providing we don't break in, don't do any damage and don't pinch anything, they can't do anything but ask us to leave. That's if anyone finds us, which they won't. We can't be seen from the road. They can't have us for breaking and entering, not with me having a key – which the owner of the site gave me. Well, gave Rennie, which is the same thing.'

I wasn't too happy, but perhaps it made sense. She cut off any objection on my part by handing me the car keys. 'Go on, get in the driver's side. You're the learner. Take us there.'

* * *

I crawled through the thin Sunday-morning traffic to the old cinema site. Susie was right. It was a good place. Once we got inside, she locked up the gate so we shouldn't be disturbed. The mass of the old building rose up blocking sight of the road beyond, and blocking anyone's view of us. It looked dingy and about ready to fall down without the help of the demolition crew who'd move in eventually. Glass in the grimy windows was broken. Piping had been stripped from the outer walls, which were blackened with time and smoke. All around the yard ran a tall brick wall. On the other side of that were the rear walls and backyards of shops in the street beyond. Most of those, this Sunday morning, were probably closed. I stopped feeling uneasy about being there. Susie was the one with the key, after all. I three-point-turned until I could manage it like a pro and backed round the corner of the building without scraping the wall once. I even, though I felt guilty about it afterwards, forgot about Ion for a while.

When we parted she said quietly, 'Listen to me, Fran. If you're serious about looking for this Max character, let me help. I've got no business at the moment except for a couple of odd jobs which won't take me hardly any time. And I admit I've got an ulterior motive. If I work with you on this, you'll see me working – we'll be working together. It will give you an idea whether you could work with me in future. You might think again about joining me at the agency.'

'It could be risky,' I said after I'd thought about it for a minute or two.

151

'I've been in tight spots before.' She grinned. 'I can run fast.'

I made a decision. 'All right then, Susie. With one proviso. If I think you're getting into real danger, I will go to Morgan and tell her all I know about Ion. I've got him on my conscience. I don't want you there as well.'

It was because I didn't want to worry about Susie that I hadn't told her about the plan I'd hatched to go back to the cellar on the quiet and have a good look round. On Monday mornings the pizzeria opened at eleven thirty as usual in time to catch the lunchtime trade. But Jimmie got there earlier, at around half past eight, to let in Wally to do his cleaning. This meant that after eight thirty, although technically we weren't open for business, the burglar alarm would have been switched off. Also, I understood that Jimmie, having let Wally in, went off again, locking the street door, and got himself breakfast somewhere.

The idea of returning had come to me on Friday when I collected my pay. I am not an expert at breaking into places. I don't want you to think that. But I've climbed in and out of a few untenanted houses in my days living in squats. Bathroom windows are often overlooked when people secure a premises and they seldom have safety catches, at least not in old buildings.

The so-called staff restroom at the pizzeria was at the back of the building. Some time in the distant past an extension had been built on there. It had been done on the cheap. Most of it now formed part of the kitchen. A small area had been bricked off for staff use and was accessed by a door beyond the stairs down to the cellar, and round a corner. The window of the staff toilet, attached to the restroom, was closed by a simple little metal arm with holes in it, fixed to the frame of the glass. It popped over a metal peg on the lower inside ledge of the outer window surround. There was also a little swivel handle halfway up one side which was supposed to slide into a groove in the outer frame. But that had been painted over by a careless decorator and, as a result, it was stuck in the open position and wouldn't swivel at all. The frame around the glass didn't fit well against the outer window frame. It was old and the hinges were loose. If I got there around nine, after Jimmie went off to breakfast and before Luigi or Mario turned up, I might be able to effect entry through the toilet window and sneak down to the cellar. Wally would be cleaning either the customer toilets or the restaurant and kitchen floors. I could have a good rummage round undisturbed. I slipped a long nail file into my pocket and set out.

My first move was to observe the pizzeria from the other side of the road. Sure enough, at a quarter to nine, Jimmie came out and strolled off down the road to find the sort of place that sold greasy fry-ups and strong tea. Through the window I could see Wally pushing his mop back and forth in the restaurant. A cigarette dangled from his withered lips and, as he swept, ash fell on the the newly cleaned patch. He left it there as he moved on to the next bit. I made my way round to the back of the building and got in over the wall to the roof of the shed, just as Ion had done on that first morning I'd met him. As I did, an idea came to me which ought to have occurred before. I'd been assuming Ion had slipped into the restaurant during opening hours, from the street. But surely it was much more likely he'd done just as I was doing. He'd watched from the street, worked out the early-morning routine, waited for Jimmie to leave and then nipped round to the back. I might have guessed, when he admitted to coming over the wall and shed roof, that he'd done it before. He wouldn't have known about the loo window. But he might have struck lucky and found the kitchen door unlocked by either Jimmie or Wally.

I dropped to the ground and made my way to the kitchen door, just to check if it was open. That would make everything easier. But it was still locked so I had to get in via the toilet window as planned. I had decided that, if by any piece of bad luck Jimmie came back and caught me, I'd spin him some yarn about taking off a ring in the restroom to wash my hands, and forgetting it there. Not many people would buy a story like that, but Jimmie just might.

I left my plastic carrier with my uniform in the shed. Equipped with a wooden box I found in there, I reached the wall of the staff toilet without being challenged. I climbed on the box, reached up and slipped my nail file between the two frames. I felt it come up under the metal arm and stop. I gave it a good shove upwards. The metal arm leapt off the little peg and crashed down again free of it. Nothing now secured the two parts of the frame together. Frankly, it was a doddle. I pulled the window open and, hauling myself up, managed to wriggle through the gap. I am on the small side and weigh just over seven and a half stone. Getting down to the floor on the further side was the most difficult bit and I nearly went head first into the toilet. But fortunately it had an old-fashioned high cistern connected by a pipe to the toilet bowl and I was able to grab this pipe to prevent my headlong fall and scramble down with nothing worse than a couple of scraped fingers.

I opened the door of the restroom, crept to the corner and peeped round it, down the corridor. Wally wasn't to be seen. I tiptoed down the cellar stairs.

Down there it was as gloomy and unfriendly as before, despite the efforts of the single light bulb. Wally had been there to collect his brush, mop and bucket and had fortunately left it on, so I had no need to risk attracting attention by switching it on myself. I knew I hadn't much time, although I wasn't too worried about Wally finding me. I'd prefer it if he didn't, but he wasn't likely to tell Luigi or Mario if he did. However, avoid complications, that's my motto. (Ganesh says the reverse is true.)

I started off at the far wall and worked my way back towards the stairs so that the longer I was down there, the nearer I was to my route out. I braved the corners, the possibilities of wildlife and the spine-tingling soft touch of huge hanging cobwebs. Carefully I shifted dusty boxes and miscellaneous junk. Some of it seemed to date from the days of the Hot Spud Café. I recognised the metal containers which had held the fillings for the spuds. Try as I might, however, I couldn't find anything suspicious. I moved tins of olive oil and opened boxes of cheap wine. I studied the racks of dearer wine, pulling out the bottles to see if anything was hidden behind them. I nearly upset a tower of tinned tomatoes. Nothing.

I couldn't stay down here much longer. Wally would be back soon. I made a cautious ascent to the top of the stairs. There was still no sign of Jimmie but Wally was in the customers' toilets, clashing his bucket about. I scampered back to the restroom and into the loo there. I climbed on the toilet seat and struggled out of the window. This time I did fall, and landed in a heap on the ground. Fortunately I didn't do any harm, only bruised my behind. I returned the box to the shed, collected my plastic bag, made my way back over the wall and headed for the nearest coffee shop. There I sat with a cup of latte until I reckoned I could safely return to the pizzeria. At eleven ten, I walked boldly in through the front door.

Mario had arrived meantime and was stomping round the kitchen in a foul mood. He didn't ask me if my cold was better or say he was pleased to see me back. He just began straight away with, 'That Bronia has walked out. She didn't give a proper notice in or anything, didn't say a bloody word. She just left this!' He brandished a slip of paper. 'Left a note stuck to the oven door. She's got another job, the little cow. What am I supposed to do?'

I opened my mouth and shut it again. I hoped he didn't find out I'd known about Bronia going for another job. I wished I had the nerve to ask him why he was worrying about staff shortages. He was the cook. All he had to do was run his kitchen. Waitresses were a problem for the manager, Jimmie.

'I can't help you being in that play,' Mario was saying. 'You can't have any more time off. That schedule –' he pointed at the schedule pinned to the wall on which Bronia and I had arranged our shifts around Po-Ching's – 'that's worth nothing now. Where am I going to get another waitress at short notice?'

'There's only a couple more rehearsals, plus the dress rehearsal, and then it's the performance. I don't need many more evenings,' I managed to get in. Boldly I added, 'And I'm not giving up the two rehearsal evenings, not at this late stage in the play. We haven't got much time to iron out all the little problems.' Artfully I added, 'Besides, what with you and Silvio and nearly everyone I know coming to see it, the pressure's really on to get it right.'

Mario scowled at me but he didn't want to lose another waitress. Also, the reminder that Silvio was taking a keen interest in our production carried weight with him. 'Right. But the rest of the time, you'll have to work double shifts.'

I jumped in with both feet. 'Um, I might be able to find you a temporary replacement for Bronia. She wouldn't want to stay on, just for a week or so. It would give you time to recruit someone else permanent.'

Mario folded his arms and leaned back against the worktop. 'What does she look like?'

'Does it matter?' I asked, annoyed by this sexist attitude. 'We don't walk round in bunny costumes.'

That forced a grin from him. 'Pity about that. No – I mean, she's not got tattoos or stuff like that? The customers don't like it.'

'No,' I said. 'She's blonde and curly-haired.'

He raised his eyebrows. 'Tell her to stop by.'

It occurred to me that getting Susie Duke a temporary job as a waitress at the pizzeria might not be the most sensible idea I'd ever had. It was a strictly spur-of-the-moment thing. But I'd accepted her offer of help in the matter of Ion and, well, she might notice something I'd missed. She was the professional, after all.

'I'll just go and change,' I said, heading back towards the restroom. I remembered to close the loo window, reflecting it had been a lot of effort for nothing.

I phoned Susie immediately I'd finished my shift and told her about that morning's escapade.

'Blimey, that was risky,' she said admiringly.

'Not really, I knew Jimmie went for breakfast and only Wally would be around so early. I couldn't have tried it if Mario or Luigi were there. They'd have nabbed me for sure. But Mario doesn't get there before ten thirty, neither does Luigi.'

I then confessed I'd volunteered her as a waitress and that Mario was expecting her that evening. I wasn't sure how she'd take it. However, she seemed to think it was a good idea. Her enthusiasm made me nervous. I stressed to her she was undercover and on no account must she mention the Duke Detective Agency.

'Or we're both dead,' I said.

I did wonder, as I made my way to The Rose that evening, how she would be getting on in her new job waiting tables, but once I got to the functions room, our theatre, all thought of anything other than the play was wiped from my mind.

Everyone was assembled. They stood in a mutinous gang as Marty stormed up and down in front of them, obviously in a foul mood. His nerves seem to have cracked, now we were so near the big night. He was haranguing them on their inadequacies and greeted me with a sour, 'Where have *you* been?'

As the evening wore on, he got worse. Nothing anyone did or suggested was right. Ganesh developed a fit of the sulks and sat in a corner with his arms folded when not required on stage, speaking to no one, not even me. Carmel, the red revolutionary of our number, was the first to decide enough was enough. She turned on Marty and yelled at him that he could keep his sodding play.

The rest of us, now that she'd made a stand, joined in and made the point that we were all volunteers who'd given up much free time against little hope of reward and we were doing our best.

'Best?' shouted the distraught Marty. 'Do you think that when a director is explaining to the top actors what he wants, they turn round and say, stuff it, we're doing our best?'

'We are not the Royal Shakespeare Company!' screeched Carmel.

'Too right!' retorted Marty.

At this the whole thing threatened to descend into an unseemly brawl. Owen and Nigel voiced forceful objections to being treated in this way and proposed immediate strike action. Carmel looked ready to punch Marty on the nose.

Ganesh said calmly, from his corner, 'This is unprofessional. We should sit down and discuss our problems properly.'

I was afraid, for a moment, that they'd all turn on him, but the aggression seemed to seep out of the atmosphere. We all pulled up chairs in a circle and managed a fairly sensible talk-through of all the little glitches which were worrying Marty.

I was sitting next to our director and I did have concerns that he was headed for an early heart attack. His plump face was an unhealthy puce and he was sweating.

'It's all going to be all right, Marty,' I assured him when we'd finished.

He gave me an awkward, sideways look and didn't reply for a moment. Then he said suddenly, 'I've asked all the others how they see their parts, but I haven't asked you. How do you see Miss Stapleton?'

I understood his meaning. When actors walk out on stage, they become the role they play. It's as though the natural order of things is reversed. The real-life persona is laid aside and you are the person you are presenting to the audience, or how will they believe in you? While I was on stage, I *was* Miss Stapleton. I had to understand her from the inside out.

I said, 'She's a battered wife, isn't she? We find that out at the end. She's tied herself to a pig of a man who beats her up, has already murdered once, and is planning to murder again. As part of that plot, he is insisting that she pass herself off as his sister, when she is in reality his wife. She's been getting in deeper and deeper. Apart from a couple of feeble attempts to warn off Sir Henry without being specific about the kind of danger he faces, she goes along with everything Stapleton asks of her until the very last moment, when she rebels.'

'Is she a villainess, then?'

I shook my head. 'No, Stapleton is evil but Doyle never suggests Beryl Stapleton is. She's under his influence. Doyle practised as a doctor. I bet he came across a few battered wives in his time. He understood her.'

'She goes along with his plans because she's afraid of him, then?' Marty stared at me intently. He was still sweating.

'She's certainly afraid of him. He's been violent towards her. But she's still managed to persuade herself he loves her. There are a lot of women in that sort of situation. They stay with men who treat them appallingly. The worst thing, you see, would be to have to face the fact that they weren't loved.'

Marty gave a grunt and I wasn't sure he went along with that. But I didn't suppose he'd ever come across a real-life battered wife and I had. Her name was Lucy and she'd finally run away and ended up sharing a squat with me and others.

'She's not stupid,' I said. 'She's just lost all sense of her own value and ability to make independent judgements. I also think she's deliberately isolated herself from what's going on around her. People can blot out unpleasantness to an extraordinary degree. It's only when she meets Sir Henry Baskerville, and he, obviously, is falling in love with her, that she realises just what she's helping her husband to do. That's when she rebels.'

Marty rubbed his hands on his pudgy thighs as if he wanted to wipe away the perspiration. He muttered, 'Yes, yes.'

'Of course,' I said. 'By then it's too late for her to become a heroine. Doyle realised that. Sir Henry falls in love with her, but he doesn't carry her off to a new life at the end of the story. She's still Stapleton's wife, she still shares his guilt, and she goes down the path to ruin with him. There's no question of Sir Henry continuing to love her once he knows the truth. You can feel a bit sorry for her, but she's always known right from wrong and that what Stapleton is doing is wrong. She should have spoken up at the first. It means she can never be seen as innocent.'

Marty jumped up in a quick careless movement, causing his chair to scrape on the floor and rock dangerously. As he did so, a piece of paper fell out of his pocket. Thinking it was something to do with the play, I picked it up and called to him as he strode off. He turned back and I held it out. As I did so, I saw what it was.

It was one of those printed flyers the police hand out on the street when they're seeking witnesses. This one was headed: FATAL INCIDENT: CAMDEN TOWN UNDERGROUND STATION. It stated the facts of Ion's death briefly without suggesting any cause for his fall and asked anyone who was on the platform at the time to contact the police. My skin prickled.

'Where did you get this, Marty?' I asked.

He turned an even more unattractive purple. 'Plain-clothes copper was handing them out at the Tube station tonight. I just stuffed it in my pocket.'

'I saw you the night of the incident, in the High Street,' I recalled. 'I found you by the Roundhouse, remember? We walked down the street together.'

'Yes, I do,' he said testily. 'So what?'

I took a deep breath. 'The kid I was looking for that night.' I shook the leaflet at him. 'This is the one.'

From purple, Marty turned grey. 'What are you talking about?'

'I knew this kid, the one who died. When I left you so suddenly, it was because I went running after him. We were just by the Tube station.'

'Well, I don't know anything about it,' he snapped. 'Just chuck that piece of paper away. I didn't mean to keep it. I don't want it.'

He marched off. I folded the leaflet and put it in my pocket, meaning to show it to Ganesh later. I couldn't help wondering just what we'd been talking about, Marty and I. About the play, or something else?

I did show the leaflet to Ganesh, on the way home, just as we reached the corner where our ways parted.

'They're treating it as a suspicious death, Gan. They must be.'

'Then let them get on with it,' said Ganesh.

Chapter Ten

I discovered, when I went to work at eleven thirty on Tuesday, that my misgivings about the effect Susie would have on the male staff of the San Gennaro had been well founded. Clearly, she'd been a hit. Even Mario said, 'That is one very attractive woman, that mate of yours, Fran.'

He went on to say that Pietro had fallen in love on sight and dedicated his music to her the previous evening, warbling sentimental ballads and looking like a sick spaniel.

Someone, no doubt Mario, had passed the word to Silvio that there was a new staff member. Our boss dropped by at six, as I was going off duty after a double shift and Susie had just arrived to take over. Silvio's obvious intention was to assess the new employee for himself. His eyes sparkled on being introduced to her and he was flamboyantly gallant.

'Nice old gentleman,' said Susie to me in the restroom. She was buttoning her red waistcoat. It was on the tight side and she was wearing a low-necked white blouse underneath. On me the uniform looked as if I was dressed to go to a kid's party. It made her look as if she was just about to walk on stage as Carmen. I commented as much.

'Get yourself a Wonderbra,' she advised.

'I haven't got anything to put in it.'

I wondered if Silvio had left and hoped he had. He wasn't a young man and the sight of Susie bursting from her ethnic kit might place a serious strain on his heart. I was seriously concerned that I'd done the wrong thing bringing her there. We could do without more complications caused by male hormones.

Even more worryingly, Jimmie drifted past me as I left and said, 'Funny thing, I can't help thinking I've seen that Susie around somewhere.'

'She's sort of a local girl,' I said.

'I suppose that's it. She's a bonny lassie and the type you remember. She must've come in the old spud café a couple of times.'

'You miss the old spud café, don't you, Jimmie?'

He sighed. 'I feel a wee bit useless here. When I was running the spud place, it was my own, I made all the decisions, I made up the menu, I cooked the spuds. It was hard work and I didn't make a lot of money. But I was—' He paused, flushed a salmony pink which clashed with his faded ginger hair, and said, 'I felt I was somebody, you know, hen?'

I nodded. 'I know, Jimmie.'

'Aye, well. All that glitters isn't gold, they say.'

Impetuously I said, 'Why don't you get Silvio to buy you out? You could set up another spud café.'

'Maybe,' he said.

Poor Jimmie. Nothing to do but watch TV and read the tabloid press all day. New clothes, new shades, new job, more money. No independence, no satisfaction, no heart in it.

* * *

165

I should've warned Susie to watch out for Luigi in particular, not only because he was, I'd decided, a nasty piece of work, but because I should have known he'd fancy her. As it was, she'd found out about him straight away. The moment she walked in the place on Monday night, she told me, Luigi went into Latin lover mode. Realising every other male in the place was fantasising about the new help, he made his move quickly.

'I'm going clubbing with Luigi tonight, after we pack up here,' said Susie to me as we parted on Tuesday. There was an undeniable glow of triumph in her face.

'Is this wise?' I asked in some trepidation.

'Don't worry,' said Susie. 'I can look after myself.'

'I hope you're sure about that.'

'Do me a favour. I mean . . .' She primped her curls. 'A girl doesn't mind a man fancying her. But I'm not stupid. I know that sort is generally trouble. They get possessive – that's before they dump you. It's sort of one-way traffic. But I can handle him.'

She seemed to know all about it. She'd always appeared to dote on the late Rennie Duke. Now I was beginning to wonder.

'I thought you'd be pleased,' she said. 'It's a great opportunity to learn something. Fellows like that, they always want to boast and impress a new woman in their lives. He might say something interesting.'

I pointed out as tactfully as I could that Luigi would be suspicious if Susie started asking too many questions.

'I'm not an amateur,' she said huffily. 'And I won't need to ask a lot of questions. I told you, that sort shoots his mouth off to make an impression.'

* * *

We were both off shift on Wednesday morning. Susie appeared on my doorstep at eleven, looking slightly hung-over, and collapsed on the sofa.

'That Luigi,' she said. 'I reckon he's got an extra pair of hands.'

'I warned you,' I said, handing her a strong cup of coffee. 'Did he say anything interesting? I mean, about the pizzeria? Spare me the details of your private life.'

'He didn't get anywhere,' she said, taking the coffee. 'He's got hopes. But he's going to find out that's all he'll ever have.'

She sipped the coffee and put down the mug. 'He was sort of funny about the pizzeria,' she said thoughtfully. 'He doesn't like Mario. There's some sort of dispute between them. Then I overheard a scrap of conversation he had with someone on his mobile phone. I'd nipped into the Ladies' to fix my make-up. When I came back, Luigi was nattering away with the phone stuck to his ear. He didn't see me or hear me come up. He was speaking English. He sounded impatient. He said, "It's all arranged. The paperwork's done, everything. It'll just go through like the last lot." I thought it best then to make myself visible. If he'd turned round and found me standing there, listening, it would have been tricky. So I just walked up to him, all smiles, and said, "Here I am!" He said to the person on the phone, "I've got to go," and he closed the phone down. He didn't say anything about it to me and I didn't ask.'

'That's it!' I exclaimed. 'They're bringing in another lorry with more people hidden in it.'

She frowned. 'What did he mean about paperwork?'

'For what the lorry should be carrying. I don't know, fruit, vegetables, cut flowers, whatever lorries do bring from the Continent.'

'Perhaps,' she said doubtfully. She drained her coffee. 'It was a good evening out, whether it turned up anything or not. I hadn't been clubbing in years. Rennie wasn't into that sort of thing. He reckoned the strobe lights gave him headaches. Now then, Fran. How about going over to the old cinema yard and practising emergency stops?'

'Give it over,' I said wearily. 'I've got dress rehearsal Friday night and the performance on Saturday. I've got to go through my lines.'

'You mustn't stop practising, Fran. You'll lose your touch. Tell you what, we'll get up early and go and do a couple of hours' practice before either of us goes to work tomorrow.'

'What?' I stared at her in dismay. 'Susie, it's flipping cold in the early morning and it's dark!'

'So what? The car's got a heater and it's got headlights. The street lights shine over the wall into the yard. It won't be really dark, just a bit gloomy. Come on, you can roll out of the sack at six for once, can't you?' She stood up. 'I suppose I've got to go home, then, and leave you learning your lines or whatever. I'll see you at work.'

As I hadn't to be at work until six, I walked over to the newsagent's to see Hari and Ganesh. I didn't want Gan to think I was avoiding him.

Between customers, we talked about the play, Hari waxing lyrical about life on the stage. People who don't know anything about it often do. But there are more actors like me, kicking their heels, than there are in full employment.

Ganesh seemed quiet, preoccupied. I asked if he felt confident about his lines. He said he did. Was it the costume which worried him? No, he'd managed to persuade Marty he didn't need to wear the bowler hat. Well, I asked, is it the dress rehearsal? I realised the last rehearsal had been awful, complete chaos. But now that was out of the way, the dress rehearsal would be OK.

He drew a deep breath. 'It's not that, either. I'm a bit concerned about the actual performance, in front of an audience.'

'Gan, we all suffer stage fright. It will be fine.'

He leaned forward and said fiercely, 'How do you know? I'll tell you what's really worrying me about it. It's that dog.'

'Oh come on, Gan. Irish Davey's trained it to run across the stage. You saw it do it. No problem.'

Ganesh snorted. 'You know what they say. Never act with children and animals.'

'Only because they steal the scene. Relax, Gan.'

He sat on the stool behind the counter, anything but relaxed, and stared at me in a way which made me nervous. In the background, Hari muttered to himself over some paperwork before disappearing into the storeroom to check something out. He always seemed to have paperwork problems connected with the business. Ganesh has this idea that he and I might go into business together one day. He wants us to run a dry-cleaning place. No chance. I've seen the hours Hari puts in.

'I went past the pizzeria Monday night, after I left you,' Ganesh said, still fixing me with that look.

My heart sank. I'd forgotten his route home to the shop would take him that way.

'I just glanced through the window to see how much business they were doing. There was a new waitress. It's a funny thing, but she looked very like Susie Duke.'

'Ah,' I said. 'I was going to tell you about that.'

'Were you? You haven't said anything so far and you've been here for the past hour.'

'We were talking about the play. Don't be difficult, Ganesh. Susie hasn't got much work at the moment in her business. Bronia left suddenly to take up her new job. Mario was rampaging round the place making a fuss about being short of staff and saying I'd have to work double shifts. I haven't got time to work double shifts! I suggested Susie – just temporarily.'

'And do they know about the Duke Detective Agency?'

'Come on,' I said. 'Do me a favour. Of course they don't.'

Ganesh leaned forward and jabbed a finger at me. 'You,' he said, 'are living very dangerously. I know what you're up to. You're still trying to track down that Max. You couldn't drag me in so you've dragged in Susie Duke.'

I denied it hotly. 'Susie wanted to help.'

I almost told him about Susie's date with Luigi but that didn't seem like a good idea. Instead I said, 'Susie also thinks there's something going on, something secret. She overheard Luigi on his mobile. He was talking about paperwork being ready and bringing a new lot through.'

'It's a business!' snapped Ganesh. 'All businesses have paperwork. Look at Hari. How do you know he wasn't talking about jars of olives?'

I didn't, of course, so I just stood there looking mutinous.

He tapped his fingers on the counter. 'I don't want to quarrel with you, Fran. I don't like rowing with you at any time and I certainly don't want us falling out just before the performance. We've all got to work together on that play and not go squabbling like Monday night. If you and I aren't speaking off stage, it'll show on stage. So for that reason, and only for that reason, I won't say any more now. But once we've done the play on Saturday, once it's all behind us, you and I are going to have a long talk.'

'You're not my father!' I snapped. 'I don't have to listen to you lecture me.'

'No,' he said. 'I'm your friend. I care what happens to you. Probably the only person who does.'

That was a sobering thought. He was right. There were a few people who might be sorry if I came to harm, but none who'd really grieve for me except Ganesh. I was about to say I realised that and appreciated his caring, when he spoke again and spoiled it.

'Unless you think your new pal Susie Duke will shed tears when she hears someone has knocked you on the head and tipped you in the canal – or in front of a train.'

'I'd hate to think,' I told him, 'that you were jealous of Susie. Why don't you like her?'

'Who said I didn't like her?' He glowered at me. 'She's all right. But she's got an ulterior motive in being so

171

friendly towards you. She wants you to work for that crummy detective agency she runs.'

'I know that!' I defended Susie. 'She's upfront and honest about that. She's not being underhand.' I drew a deep breath and added, 'I am always careful—'

'Hah!' exclaimed Ganesh loudly, causing Hari to pop his head out through the storeroom door and look round the shop in alarm.

'I care about my own safety! No one,' I went on, 'is going to knock me on the head and tip me in the canal – or anything else.' I hoped this was true.

Ganesh folded his arms. 'All right. But just remember this. Susie was married for goodness knows how many years to Rennie Duke, who was a seedy, devious, untruthful little snoop. Keep company with someone like that for long enough, and some of it has to rub off.'

I thought about the key Susie had kept, which had allowed us on to the old cinema site – but I didn't tell Ganesh about it.

I wasn't very happy when I made my way to work that evening. Quarrelling with Ganesh always gets me down. I know we hadn't actually had a full-blown stand-up fight, but we'd parted on frosty terms. I wasn't prepared to take all the blame for this. Ganesh's superior way of lecturing me had annoyed me. He didn't have any right to tell me what to do. On the other hand he cared about me and, if he was in a bad mood, it was because he was worried about me and not just about Irish's dog.

I was also annoyed because he'd suggested I couldn't hold my own against Susie Duke, that I'd be influenced by her. This was insulting to me. What was I? A kid? No, I was nearly twenty-two, I'd looked after myself since I was sixteen, I'd mixed with every kind of person and learned to be streetwise in the cause of self-preservation. So, I told myself, I can handle the situation. I know what I'm doing. I'll make out all right.

Yes, sneered a voice in my brain, *like you've done all through your life. Falling out with authority at every turn and messing up everything you've ever started to do. Not to mention getting yourself into situations like this one. You should have walked out of the pizzeria after the first week, when you realised something wasn't right about the set-up. You should never have promised Ion you'd help him. Probably you should never have agreed to be in that play.*

I was rather startled at finding myself thinking the last thing. The play wasn't ever going to take the world by storm, but once we'd got all the problems with it ironed out it should be a good production of its kind. Marty's script, though difficult to decipher, was a good one. He had talent as a playwright. I hoped that one day he was successful with his own original work, not just doing adaptations of well-known stories to please someone like Freddy.

The trouble was, in real life, you have to compromise. I've never been good at that. I put it down to my Hungarian blood. We Magyars aren't content to settle for less than we really want. All or nothing, that's our motto. We were always the cavalry, charging straight at the enemy. Grandma Varady believed in going straight at a situation. When I was expelled from school, we had to hold her down to stop her marching round there to tell the headmistress what she thought and to insist I was reinstated.

Then there was the time I was nudged off my bicycle by a car driven by someone who'd only just arrived in the country and hadn't got the hang of our traffic rules, like driving on the other side of the road to every other nation. I was brought home in a police car. The driver of the car which had hit me followed behind, to explain and apologise. Poor man, he was so upset. He'd been driving for over twenty years and never had an accident. He'd only been in the country twenty-four hours. I wasn't hurt. Dad was ready to forgive the driver. The police didn't want to charge him. But Grandma Varady hit the roof. The result was the driver withdrew his apology and got stroppy. The police turned nasty. Dad tried to intervene and got it in the neck from all sides. I was so embarrassed I slipped away while they were all going at it hammer and tongs, and stayed out for the rest of the day. Grandma had a point, because the front wheel of my bike was bent and useless. But, as you see, nothing in my upbringing educated me into accepting anyone else's point of view without a good argument first, or to do all those little deals in life you have to do if you want to be friends with people you meet every day. That's the risk with 'all or nothing'. You may just end up with nothing.

We had an exceptionally busy evening at work and that stopped me thinking about anything. I did hope, in the hurly-burly of rushing back and forth to the kitchen, that Susie would forget about the early-morning driving lesson. I was even less inclined to keep on with the driving, at least for the moment. Something else I should have thought more about before I accepted. But as we parted outside the pizzeria that night she pointed a pink-varnished nail at me and said, 'Six o'clock tomorrow morning. I'll pick you up.'

'Oh, great,' I mumbled.

'Hey,' said Luigi, materialising from somewhere in a snazzy jacket with the collar turned up, and jangling his car keys. 'I'll give you a lift home, Susie.'

He didn't offer me a lift. I walked.

Forget the rising sun and larks singing. Six o'clock in the morning at the end of February is not a nice time to be up and about, not in London, anyway.

Susie appeared at my door, clad in a pink puffa jacket and woolly hat, apparently full of beans.

'How did you get on with Luigi last night?' I asked. 'After he gave you the lift home?'

She stared at me wide-eyed and innocent. 'He gave me a lift, that's all. I told him I was really tired. I didn't ask him in for coffee or anything.'

Oh yeah? snarled that inner me. Well, it was Susie's problem, not mine. She'd let herself in for it.

The night sky above had that luminosity which comes from absorbing all the light beamed up from below. At street level the curious half-dark of big cities is even more obvious. It's a night world that is never really dark, yet the darkness is there, swirling in alleys and shop doorways with an almost tactile quality to it. Perhaps lost souls wander in a similar gloom in some mythical Underworld somewhere – although there are plenty of them wandering the streets of London, come to that. London at night is the kingdom of Dis.

It had rained around three that morning. I'd heard it pattering on my windows. The wet pavements shone dully beneath the yellow lamplight. The wind bowled rubbish along them. Papers rustled round my feet. An empty can rolled noisily into the gutter. Someone had chucked a polystyrene box half-filled with uneaten chicken tikka into our porch. Someone else, or perhaps the same person, had thrown up outside the next-door gate. It was bitterly cold.

But there are always people about in a big city, even at that unearthly hour. Some of them are the lost souls I mentioned, some respectable citizens who start work early. As Susie and I drove towards the old cinema site, we passed huddled figures plodding along or hunched in miserable queues at bus stops. Each person was wrapped up to the ears against the cold and enclosed in a personal world of discomfort and resentment. They looked neither to left nor right. Occasionally a brightly lit bus cruised down the main roads, shining in the gloom like a liner at night on a dark and hostile ocean. The passengers had wan, sleep-puffed faces.

Around the old cinema it was quiet. Such businesses as there were in the area didn't open before nine. Susie, still exuding an optimism which was positively indecent at that time of day, unlocked the padlock and pushed open the gate. I drove through. She pushed it shut behind me.

'Just in case,' she said as she climbed back in the car. 'Now then, you drive round the yard here and when I slap my hand on the dashboard, you stop – immediately.'

'This is ridiculous,' I said.

'No, it's not. You're getting experience of driving in poor light as well. It's not that dark, not really.'

To be fair the surrounding street lighting and illuminated shop windows meant that the yard wasn't pitch
black. But it still appeared as a big gloomy sinister void.

'I can't see what's out there, beyond the headlights, not
properly,' I muttered rebelliously, peering through the
windscreen.

'No, so be ready to stop suddenly even if I don't slap
the dashboard.'

I drove round the yard very slowly once to get my
bearings and check the far corners. They might conceal
some old hobo who'd climbed in to doss undisturbed, and
was liable to lurch out under my wheels. But it seemed we
had the place to ourselves. My eyes adjusted to the shadows
and it didn't seem so dark and frightening after all.

I made emergency stops three times in response to Susie
hitting the dashboard. Then she ordered me to pull up
under the lee of the far wall. I glanced at my watch. It was
just on seven-thirty. Dawn was breaking slowly in the sky
above us, which now had a thin, dirty navy-blue tinge to it.
She began digging in a canvas bag she'd brought along
and produced a thermos flask, two plastic cups and a copy
of the *Highway Code*.

'Have a coffee,' she said. 'Warm us both up. Then I'll
ask you some questions.'

I accepted the coffee and we sat in silence drinking it. I
wasn't thinking about the *Highway Code*, although I should
have been.

'Susie,' I said at last. 'I saw Ganesh yesterday. He's
really dead against my working with you. He's found out
you're waiting tables at the pizzeria. He's a bit miffed with
me at the moment.'

'He'll get over it,' said Susie comfortably.

'You don't know Ganesh,' I said. 'He never gives up. He never forgets anything. I've a feeling he could be pretty unforgiving if I did anything really wrong. He . . .' I hesitated. 'It sounds daft, but he's got a sort of respect for me. He thinks I do stupid things. But he also thinks I'm an OK person. I don't want to let him down.'

I don't know what Susie might have replied to that. There was a distant rattle and scrape of metal. From the far side of the dark cinema block the beam of headlights suddenly fell across the yard.

'Bloody hell!' gasped Susie. 'Someone's coming in here! Quick!' She grabbed my beaker and stuffed it and the thermos into the bag. 'C'mon, Fran. Don't just sit there! Kill the lights and get out of the car!'

She was exiting the car on her side as she spoke, canvas bag slung over her shoulder. I switched off the lights and scrambled out. My side was next to the wall and I had only just enough room. I squeezed between car and wall, scraping my clothes on the brickwork, and ran after her. It struck me, as I did, that she seemed to have forgotten that, according to her, whoever it was could only ask us to leave. When I got a chance, I'd ask her again to give me her rundown on the law of trespass.

She'd headed for the cinema itself and seemed to know what she was doing. I could just make her out and then she dived behind a skip full of rubbish. I scuttled behind it too, thinking this was where she meant us to hide. I had time to decide it wasn't a very good hiding place, but when I got there Susie had disappeared.

'Fran!' I heard an urgent whisper from above my head.

I put out my hand and felt a metal rung beneath my fingers. There was a ladder, part of a fire escape, fixed to the wall. Susie had already shinned up it and I followed.

I was putting my faith in her and also in the ladder being fixed firmly enough to take the weight of both of us. I don't like heights very much and was glad of the poor light, which meant the ground was indistinct. Even with my dislike of heights, the arrival of unknown visitors would have sent me up that ladder. I had a feeling whoever they were, they wouldn't be pleased to find us there, and asking us politely to leave wouldn't be their reaction.

I reached the top of the ladder and a parapet. Susie's arm came out of the murk. She seized my shoulder and hauled me over the edge on to a flat piece of roof. She was panting noisily and so was I. I hoped they wouldn't hear us down below.

We crawled along the roof below the parapet and peered over the edge. A lorry had driven into the yard and stopped directly below us. The driver jumped out. His headlights had reflected off Susie's car and he was on his way to investigate it. We watched as he walked round it and peered inside. Then he went to the rear and stared thoughtfully at the boot lid. Susie had left it all unlocked, but he didn't touch the vehicle, much less try to open any part of it. He was cautious. I guessed he was thinking it might be booby-trapped. I found myself wondering if he'd ever served in the army and been stationed in Northern Ireland.

He had learned all he could from just looking at the car. He walked away into the middle of the yard and stood, hands on hips, staring round him, looking for the person or persons who'd brought the car in. Then he began to walk slowly towards the cinema. In a moment he'd see the skip and, if he investigated further, he'd find the ladder.

Just then, however, more headlights gleamed in the gloom and a car entered the yard. It parked on the further side of the lorry and although we heard the slam of a door as the driver got out we couldn't see him.

The lorry driver turned back and went to meet the newcomer. Both were now behind the lorry, presumably in conversation.

'What do we do now?' I whispered to Susie.

'Hang on a jiff,' she said. She sounded remarkably calm. 'We might learn something.'

We did that all right. The driver had climbed up into his cab from the passenger side and switched off his headlights. The car driver had killed his. It was still gloomy down there, if not really dark. The wind nipped spitefully at my earlobes. I wished I had a woolly hat like Susie's.

Driver and newcomer were now proceeding towards Susie's car. I drew in my breath. Because there were no longer lights below, I couldn't make out any detail of the two figures. All I could see was two dark grey outlines. The tall one I knew was the driver. The other was not quite so tall and in shape quite different, a massive rounded body on stubby legs like a kid's stuffed toy. The effect was increased by the shapeless hooded jacket which covered his bulk and his head.

'A fat man!' I said more loudly than I intended and winced when Susie dug me hard in the ribs. 'Sorry, Susie,' I hissed.

Cautiously we peered over the edge again. The men

were talking together by Susie's car, deciding what to do.

I heard the driver say, 'Probably nicked.'

The other man said something in a low voice. I couldn't catch the words.

'Yeah, yeah,' said the lorry driver. 'I'll take a good look round before I go. But I want to unload them now. It's getting too light. There will be people about. I want 'em off my rig and out of here.'

Susie touched my arm. 'Follow me,' she breathed into my ear.

'No,' I whispered back. 'I want to see what he's got in that lorry. You heard, he's going to unload it now.' My spine tingled and butterflies were doing the can-can in my stomach.

'It'll be cigarettes or booze . . .' she muttered.

But she was wrong. Somehow I'd known she was. As soon as I'd seen that portly shapeless figure I'd guessed what to expect.

The driver released the doors at the back of the lorry and called something inside. A figure dropped out, jumping to the ground and moving a little distance away, then another. When I was a kid my dad used to amuse me by drawing stick figures, one on each page of a small note-book. Each figure was caught in a frozen moment of action, like photographic stills. When Dad riffled through all the pages of the notebook, the stick figures appeared in rapid sequence, giving the illusion of movement: a running man, a jumping horse. I expect you've done the same sort of thing. I was reminded of it now as the dark little stick figures each repeated the movement of the one before, emerging from the body of the lorry, jumping, running to one side. I counted some dozen in all. They stood in a huddled group, waiting.

I dug Susie in the ribs. 'Luigi's phone call . . .' I breathed. 'I said they were bringing another lot in!'

The driver was pointing in the general direction of the exit. The men – I thought they were all men but one or two were very slightly built and might have been youths or women – began to murmur together. The ominous silhouette of the fat man reappeared and beckoned to them. They trotted trustingly after him, out of sight, like the kids after the Pied Piper of Hamelin.

When the fat man had led them all away, the lorry driver closed up the rear of his rig and climbed into the cab. After a few moments, the fat man returned alone. He walked down the far side of the lorry. The driver and he must have had some conversation. A car door slammed. The fat man reversed his motor past us and three-point-turned beautifully so that he could drive down the side of the building and out. When he'd gone, the driver climbed down from his cab and started out again towards the old cinema.

'Now!' ordered Susie.

This time I followed her. We scrambled across the roof, up and down, round pipes and over brickwork. Eventually she stopped and pulled at what it was now light enough for me to see was a trapdoor. It creaked up and open. She slid through the opening into the dark pit beneath, and stopped with her head sticking out and one arm held upwards, propping up the trap.

'Grab hold of it, Fran, and come on! There's a ladder.'

If there'd been less urgency about the situation, I'd have hesitated. As it was, I grabbed the edge of the trap in one hand and felt over the edge of the frame with the other. There was a ladder there all right.

I scrambled over and let the trap fall above my head, hoping the clunk it made wasn't audible to the driver prowling round below. The light was abruptly cut off, leaving me in real darkness. I don't know to this day quite how I got down the ladder to the floor. When I reached the bottom, I found myself illuminated unexpectedly by a pencil ray of light. Susie had a torch. She must have had it in the canvas bag. She was a pro, all right.

'Where are we?' I asked. 'I mean, I know we're inside the cinema, but what now?'

'This way.' She set off. The torch beam bobbed along a corridor. She came to a door and pushed it open.

We found ourselves in a small room. My foot struck something on the floor with a metallic clink. She focused the torch beam downwards and I saw a round flat metal can of the sort spools of film are kept it.

'Old projection room,' she said briefly. 'We're all right here. Even if that driver finds the fire escape, he won't fancy climbing up it. If he does, and gets on to the roof, that's as far as he'll go. He won't know the layout.'

'You know it, it seems,' I said drily. 'You seem to know the whole building like the back of your hand.'

'Yeah, well, I've been here before, haven't I?' She spoke casually.

A lot too casually for my liking. Things were coming together in my head and I didn't like the picture that was forming. I remembered my suspicion, when Susie first showed me the key to the gate, that Rennie had kept it because he intended to steal the odd item from the building. I'd assumed that if he had, Susie had known nothing about it. But Ganesh's voice echoed in my ears, pointing out that years living with Rennie must have had some influence on his wife.

'Susie,' I said quietly. 'Tell me the truth. How come you know the way in and out of this building so well?'

'I told you.' She sounded surprised. 'Rennie did a job for the bloke who bought it. He reckoned his business partner was cheating on him. It meant keeping observation. Well, we couldn't do it from outside, could we? We'd have been spotted. So we did it from here, the perfect place, really, see?'

She flashed the torch beam around the walls and brought it to rest on a square aperture. I followed her to it and she shone the torch through it and downwards.

I had the impression of a vast emptiness. I couldn't see the bottom, but the torch beam caught the curved frontage of a balcony.

'The auditorium,' said Susie. 'From up here we could watch anything that went on down there. We took turns, Rennie and me, sitting up here, waiting for the bloke to turn up and start moving stuff out. Twenty-four-hour watch it was, but we got the evidence. Rennie took pictures of him loading the stuff into a van. He leaned over that parapet and snapped him from above. Neat job, that was.'

'You sat up here at night, watching, on your own?' I gasped.

'Oh no, fair do's. Rennie did the night shifts and most of the day shifts as well. I just took over for an hour or two in the middle of the day to give Rennie a chance to go home, shower and fry up something to eat. He could kip up here. He brought a sleeping bag. Brought his sandwiches as well. Home from home, he used to call it.'

Susie gave a sentimental sigh. 'They were good days, Fran. Rennie and me, working together. We were a team.'

Her voice became dreamy. 'Anyway, I didn't mind being here all alone during the day. See, I felt I knew the old place. My mum, she'd worked here as an usherette when the cinema was in its glory days. She was sixteen when she started the job and she told me all about it.'

She broke off. From above our heads came an ominous creak and a crunching noise. It was repeated.

'Susie,' I whispered. 'The driver, he *is* up there.'

'Up there isn't down here,' she replied with that optimism of hers which was beginning to irritate me. But she killed the torchlight. 'He won't wander about up there indefinitely. The whole structure's wonky. He'll be frightened of an accident. If he breaks his leg he'll be stuck. Time is against him. It's light now outside and he won't want to hang around and have someone notice the lorry. If he can't see us, he'll call it a day. Trust me,' she hissed.

I had little choice. We heard a bit more movement and then silence.

'He's gone,' whispered Susie. 'But we'll just wait a while to give him time to get clear.' She switched on the torch and flashed its beam over my huddled figure. 'Come on, cheer up.' When I just grunted she went on, 'I wish I could've seen this old place in its heyday, like Mum saw it. It was just like a palace then. The seats were red plush. All the ornamental bits and carving were gold. There was a cinema organ. It rose up out of the floor before the show began, with a chap sitting at it and playing away for all he was worth. He played the hits of the day and things like the "Blue Danube" waltz that everyone knew. Then he'd sink back out of sight as the lights went down. The beautiful big velvet curtains across the screen were drawn back with a rustling noise and everyone would settle down. You could feel a buzz of anticipation, Mum said. The screen would show that big brass gong and the muscleman striking it with a hammer. My grandad told me the bloke hitting the gong was Bombardier Billy Wells, an old-time boxer. But I don't know if that was right. It was like being in a magical world, Mum reckoned. She got to see all the films, got to see them over and over again, but she didn't mind. In the interval the lights would go up. The courting couples would spring apart. She'd go along between the aisles with her tray of ice cream and little boxes of orange squash. She had a proper uniform with a little hat.

'Later on, of course, the place got run-down and tatty. Audiences dropped off when the television came in. Before that, Mum told me, they'd queue round the block to get in, not just for the big films, but any film. Then they closed it. Cinemas were changing. They had to, if they wanted to survive. This old place didn't meet modern regulations on safety and it only had the one screen. It'd have cost a lot to turn it into a modern multi-screen complex with all the trimmings. Even if they had, I suppose it would have been superfluous. It sort of got made redundant. Mum wasn't still working here then, of course, when it closed, but I remember how sad she was. That's why this old place is like a friend to me.'

I clambered to my feet and went back to the aperture. I poked my head through. In the darkness something creaked, filling me with a momentary panic that the driver was back and inside the building, but it was only the woodwork. The air was stuffy, full of dust and overladen with the sour memory of nicotine from the days when everyone puffed away in the cinema. I thought of Susie's mother in her usherette's uniform and with her tray, walking down the aisles with her torch flashing along the rows – and her daughter, years later, sitting up here with her little torch and a packet of sandwiches.

'Funny thing,' came Susie's voice from behind me. 'We never had any money when I was a kid. But when you look back at childhood, it seems like everything was warm and comfortable then.'

I considered my own childhood and the drama of my mother's departure. Despite that, I hadn't felt unloved because Dad and Grandma made sure of that.

Susie said, 'Rennie and I were pretty skint quite a lot of the time, too, but we were never miserable.' With a change of tone, she added, 'But you don't make many friends in the detection business. I wouldn't tell you otherwise, Fran.'

We sat in silence for a while, drinking the last of the coffee from Susie's thermos. It was a bit stewed and unpleasant.

'What do we do now?' I asked.

She shone the torch on her wristwatch. 'I reckon it's safe to go.'

'What about the car? Now they've seen it, they'll know the registration number and be looking out for it.'

'Yes, that's bad,' she agreed. 'I think I'll leave it here and report it stolen.'

'Would that work?'

'Well, the alternative is to drive it home, lock it in my garage and not use it until things settle down. We'll cut out the driving lessons for a while.'

After a moment I said, 'At least now we know Ion told me the truth.'

'You mean the fat bloke? You don't know it was the same one. You didn't hear a name.'

'Come on,' I replied impatiently. 'How many organisations are there in the area, running in illegal immigrants in lorries and coordinated at the drop-off point by a fat man? We saw Max down there. It means he's local. That's how Ion came to see him in the street. He's around here somewhere and if he is, I can find him.'

'Not without a better lead than you've got. Believe me, I've traced people. You've got to have something to go on. At least a picture or a look at his face. All you've got is that he's fat. A ticket from a speak-your-weight machine could tell you that.'

I noticed that from 'we' she'd gone back to using 'you'. She was worried about the car.

When we emerged on to the roof again it was daylight. It revealed just what an obstacle course it was up there and what a bad state the roof was in generally. Fortunately I'd had no time to notice that during our flight earlier. I understood the driver's reluctance to linger up here, clambering over rain-wet surfaces. Climbing down the fire escape in broad daylight was worse than shinning up in the gloom. I was thankful when we got to the ground.

Susie walked round the car, frowning.

'Perhaps,' I said, 'they won't be able to trace it to you.'

'An outfit like that,' she said, 'has got to have a bent copper or two in its pocket to look it up on the computer for them. If they're thorough, they'll trace it to me all right. Even if I reported it stolen, they wouldn't believe it. Not once they found out about the detective agency.'

It was a disquieting thought.

Chapter Eleven

We discussed it some more without reaching any decision and in the end, as the surrounding area woke up, the roads filling with traffic and the pavements with pedestrians, we drove back to Susie's block of flats.

It was a short but tense journey. Susie was worried about the traffickers tracing her car. I was filled with the conviction that I'd seen Max, seen him with my own eyes. It gave me the most extraordinary sensation: satisfaction because my belief in Ion had been justified, mixed with something akin to panic because the moment was drawing near when I'd have to tell my story to Janice Morgan. I was wound up like a clock spring. We locked the car away in the graffiti-covered garage. Then we went up to Susie's place for a cup of tea.

I hadn't been inside Susie's flat since the days following the death of her husband. On my last visit, my driving lesson, I hadn't had time to socialise. I noticed, as we made our way up there, that little appeared to have changed since the last time I'd set foot in the block. The lift was still, or again, out of order and we had to toil up the stairs. The staircase had the same stale smell. Ascending through its concrete bareness was depressing and eerie, like being in some futuristic maze. As we turned to trudge up the last flight, some kids ran down past us. They forced us back against the walls and, whooping and yelling, their pinched little faces twisted in unholy glee, clattered on downwards.

'That Darren Murphy and his brothers,' said Susie. 'They're maniacs. The whole family's raving mad.' She sounded philosophical about it. She added, 'Still, if you live here, it helps to be a bit mad.'

The wind cut icily along the open balcony in front of the flats at each level. I supposed the blocks had been built in the sixties when this sort of development had been confidently expected to solve the housing problems of the big cities: a triumphant social experiment. The planners might have thought that, but not the people who actually had to live in the flats. Many of these blocks had been torn down in the years since then, but here they'd survived. The day the bulldozers moved in, everyone would be cheering.

At Susie's flat someone had cleaned the graffiti I remembered from the outside wall. But another local artist had been along with his can of aerosol paint and re-decorated it with a fresh lot. The jumble of letters didn't consist of personal abuse in the way the previous scrawled messages had. Rennie hadn't been popular. This time, the new artist (perhaps one of the Murphy brothers) had confined himself to his own name and a crudely drawn unflattering image of a man in a rocker's jacket. The artist himself? An admired pop star?

'I keep telling the council,' said Susie. 'They promise to come round and clean it off but they don't bother. You can't blame them. Someone would only come along straight away and spray another lot.'

Inside the flat was tidier than when I'd last been here but otherwise unchanged, the same suite covered in blue velvet-type fabric, the line of posturing flamenco dolls. The cross-eyed china cat inside whose hollow body Rennie had apparently hidden his personal insurance certificate now held pride of place on an occasional table. Beside it was a photograph of the late Mr Duke, wearing shorts and a luridly patterned shirt. There was also a pot plant with dark green leaves and tiny orange flowers. The whole thing was clearly a shrine to Rennie's memory.

It did occur to me that, when Susie had told me she hadn't invited Luigi up here for a coffee, she'd been telling the truth. Even Luigi, I fancied, would have found the memorial table put a bit of a damper on his passion.

'That's the British answer to any problem, isn't it?' Susie called wryly from the kitchen where she was plugging in her electric kettle and rummaging in the fridge for milk. 'Make a pot of tea.'

'Yeah,' I agreed absently, studying Rennie's picture. Even in a holiday snap he managed to look shifty.

She carried the tray with the mugs into the living room. 'Do you want a drop of something with it, Fran? For the shock? I've got whisky.'

'Not at this hour of the morning,' I said. 'Thanks all the same.'

Because of our early start, it was still only just after nine. Having been up since the crack of dawn, I would have been starting to flag if it hadn't been for the adrenalin still coursing through me. We didn't need to be at the pizzeria until half past eleven and I hoped the buzz kept me going until then.

'Right,' said Susie, plonking a cup of tea down in front of me. 'We haven't got much time and we've got to sort this out. We agree a plan of action and we stick to it.'

'Marty's making us run through our weak points in the script tonight,' I reminded her. 'They're all turning up at my flat. I must be there.'

'Forget that. That's not until this evening. What we need to decide is what we do this morning, before we go to work. That's the most important thing. We've got two hours to make up our minds and do it.'

I picked up the meaning of that. 'You're talking of going to the police,' I said. 'It's easy for you. You didn't hold out on Morgan as I did. You didn't have her sitting on your sofa urging you to confide and burbling about places of safety.'

'Fran.' She leaned forward. 'I'm a professional. I run a business here. If I come across something really dodgy in the course of my work – and it doesn't have anything directly to do with a client – I have to inform the cops. Those people getting out of that lorry, that was well dodgy. You told me that Inspector Morgan is investigating a gang running in illegal immigrants and based in the area. Both of us, Fran, we both need to tell her about this.'

'Then you're going to have to tell her about Luigi's mobile phone call. He could even have been talking about this very lorry. And I,' I finished firmly, 'will tell her about Max. I'm not leaving out the bit about Max.'

'Are you going to tell her you were on that underground platform and saw your little friend take a dive in front of a train? You either tell the cops everything or you tell them nothing,' she retorted. 'If you tell them half a story and they find out the rest somehow themselves, you're in trouble.'

'I'm in trouble, anyway,' I said gloomily. 'For not telling Morgan when she came to see me.'

She shook her blonde curls. 'You've got an excuse. You were in shock. You'd witnessed the terrible sudden death of someone you knew. You cannot be expected to have been of sound judgement that evening when she called round. You didn't expect her, did you?'

I shook my head.

'Right, she turned up unexpectedly, uninvited, at a time when you were not yourself. She can't grumble if you didn't bare your soul. That's your best defence. Stick to it.'

It sounded all right when she said it. I didn't know if Morgan would buy the excuse. Parry certainly wouldn't. But the decision had been made for me. Susie was going to the police and I had to go with her. I'd held out on Morgan once, but I couldn't do it a second time.

Again Susie's attitude niggled me. She was a great one for handing out advice. Join the Duke Detective Agency, Fran. Learn to drive. Trespass on the locked-up premises of the old cinema. Try to convince Morgan that Ion's death has left you near a nervous breakdown. At this rate, I would end up with a nervous breakdown, only I hadn't got time for one. I could almost see Ganesh's ghostly presence standing beside me with an 'I told you so' expression on his face.

We got to the cop shop just before ten. I had a speech ready, demanding to see Inspector Morgan and no other officer. It was a condition I'd already insisted on to Susie. But bad luck was in the ascendant. A contrary star sign must have collided with my own. Wayne Parry was lurking in the reception area, chatting up an unimpressed woman officer on the desk. When he saw Susie and me enter, he stopped, looked surprised for a couple of seconds and then smirked, as if he'd known all along I'd eventually take up the invitation to drop by.

'Hello,' he said in his genial way, 'Look what the cat brought in.'

'Speak for yourself,' snapped Susie.

'Not you, love. This one.' He pointed at me. 'What have you done now, Fran? Got yourself into a fix and want us to get you out of it?'

This was too near the truth to be welcome. 'It's Miss Varady to you,' I retorted, taking my cue from Susie. If one of us was going to be stroppy we might as well both be. 'We'd like to talk to Inspector Morgan.'

'Would you now? What would that be about, I wonder? How about having a nice little chat with me in the interview room?'

'Forget it,' I said. 'This is for Morgan's ears only.'

'All right, Moneypenny,' he said. 'I'll tell the inspector. But she'll want to know what it's all about, just generally.'

'Just generally, I'm not saying a word to you. You can tell her it follows on the visit she paid me recently.'

He gave me a thin smile and told us to wait. We sat down on an uncomfortable bench. The desk officer ignored us. Coppers came in and out. They ignored us. A man came in and began a loud complaint about his car being towed away. They sent him along to the traffic section.

Parry came back and said Morgan was busy. We could either talk to him or carry on waiting.

'We're not talking to you,' I said. 'Nothing personal. But Morgan came to see me. Both Susie and I have to get to work this morning by half past eleven and we can't wait any longer. Go back and tell Morgan it's now or after the weekend. Tonight I've got a rehearsal at my flat. On Friday I've got to go to work and to the dress rehearsal at the pub in the evening. On Saturday it won't be convenient because not only have I got to go to work during the day, but it's the real performance in the evening.'

Parry went away again.

'Perhaps we could talk to him, Fran,' whispered Susie.

'No way. Morgan's playing one of her games. She's guessed I didn't tell her something at my flat that I've decided to spill the beans about now. She's letting me know that if I muck her about, she can muck me about.' I folded my arms and stretched out my legs. The desk officer gave me a sardonic look.

Parry returned. 'OK, she's got a ten-minute window.'

'A *what*?' I asked, and he had the grace to blush.

In the end, Parry sat in on the conversation anyway. The four of us huddled in friendly proximity in the cramped interview room. I'd been in this room before and its dark green-and-cream-painted walls didn't look as if they'd been redecorated since my last visit. I recognised some of the pockmarks and scratches in the paint and noted some new ones. A very young, ginger-haired PC in a woolly pullover brought us tea. I was awash with tea already and feeling peckish. I hadn't had any breakfast. I asked pathetically if there was any chance of a bacon roll from the canteen.

'You've got a nerve,' said Parry, almost with respect.

'Tell them to send down two bacon rolls and charge them up to me,' said Morgan.

'Thanks,' I said, 'really.'

'I'll claim it as expenses,' she said. 'Now then, what's it all about?'

Susie and I explained, taking turns. I went first and told them about my initial meeting with Ion and the tale of his search for his missing brother. I told them about the fat man he'd seen in silhouette and his hearing the man addressed as Max. Ion had believed Max was connected with the pizzeria because he'd followed him there and seen him go into the corridor where the office door was – but it was strongly possible he'd mistaken the door to the toilets for the office. I knew Ion had been on the premises and even down in the cellar. For my part, although I'd tried to find out if it was true there was someone called Max connected with the San Gennaro, so far I'd drawn a blank. On the other hand, I'd long had suspicions about the place where I worked.

'Why?' ask Parry at this point, when I paused for breath.

I explained as best I could, confessing my suspicions were largely based on Jimmie being so clearly out of the loop and in no way an active manager. Parry snorted.

'I know 'im,' he said. 'He used to sell those spuds. He was always dodgy.'

'So do I know him,' I said. 'And he isn't crooked. Not big-time, anyway, not like we're talking about. If there is something going on at that pizzeria, Jimmie knows nothing about it.'

Parry looked unconvinced. I was worried. One reason I'd been so reluctant to tell the police of my suspicions was because I hadn't wanted to make trouble for Jimmie.

'If,' said Parry, 'if he's not really the manager, why is he there, eh? Perhaps he's doing a different job, one you know nothing about.'

'He's there to be the fall guy!' I insisted. 'He does nothing all day but watch telly and read the tabloids.'

Susie broke in with, 'Fran's right about that pizzeria. I've been working there, just a short while, but at least someone at the place is into something. I had a date with the barman.'

She explained about Luigi's phone call and I could tell they were interested in that. They exchanged significant glances. Morgan tapped the end of her biro on the table. Parry relapsed into silence. They were both looking at me.

I was even more worried because the moment had come for my big confession: that I'd been on the underground platform and seen Ion fall in front of the train. I took a deep breath and blurted it out, adding that I'd not, definitely not, seen how he'd come to fall.

The bacon rolls turned up at that point, which was a fortunate interruption as Morgan's face had turned rather red and I could see she was about to bawl me out in a big way.

The food interval enabled her to get control of her emotions. She'd remembered you don't start yelling at a witness before she's finished her tale. You wait until afterwards.

While I licked grease off my fingers, Susie took up the story. She explained about the driving lessons and why we'd gone to the old cinema site, and how we'd been interrupted by the arrival of the lorry and hidden on the roof.

At this point, Parry stopped sucking his teeth to ask, why hide?

'We didn't know who it was, did we?' she retorted.

'Not because you were trespassing?'

'No! And we weren't. I've got the key.'

Morgan cleared her throat, gave Parry a warning look and indicated we should continue. 'What happened then?'

Susie told them about the men jumping from the lorry and they both sat up like a couple of gun dogs. I finished off the whole thing by telling them I was sure I'd seen the fat man, Max. Unfortunately, I couldn't give a better description of him.

Morgan stopped tapping her biro on the table. She said, 'I see,' but that was all.

This was apparently some signal to Parry. Either it was the way they worked together, or she just didn't trust herself to speak.

'Let me get this right,' said Parry. 'You and Mrs Duke broke into the yard at the back of the old cinema to practise your driving skills, Fran.'

'I told you, we didn't break in!' snapped Susie. 'I've got the perishing key. Look!' She delved in her pocket, took out the key and flourished it under his nose.

Parry's bloodshot gaze fixed on it disbelievingly.

'And does the owner of the premises know you've got this key?'

'He should,' said Susie. 'He gave it to Rennie, my late husband.'

'Yeah, I remember your old man,' said Parry, sarcasm dripping from his moustache.

Morgan stirred and took charge. 'Perhaps, Mrs Duke, you had better leave the key with us.'

'Why?' demanded Susie.

'Because,' I said, 'they'll go round to the yard and try it to see if it really is the key.'

'Thank you, Miss Varady,' said Morgan, managing to sound both exasperated and wearily patient at the same time. 'We shall of course check your story. You'd hardly expect otherwise. I'd also like to be sure neither of you will be tempted to return to the area.'

'For your own safety,' added Parry sanctimoniously.

'Also,' went on Morgan, 'I suspect that if the owner gave it to the late Mr Duke, as you claim, he's forgotten and hasn't noticed it wasn't returned. I'd like to nudge his memory and see if he can recall giving it to your husband.'

'Remind him,' said Susie, 'Rennie did a job for him. I'm not giving you details, that's client's confidence. But that's when Rennie got the key.'

'While you're about it,' I added, 'ask him if he's given a key since then to anyone else, like any lorry drivers.'

'Thank you again, Miss Varady,' Morgan returned. 'I think I can manage the investigation into this matter without suggestions from you.'

That annoyed me, considering the serious discussion Susie and I had had about coming here in the first place. Being here was, for me, a rare instance of my brain controlling all my basic instincts. I should've stuck with instinct. I thought, right, then. I'll keep my ideas to myself from now on!

'Now then, Miss Varady.' She was still being formal. That meant she was really mad at me. 'When I spoke to you recently you denied any relevant knowledge of illegal immigrants or suspicious activities in the area. Despite the evidence of the security camera placing you at the Tube station, you adamantly denied witnessing Ion Popescu's death.'

I was startled to hear her give Ion his full name like that. She must have found out quite a bit about him. Even I hadn't known his surname. I felt uneasy. Here sat Susie and I, telling everything we knew, and there sat Morgan and Parry, in possession of an unknown amount of information. We were giving our all. They had been giving nothing away. That Morgan mentioned a name now wasn't a slip of the tongue. She'd wanted to give me a jolt, make me uncertain. She'd succeeded. I rallied as best I could.

'You didn't mention his name,' I defended myself. 'Anyway, I only knew him as Ion. How do you know his name? I thought illegal immigrants had false papers or none at all.'

'He had a letter in his pocket, from home,' said Morgan briefly.

That might have been true, or not. It was what she chose to tell me and I had to accept it.

'You were there when he died, Fran, and you're a witness. You know that and you know you should have told me at once.'

Her voice was coldly inquisitorial. The years fell away and I was up in front of my old headmistress again, charged with some heinous crime against school rules. I told myself I wasn't twelve years old again. I was a citizen of twenty-one, tax-paying at the moment because of the job at the pizzeria, law-abiding, well, fairly, and here to do my duty and aid the police in theirs. This didn't have to be all one-way traffic. They had to take my point of view into account and not just sit there forcing me to adopt theirs. Susie nudged my foot with hers by way of reminder.

'I was in shock when you called round,' I said. 'I wasn't thinking clearly.'

Parry's eyebrows twitched. Surprisingly, Morgan said, 'I'll accept that in view of the fact that you and Mrs Duke have come forward now.'

Whew! I must remember that shock excuse.

'I never met the kid,' said Susie quickly.

I went on, 'I was only a witness in the sense every other person on that platform was. I didn't see how he fell and that's the truth.'

'You're not a witness as everyone else was. You knew him. You knew he'd been behaving in a way you considered dangerous. Did you consider him suicidal?'

'No,' I said. 'He was looking for his brother.'

'So, do you suspect he was pushed?'

'Yes, but a suspicion is all it is. I tell you, I didn't see how he fell. I didn't see anyone else on that platform I recognised. I hope,' I added, 'no one else on that platform recognised me.'

She didn't rise to that one.

'Now, about this fat man. You say Popescu claimed he'd heard the driver of his lorry call the man Max. But he was some distance away, behind a hedge, according to the tale he told you. The story really doesn't hold up, does it? The boy was frightened, he'd had a stressful journey. He was tired, hungry, didn't know where he was. In panic, people imagine all sorts of things.'

'Max exists,' I said obstinately. 'I saw him for myself this morning, standing by the lorry. There's no doubt about it, not in my mind.'

Parry uttered a sort of growl indicating disagreement.

'I think Sergeant Parry means,' said Morgan with a faintly irritated glance at him, 'that even if what the boy told you was correct, you can't be sure that the man you glimpsed this morning was the same one. You told us the light was poor. You were above him, hiding on a roof. You were panicking a bit yourself. He wore a hooded jacket and his face wasn't visible to you. You didn't hear anyone address him by name.'

'It was Max!' I shouted. I was getting pretty peeved by now. 'Look,' I said. 'First you want me to tell you everything. Then you tell me you don't need my input. Next you grumble because I didn't tell you the whole story when you came to the flat. Now I tell you I saw him and you say I'm wrong. Can you make your mind up?'

'If he was even called Max,' put in Parry. 'And the kid hadn't got that wrong.'

'See!' I bounced off my chair in frustration. 'You don't believe it, anyway.'

'Calm down,' advised Morgan. 'We'll investigate everything you've told us.'

'Does it tie in with what you already know?' I asked hopefully, not really expecting to be told.

I wasn't. I just got an old-fashioned look from Morgan. 'From now on, Fran,' she said. 'I expect full cooperation from you. Leave us to make what we want of your information and no detecting on your part, right? Leave it to us, the professionals. You, too, Mrs Duke.'

'I'm a professional as well. I know the rules!' retorted Susie.

'Good, stick to them,' said Parry.

'Right,' I said as Susie was bristling and this threatened to develop into a slanging match. 'Then can we go now? We've got to be at work by eleven thirty. We've only got twenty-five minutes to get there. We'll need a lift in an unmarked car and I've got to go home first and get my uniform.'

'Anything else?' snarled Parry.

'What about you, Susie?' I asked her.

'Got my uniform in my bag,' she said absently. 'Listen, I'm not worried about any flipping job. I'm worried about my skin. What if they trace my car? Are you going to give me protection?'

'I hardly think it's come to that, Mrs Duke,' said Morgan. 'But if you're worried, perhaps there is a friend or relative you could go and stay with for a few days? Let us know where we can find you, naturally.'

'I can go to my sister in Margate,' mumbled Susie. 'Provided she doesn't know why I'm there.'

'Fine. Leave the address with Sergeant Parry.'

'I'll go today,' Susie said. 'Right now. Fran, you'll have to tell them at the pizzeria I can't come in any more. I'm sick. I was only hired temporarily, anyway.' From under her seat she scooped up the plastic carrier she'd brought with her and thrust it into my arms. 'Here you are, this is my outfit. You can give it back to them. I shan't need it.'

I thought this wouldn't go down well with Mario or Luigi, but she was right. She had to stay away from the place.

Eventually Susie set off home under her own steam and Parry drove me to my flat to get my uniform.

'How long have you been mates with Susie Duke?' he asked as we threaded a way through the traffic.

'I met her when her husband died.'

'Doesn't explain why you're bosom pals now.'

'We are not bosom pals,' I told him. 'We just happen to be working at the same place at the moment, waitressing.'

'I thought she was still running that iffy detective agency.'

'She is, but business is slow. It isn't iffy. Susie is on the level.'

'And she's teaching you to drive, right?'

'Yes, but only because she's grateful I found out who killed Rennie.'

'You did, did you?' he retorted sarcastically. 'All on your little lonesome?'

'Yes, I did and yes, alone!' I can do sarcasm, too. 'If it wasn't for me, you coppers would still be wandering around getting nowhere. I told you who did it.'

'We'd have got to him eventually.'

I allowed myself a superior, 'Hah!'

We'd arrived at my flat. I didn't let him in. I didn't have time for any more chit-chat and enough people had been tramping through my home. I didn't need Parry in there. It was like perishing Waterloo Station already. I dashed in, grabbed my uniform, rushed out and jumped back in his car. He had less to say on the short journey to the pizzeria.

He dropped me nearby but far enough away to avoid being seen by any of my co-workers.

'One of them might recognise you,' I warned.

'You want to be careful, Fran,' he said to me as I climbed out of the car. He was leaning towards the open door, his left arm resting on the back of the passenger seat I'd vacated. 'These people-traffickers are serious villains. They've been making a lot of money out of bringing people in and they have a neat little operation set up to do it. They won't want anyone rocking the boat. You might be small fry, but you can cause them problems. If they find out how much you already know, you're in trouble. The police don't want anyone rocking our boat, either. A lot of time and effort has been given to this investigation. We're getting close. You could upset the apple-cart.'

I could have pointed out that he was mixing his metaphors but the niceties of the English language mean nothing to Parry. Nor do any other niceties.

'I know!' I said crossly. 'I'm not an idiot.'

'You remember what happened to young Popescu.'

'I'm not likely to forget!'

For a second or two he seemed to hesitate and I had the impression he'd been on the point of telling me something else, but then changed his mind.

'I'll be seeing you,' he said, as he let in the clutch and drove off.

I yelled, 'Not if I see you coming first!' after his car but obviously he couldn't hear me. A couple of passing skinheads did, though, and were greatly amused.

'Given the poor bloke the elbow, darling?' they enquired.

I glared at them and stomped off. I could hear their laughter following me down the street.

'What d'you mean? She's not coming any more!' yelled Mario. 'Just like that? What am I supposed to do? Wait tables myself? What's wrong with her?'

'She's sick,' I offered.

'With what? Is she another one with a bad cold?' He gave me a nasty look.

I gave him an innocent one. 'Yes, I think she caught it from me.'

'Bloody women!' moaned Mario and set about punching the pizza dough in a way which made me very nervous.

'You remember I can't work this evening? All the cast is coming to my flat,' I ventured.

Mario told me very rudely what I could do with my play.

In the end I got Po-Ching's phone number from Jimmie. I rang her to ask if she knew anyone at all who could wait tables and come in that evening. She said she'd bring a cousin along.

'That's all right, then,' said Jimmie, the only unruffled one among us. Ignorance, as they say, is bliss. Seriously he added, 'Let's hope she doesn't catch this cold that's going round. You know, I don't feel so well myself.'

I left him peering into a little mirror, pulling down his lower lids to see if his eyeballs were bloodshot, sticking out his tongue and trying to see the back of his throat. If he didn't watch out, he'd dislocate his jaw.

Chapter Twelve

I got off work at six when Po-Ching and her cousin turned up. The cousin was a cheerful-looking girl with one slight drawback. She didn't speak much English. In fact, apart from 'Hello' and 'very good' she didn't speak any.

Mario had given up being furious and now just stood in the kitchen, banging his forehead despairingly with the palm of his hand.

I suggested that we give the cousin a menu card with all the items numbered. That way, she could indicate to the customers that they should point at what they wanted, and all she had to do was tell Mario whichever number it was.

'Like in a Chinese restaurant,' I encouraged. 'It'll be all right. If a customer asks her about anything on the menu, she can say "very good", and if it gets complicated she can ask Po-Ching.'

Mario gave me the look of a man for whom life had lost all meaning. I felt quite sorry for him. Perhaps he was just a pizza cook and not a villain after all. Perhaps I was wrong about the involvement of the pizzeria in any skulduggery. What had I to go on? That they wouldn't give Jimmie any responsibility – but hey, if you were opening a new business and you wanted it to be a success, would you put Jimmie in charge? They'd made him titular manager because he'd owned the previous business and was Silvio's partner. They had to do something with him.

I couldn't overlook the existence of the fat man, Max. Now that I'd seen that sinister rotund figure for myself, I knew Ion hadn't imagined him. But had he imagined Max's visit to the pizzeria had involved going into the office? Despite Ion's insistence, I still felt it possible that he had been mistaken about that. Ganesh, Susie, Morgan and Parry, all thought Ion had got it wrong. To tell you the truth, I, too, was secretly hoping he had got the wrong idea about that part of the story. If Max had really visited the office it seemed to involve Jimmie, and that was something I just refused to believe. But without that one fact, the link with the pizzeria was broken. Anyone can walk in and use the customer toilets. He may be the biggest villain in the world. It wouldn't make the pizzeria guilty. I wished I had been able to turn up something in my search in the cellar. That was what I wanted, something specific I could show or tell Janice Morgan.

I eyed the distraught Mario, now prowling about his kitchen, nervously picking up and putting down knives in an unsettling manner. He had shouted violently at Ion when Ion had appeared at the back door, enquiring about his brother. But Mario shouted at everyone. He might only be a pizza cook but like those celebrity chefs you hear about, he was temperamental. Right now he looked suicidal.

'Honestly, Mario,' I repeated. 'It will be all right.'

'Go to your rehearsal,' he said hollowly.

The gathering at my flat wasn't until eight thirty. Ganesh couldn't get there before that because Hari needed him. Carmel also couldn't get there earlier because the manager of her supermarket refused to let her change her shift, insisting she work until eight or collect her cards. Carmel, it seemed, had had several disagreements with this manager and the threat to sack her was nothing new. This time, however, she thought he meant it. She was plotting revenge but, in the meantime, needed the job. I didn't tell Mario I had two and a half hours in hand. He'd have had me waiting tables until the last minute, end of shift or no end of shift.

'Cheerio, everyone,' I said.

Luigi didn't answer because he was being grumpy over Susie not coming in any more which meant he wouldn't get another chance to work his seduction technique. Her other admirer, Pietro, played tuneless snatches on his accordion and looked glum. Jimmie had gone home early to take some aspirin and drink lots of tea and whisky.

'I hope it all goes well, Fran,' said Po-Ching.

'Very good,' said the cousin.

It wasn't very good, that was the problem, and I had two and a half hours to brood on it. I decided to ring Susie when I got home and check that she'd left for Margate. I was worried about her, chiefly because she was worried herself. Susie, together with the late Rennie, had been in and out of many a scrape and was used to walking close to the edge. But this time, she was scared.

I went out into the hall to the payphone and tried to reach her. At her end, the telephone just rang. No one answered. She hadn't left the answerphone on. She must have gone to Margate, just as she'd said she would.

On the other hand, she might just not be picking up the phone, afraid who might be on the other end of the line.

Dissatisfied though I felt, I forced myself to leave it at that.

By eight forty-five the cast had assembled in my flat. Marty mostly wanted to concentrate on the scenes in which Carmel appeared, because she was still inclined to improvise her lines. As I didn't appear in any of these scenes, it was a bit boring for me and I began to think that, after all, I needn't have bothered to be present – or at least, I needn't have had them all over here in my flat.

Carmel, true to type, had arrived in the usual grumpy mood.

'I had another barney with the manager!' she announced.

'I feel sorry for the poor bloke,' muttered Ganesh.

She soon got fed up and resentful of the fact that more fuss was being made about her lines than anyone else's.

'You're picking on me,' Carmel accused Marty.

'No, I'm not. You keep messing the lines around.'

'Yes,' put in Nigel. 'And it really throws me off my stride.'

'Well, it shouldn't,' said Carmel, glowering. 'You've got to be able to think on your feet when you're in the theatre. Anything can happen out there on stage.'

'Anything can,' argued Marty. 'But with proper rehearsal, the likelihood is cut to the minimum. Now, we'll take the scene where the butler and his wife, the Barrymores, confess that the escaped convict on the moor is really Mrs Barrymore's brother . . .'

They wrangled on until Carmel sat down and went on strike. 'I'm not doing it any more. I'll be all right on the night.'

'You'd better be all right tomorrow night at the dress rehearsal,' Marty snapped at her. He'd had enough.

As a row was about to erupt, I made everyone coffee. Then they all went home except Ganesh.

He settled down on my sofa, resting his back against one arm, and with his feet propped over the other arm. 'You've got something on your mind, haven't you?' he asked. 'I mean, besides this play.'

I thought about the lorry and the stick-figures jumping from it. I was tired of keeping things from Ganesh. I wanted to tell him and I did.

'I went to the police today. I told them all about Ion and the pizzeria, and that I was on the Tube platform and saw him fall.'

He raised his eyebrows. 'I see. How did they take it?'

'Not too badly, considering. I didn't just decide to go to them out of the blue. Something made me.'

'Ah,' said Ganesh. 'Something else has happened, has it?'

'Yes.' I told him about Susie's early-morning driving lesson and our adventure at the old cinema. 'The police have advised her to stay away from the area for a while. She's gone to see her sister.'

He looked sober. 'Convenient for her. Susie Duke's skipped out of town, in other words, and left you to carry the can.'

'That's not how it is, Ganesh. She's afraid they'll trace her through the car. They don't know about me being there.'

'Well, I'm glad you told Morgan about Ion,' Ganesh said after a pause. 'Because his death is the subject of a police investigation and you should cooperate. I'm still not sure you should have said anything about the pizzeria. You don't have any proof of their involvement.'

'I know. I'm starting to have doubts myself, to tell you the truth. It sounded pretty thin, even to me, when I told Morgan and Parry,' I confessed. 'I just wish I knew why Morgan was asking about the pizzeria when she came round to see me that evening.'

'Anyway . . .' Ganesh cheered up. 'I can't say I'm sorry Susie won't be around for a while. I always thought she'd get you into more trouble and, sure enough, she did. She can stay away as long as she likes as far as I'm concerned.'

'I thought that's how you'd feel,' I said.

If she had, indeed, left London. I really wished I knew for sure.

I worked through from half-eleven in the morning until six in the evening the next day, Friday, and went home feeling shattered. It wasn't just running around the pizzeria, although we had been busier than normal. Even the afternoon, when I'd been sole waitress, had been a rush. The accumulation of events was taking its toll on me and my feet were complaining. I was sure I was developing bunions to rival those of Sister Mary Joseph, and dreading the dress rehearsal. I was looking forward to getting home where I could rest up for an hour or so. With luck, I'd then feel better.

However when I got indoors I found Erwin, in his black leather jacket and pants and gold chains, sitting on the stairs yelling into a mobile phone.

'What do you mean, they cancelled? They can't friggin' cancel. Listen, man, that's a regular gig – I know there wasn't anything on paper, there never is! They told us they wanted us every Friday and Saturday, February through March.'

The person at the other end was speaking. Erwin looked up at me and waved a hand in salute.

I left him to it and went into my flat. I'd just got my stuff together for the rehearsal and was deciding whether I wanted scrambled eggs or tinned ravioli for my supper when there was a knock on the door.

It was Erwin, still steaming gently with rage. 'Hey, Fran,' he demanded. 'You know The Rose pub, don't you?'

'Only too well,' I told him. 'I'm going to a rehearsal there tonight. Were they the ones who've let you down?'

He shook his head. 'Not them. Another place, down Battersea way. This Rose pub, what's it like? I mean, what kind of audience does a band get there?'

'If they like you, they're fine. If they don't, they'll chuck things at you.'

'How about the landlord? Is he on the level? Does he pay up?'

'I suppose so,' I said. 'I don't know. He has bands or stand-up comics or singers most weekends. Only this weekend he won't, because it's our play. It's the dress rehearsal tonight and we're doing it for real tomorrow night. Freddy, the landlord, has sold a lot of tickets to the regulars. As far as I know, he's fair about paying up. I hope so, because if there's any money over after our play, he's supposed to share it out among the cast.'

Erwin rubbed his chin. He wore a lot of gold rings too; at least, I supposed they were gold. He might just have got the lot down the market.

'This place at Battersea, we thought we had a regular gig set up there,' he said. 'But they dumped us. Just said they don't want us no more. Just like that. Like musicians, they're nothing, you can just tell 'em, we don't want you. Like musicians, they don't have to work, earn money, pay rent, eat.'

'Lousy,' I sympathised.

'So now we need another engagement, preferably long-term, at least monthly. This Freddy, the landlord at The Rose, we heard he hires bands sometimes.'

'Like I said, he has a lot of live music evenings there, when he's not got stand-up comics or variety acts. He's sort of stage-struck,' I explained. 'That's why he puts on all those shows upstairs in the functions room, pantomime, music hall, our play, anything. I think he's got a sort of dream that someone famous will one day appear on the telly and tell the nation he got his first break at The Rose pub.'

Erwin nodded. 'We thought we might check him out. Take a look at the place first, then see if we can't get him to hire us for a night to begin with, with the option of a regular arrangement if we go down well. Even if he doesn't pay much, it keeps us in the public eye, you know? People hear us and if they think we're good, they tell other people and who knows, someone else might give us work. You've got to be out there doing the gigs, Fran. If you're not, some other band is. It isn't just about earning the money, it's about not being forgotten.'

'Acting,' I informed him, 'is also an overcrowded profession.'

He eyed me speculatively. 'Tell you what, I'll come over tonight to watch your dress rehearsal and take a look round at the same time. Get the feel of the place. If I'm just there as one of your mates, the landlord isn't going to try and spin me some line. I'll be, you know, undercover.'

'Sure, Erwin,' I said. 'But, if you don't mind me saying so, you won't be undercover in that outfit.'

He promised to dress casual. With that, he said he'd see me there sometime after eight and left.

I'd lost interest in any food. I put the ravioli tin back in the cupboard and began thinking about Susie again. I was still worried that something might have prevented her from leaving London. I regretted I hadn't checked on her the previous evening. I went into the hall and tried to phone her flat one more time, but still no one answered. It was no good. I couldn't just leave it at that. I'd take a leaf from Erwin's book. I'd go without my rest, walk over to her place and check out the situation in person. With Susie buzzing about my brain, I wouldn't be able to concentrate on the play. I'd just nip quickly over there and settle my fears.

It had long been dark by the time I got to the flats. The lamp-posts sent out a glimmering inadequate light. In the gloom, I spotted the Murphy brothers and their mates, hanging around the garages, kicking a ball about, and plotting what sort of mischief they meant to get into that night. A tall blonde came shimmering towards me through the shadows and I thought it might be Susie, but it wasn't. It was a sharp-faced girl with the pale skin of the heroin addict. She wore a smart suit with a slit in the skirt which just about let the onlooker glimpse the tops of her hold-up stockings. When one set of people is winding down for the day, another set is getting ready to go to work. I wondered where she was based. She didn't look cheap. She wasn't off to stand about on street corners. She was more the sort that guests in expensive hotels phone out for. Sent-in sex like sent-in pizzas.

I pushed open the entry door to Susie's block and stepped inside. The downstairs light was broken, and the inner hall so murky I almost collided with a man coming out. He was big, tall and muscular, but I couldn't see his face. He wore dark clothing, a tracksuit, hooded top pulled well up over his head hiding his features. In addition he kept his head tilted down: a man who didn't want to be recognised. He slipped past me and, as he did, I had an impression of a familiar, if faint, odour. Then he had disappeared into the night at a jog-trot. I felt a tingle of fear run up my spine. Some people you can sense are dangerous. It ripples off them in waves. I shook myself and ordered myself not to start imagining things. It was a local fitness freak, out for his evening jog.

I stumbled up the first flight of stairs in the dark and found to my relief that lights in the upper part of the building were working. The Murphys were outside by the garages, but there would be others like them, and I didn't want to meet them, a stranger and alone, trapped in the confines of the stairwell.

On Susie's balcony, however, even with the lights working, visibility was poor. A blueish flicker behind the drawn curtains of one flat indicated someone was in there watching television. There was no other sign of life. Susie's place was at the far end. Its windows were dark but even so I started to walk towards it. I'd almost reached it when the world exploded.

Chapter Thirteen

The noise was deafening. Susie's front door blew outwards, all of a piece, straight off its hinges, taking with it the protective security grille. Grille and door flew over the balcony out of sight. At the same time, a giant fist struck me in the chest and sent me flying backwards. I bounced off the wall and then off the balcony brickwork and finally finished up, dazed and winded, in a tangled heap by someone else's front door several yards away. Flames were leaping out of the open doorway of Susie's flat and licking hungrily at the curtains of the living-room window. There was a dull roaring sound in my head which might have been the flames catching hold in her flat or just the reverberations from the explosion still ricocheting round my skull.

I knew I was yelling 'Susie!' but I couldn't hear myself for the din inside my head. I picked myself up and ran towards the flames but the heat was unbearable and drove me back.

Someone grabbed me. A man's voice shouted by my ear, 'You can't get in there, love! Come on!'

He pushed me ahead of him back down the balcony. Other people had appeared, a frightened woman clasping a wailing baby, an older woman holding a big black bag. A small girl scampered past us gripping a squirming cat. We all stumbled down the stairs. On the floor below people had poured out of their flats, clogging the stairwell and demanding to know what had happened. Like a disturbed anthill the building emptied, people scattering in all directions. We milled about outside shouting and gesticulating. The kids had deserted the garages at the offer of a free show. Led by the Murphys, they were jumping up and down, the little ghouls, enjoying the whole thing. I hoped it didn't give them any ideas for future activities, but I had a nasty suspicion that burning newspaper would be thrust through letter boxes all over the estate during the coming weeks.

A woman was shrieking and someone said the fire brigade was on its way. It arrived soon, closely followed by paramedics and then by the gas emergency team. I was rooted to the spot. I didn't know what to do. I found myself praying Susie had gone to Margate. I remembered the man with the aura of danger who'd passed me in the entry. A cold hand gripped my heart as I thought how they hadn't wasted time tracing Susie's car and she had been right to be afraid.

Someone took my arm and shook it. 'Fran!' a voice was bellowing in my ear.

I turned and saw Parry. He tugged me with him to the back of the crowd where I saw two police cars and another, unmarked one. As we came up to this last car, Morgan got out of it.

'That's Susie's flat!' I gasped. 'I don't know if she was in there or not!'

'It's all right,' Morgan soothed me. 'Mrs Duke has gone to stay with friends.'

'I know she said she was going to do that!' I shouted. 'But I don't know if she did! I tried to ring her. She didn't answer. Perhaps she didn't want to pick up the phone—'

'Pull yourself together, Fran!' ordered Morgan. 'Mrs Duke is safe. She phoned us yesterday afternoon to let us know she'd arrived at her temporary address.'

Jets of water were soaring upwards, hissing. The spray was soaking the entire area around. I could see a yellow-helmeted fireman up there on the balcony.

'You ought to let the paramedics take a look at you, Fran,' Morgan was urging.

I snapped, 'I'm all right! All I'll have is a few bruises.'

'You were lucky,' she said.

I knew that. Only a few seconds separated me from death. Just a few steps further along that balcony and I'd have arrived at Susie's door in time to be hurled with it over the balcony to the ground. I'd be a smashed body lying there amid fragments of door and grille.

Parry came up and eyed me, chewing his moustache. 'Could've been a gas leak,' he said partly to Morgan, but mostly to me.

'Don't tell me that!' I shouted at him. 'Someone put a firebomb through the letter box! There was a security grille but he could reach the slot. He did it not much over ten minutes ago.'

Parry stopped chewing and asked, 'How do you know that?'

'Because I saw him,' I said.

They both stepped forward. Hastily I added, 'I didn't see him actually do it, but I'm sure I saw the man responsible. He passed me as I entered the building.'

'Description?' Morgan asked tersely.

But I couldn't give her one. Only tell her he'd worn jogging pants and top, his face hidden by the hood. 'There was a smell to his clothing,' I added. 'Not a strong one but familiar in a way. Perhaps it was cigarette smoke.'

'A jogger who smokes?' Morgan said. 'Not part of most people's fitness regimes.'

She opened the car door and indicated I should get in the front passenger seat.

'I'm not taking you anywhere,' she said. 'But you should at least sit down.'

I got in and realised I was quite pleased to sit down. My legs had suddenly turned to jelly.

'Private detectives,' Morgan said as she joined me in the car, 'make enemies. This may be connected with what you and Mrs Duke reported and the fact that the lorry driver and the other man saw her car. It might, on the other hand, be connected with something else she's been involved with. We'll have to talk to her.'

'She'll be scared stiff,' I said. 'She won't want to come back to London until you've got this gang.'

'We're working on it,' she said. Then she added, 'Do you have to be at work this evening?'

'No – oh, heck. There's the dress rehearsal. I've got to be over at The Rose in half an hour. I must go. If you want a statement, I'll come in and make one tomorrow sometime, OK?' I scrabbled at the door release.

'When are you working tomorrow?' she asked quickly.

'Lunchtime shift. It's the play in the evening. I'd like to have taken off the whole day, but we're short-handed.'

'Ah yes, you have to be there by eleven thirty, I remember. The other staff, the manager and cleaners, presumably get there earlier.'

My mind was too full of other things to wonder why she had this interest in work schedules at the San Gennaro.

'Yeah,' I mumbled. 'Jimmie opens up about half past eight, then he goes for breakfast and leaves Wally, the cleaner, to do his work. Mario comes about ten thirty to get his kitchen started up. They're usually all there by the time I arrive.'

I hadn't told her about my early-morning visit to the pizzeria via the staff loo window and I wasn't about to. I hadn't found anything in the cellar anyway.

'Listen, I've got to go now.' I swung my legs out of the car.

'You really should let the paramedics take a look at you,' she said again. 'You – um – look a bit scorched.'

I scrabbled in my pocket for a tissue and rubbed my face. It felt sore and tender. Morgan reached up, pulled down the sun visor and revealed the little mirror on the other side of it. I peered in it. I thought I looked a bit pink in complexion but that might be from the glare of the surrounding lights.

'It's all right!' I said. 'I really must go. I'll see you tomorrow.'

'Yes,' she said. 'Fair enough. I'll probably see you tomorrow.'

I managed to catch a bus which took me nearly to The Rose. I thought one or two of the other passengers gave me funny looks but generally, they were more interested in another fire engine hurtling by, siren blaring, on its way to the fire.

I ran from the bus stop to the pub and raced through the bar, then upstairs to the functions room.

I was taken aback to find it full of people. We seemed to have collected an audience for the dress rehearsal. Erwin and the other members of his group were there, sitting in the front row armed with cans of Coke and lager, laughing and joking, obviously settled down for a fun evening. There were some workers from Carmel's supermarket and friends of Marty's, Owen's and Nigel's, who'd all come along tonight to see the play for free. I scuttled backstage and found the other members of the cast, Ganesh excepted, dressed in costume and ready to go. Denise, Freddy's wife, was also there. They stood in a group, arguing as usual.

'The heating will be fine,' Denise was promising. 'I'll get Freddy to turn on the radiators tonight. By Saturday evening the punters will be as warm as toast up here.'

Silence fell. I realised they were all looking at me.

Denise said, 'Blimey!' in an awestruck voice.

Owen said slowly, 'Speaking of toast . . .'

Ganesh appeared then from behind the curtains, saw me, stepped rapidly forward, grabbed my arms and demanded, 'What happened?'

'I – there was an explosion . . .' I stammered.

'A *what*?' yelled Ganesh.

'It's all right, Gan, honestly. I'll tell you later.'

'Where?' he demanded tersely, not releasing me.

'At Susie's flat.'

'At *Susie's* place? Even when she's not in town, she still manages to make trouble for you! When she gets back, you tell her—'

'Gan! Let go of me. It's not Susie's fault, it's mine. I shouldn't have gone over there.'

'You're sure you're all right?' he asked anxiously.

'Yeah,' said Carmel. 'How's your voice? It sounds OK. You haven't breathed in smoke, have you? It does for the vocal cords.'

'I wish something would do for yours!' snapped Ganesh.

'I only asked,' retorted Carmel.

Marty, who'd said nothing since I'd arrived and was prowling around the edges of the group, now interrupted. 'Look, I don't know what happened to you, Fran, but you're here now and if you're all right to act, let's get this rehearsal underway, or we'll be here all night. If you and Ganesh are going to talk about it, talk about it later.' He spoke sharply and his voice had moved into a higher register. He looked at me again and then away quickly as if he couldn't bear the sight.

Ganesh glowered at him but Marty was clearly in directorial mode and suffering nerves as well.

'She can't,' said Nigel, pointing at me, 'go on stage looking like that.'

They all stared at me again. Even Marty turned a reluctant gaze on me. I met it and he broke the eye contact at once. Did I look as bad as that?

Carmel said quickly, 'I'll fix her up. Get in the dressing room, Fran!'

I found myself propelled towards our dressing room between Carmel and Denise. It was an airless cubbyhole of a place which we shared with the men. Since there was no window it was hot and stuffy. The heat came from a little fan heater whirring away in a corner and the electric light bulbs over the mirror. The smell was compounded of sweat, cigarettes, the chemicals in make-up and body spray, ham sandwiches, the remains of which lay chewed on a plate, the musty odour of stale clothing and the usual yeasty stale beer smell of pubs.

'What a fug in here!' I exclaimed. 'Turn that fan heater off.'

'We put it on because it was so bloody cold,' snapped Carmel. 'Sit down!'

'It stinks in here,' I growled as the two of them pushed me into a chair in front of the mirror.

'The whole pub stinks,' said Carmel unkindly. 'I always have to wash my hair when I get home.'

'Oy!' said Denise angrily. 'It's a good job my husband didn't hear you say that. You've got a nerve. This pub doesn't stink! We open the place up every morning and air it through. We've got extractor fans going downstairs. People are smoking and drinking down there, you've got to expect a bit of atmosphere. It'd be a darn sight worse if we did food, I can tell you!'

I said nothing because I'd looked in the mirror and seen myself properly for the first time.

My face was scarlet and the hair growing at the edge of my scalp had frizzled away, giving me a bald look like one of those Renaissance portraits of society women with shaven foreheads. Nor did I have any eyebrows, as I discovered when Carmel wiped them with a tissue and they came off.

'I can fix her face,' said Carmel to Denise over my head. 'I'll use that pale green cream as a foundation. But I can't do anything about her hair.'

'I've got a wig!' offered Denise. 'I'll go and fetch it.' She hurried away.

Carmel began to slap make-up on my face. I protested I could do it myself but she ignored me. She was padded out in her costume as Mrs Hudson, mob cap, long skirt and apron, and now she said, 'Where's yours?'

'My what?'

'Costume, you idiot.'

It was back at the flat, that's where it was. 'I came straight here,' I explained. 'You see, I went to see a friend and her flat exploded.'

'Marty will go mad,' said Carmel. 'This is a dress rehearsal.'

'Look, I nearly got blown to kingdom come! You're lucky I'm here at all! Anyway, I'm not the only the who's late. Where's Irish? He's supposed to be here with his dog.'

'Marty saw him this morning,' she assured me. 'He'd got the dog with him and he said he'd be here tonight. He's not needed until almost the last scene. Before that you only hear him on tape. Denise has shut Digger out in the backyard to stop him barking when it's played. It'll be fine.'

'Will it?' I retorted, remembering what Ganesh had said about acting with children and animals.

'It's fine by me,' said Carmel. 'The less I see of that dog of Irish's the better. I don't want it hanging round here. It's not properly house-trained. It's liable to pee on the set, if it doesn't do anything worse.'

I didn't even want to think about that.

Denise arrived back puffing and carrying a large box. 'Here it is!'

She set down the box, opened it up and took out a wig-stand with a lot of bright auburn curls cascading around it.

'I wear it when Freddy and I go to a dinner dance,' she said. 'You know, any of the do's Freddy sets up for his charities. Here we go.'

Before I knew it, there I was, made up by Carmel to look like a circus clown, the whole lot set off by enough red hair to cover a sizeable golden retriever.

'Pity you haven't got your costume,' said Carmel. 'We've made you look pretty good.'

Marty stuck his head through the door. 'How much longer are you girls going to be? I want to get started. Where's your costume, Fran?'

'I couldn't bring it. There was an explosion—'

'I haven't got time for all that. You'll have to do it without costume, but you should have brought it. Honestly, Fran, I thought I could at least rely on you.'

'You can rely on me!' I snapped back. My nerves were pretty tattered by now. 'I'll manage without the costume, all right? I've been practising walking up and down in it, in my flat. It will be all right on the night. There are enough other things to worry about with this play without you getting at me over one missing costume!'

Marty seemed surprised by my reaction and backed away. He mumbled, 'All right. I didn't mean . . .' He made off.

'Well,' said Carmel, staring after him. 'What did you do to Marty to make him so scared of you?'

'He's not scared of me. I was the first person he asked to be in this play. His nerves are bad. So,' I added, 'are mine. I nearly got blown to smithereens and no one seems to think it matters a toss.'

Except for Ganesh and he was simmering like a volcano, ready to explode himself and engulf me in recriminations. As if it was my fault!

Once the rehearsal started, things went reasonably well. Even Carmel was making an effort to speak the lines as Marty had written them and not to improvise. The backdrop of Dartmoor painted by Owen and Nigel looked really good. The fireplace built for us by Freddy's carpenter mate did wonders for the opening set. To the relief of everyone but Ganesh, Irish had turned up with his dog and was sitting backstage with a can of lager, waiting for the dog's big entrance.

Denise and I stood in the wings and watched. Miss Stapleton, my character, didn't come on for the first couple of scenes, not until Watson was sent down to Devon by Holmes. Denise had been appointed prompter and was peering at the script.

'Whoever typed this isn't much good at spelling,' she hissed at me. 'Some of it doesn't look like English. What is this, some sort of Scandinavian language?'

'Marty typed it. He's dyslexic,' I whispered back.

'*Mr Holmes, they were the footprints of a gigantic hound!*' declaimed Mick on stage. His cold was a lot better or the catarrh capsules had done the trick. He sounded less nasal but distinctly hoarse. I hoped he wasn't about to lose his voice. That would really finish us off.

'Curtain!' yelled Marty at Denise, who was supposed to be operating it at this point. She yanked at the cord and the curtain swished across.

In the front row of the audience, Erwin and his mates clapped enthusiastically.

'Is that it?' asked one of the women from Carmel's supermarket loudly.

Denise, beside me, gave a sentimental sigh. 'It's going to be great, Fran.'

'Don't say that!' I begged. 'It will bring down every kind of bad luck on us. Besides, they say a good dress rehearsal is a bad omen. A bad dress rehearsal is supposed to mean a good opening night.'

'All this theatrical stuff,' said Denise. 'All these traditions, like not saying *Macbeth*.'

'Thanks, Denise. You're doing a great job,' I muttered.

'My Maxie loves it all,' said Denise.

Irish's dog had come padding up to us just as she spoke and sniffed at my jeans, smelling Bonnie. It distracted me. I thought I'd heard Denise correctly, but I couldn't be sure.

'What was that, Denise?' I asked. I touched the dog's head and he looked up at me, puzzled, sensing the tension in me.

'I said, my Maxie loves all this theatrical business. He's so much looking forward to tomorrow when you do it for real.'

'Denise . . .' I said as casually as I could, considering my throat was suddenly dry and constricted. 'Who is Maxie?'

The dog uttered a low whine.

She turned her head to look at me and grinned. 'Oh, sorry. It's my pet name for him. I mean my Freddy. He used to be a wrestler once, when he was younger, of course. He wrestled under the name of Max the Mangler. He was good, you know. A lot of people remember him and still call him Max. Freddy loved the wrestling because of the audience, all yelling and booing and cheering. That's what he likes about the shows we put on up here, the audience. Not that tomorrow's audience will yell and boo,' she added hastily. 'They'll be as nice as pie.'

'Max,' I said faintly. 'They call him Max.'

'Only his mates,' said Denise, 'and me. Everyone else knows him as Freddy. The name Max is mostly used by his pals from the old days.'

'Is that a fact?' I said slowly. 'I never knew that.'

But I knew it now.

Chapter Fourteen

Ganesh and I left the pub together and in silence after rehearsal. Ganesh was quiet because he was angry. I was bursting with my news but forced myself to say nothing until it was safe. We waited until we'd reached the bottom of the road and no one we knew was within earshot, and then we both began to speak at once.

'Listen, Fran, I've never interfered with anything you've done even if I've thought it was crazy—'

'Gan, shut up and listen to me! I've found out—'

'I've warned you repeatedly about Susie Duke and would you listen to me?' Ganesh steamrollered on. 'Oh, no. Fran Varady, the great escape artist. I told you, I told you in plain language that this time you were getting into something—'

'Ganesh!' I yelled. 'I know what you told me and I'm sorry I nearly got myself blown up. I didn't do it on purpose, you know. Will you PLEASE listen to me?'

'What?' asked Ganesh sulkily, standing in the shelter of a convenient doorway, his hands stuck in the pockets of his blouson jacket.

'I have found out the identity of Max. Max is real. Ion didn't invent him or make a mistake about him. I know who Max is.'

'Oh yes?' muttered Ganesh with a scowl.

'It's Freddy.'

'Freddy? Who's Freddy?'

'For crying out loud, Gan! Freddy the landlord at The Rose!'

Ganesh eyed me as if assessing whether the explosion might have loosened a few more screws in my brain. 'Freddy the landlord? Are you nuts or what?'

'Freddy,' I told him triumphantly, 'used to wrestle under the name Max the Mangler. Denise told me. She still calls him Max or Maxie sometimes. All his old mates call him Max. Ion described Max as a fat man and the man I saw in the cinema backyard was certainly paunchy. Or so I thought. But Freddy isn't exactly fat, do you see? It's muscle gone to seed that gives him the outline of a fat man. Freddy looks like a barrel on legs and if you saw him in poor light and didn't know it was Freddy, you'd think you'd seen a fat man. Ion did and I did.'

Ganesh was silent for a few moments and I held my breath.

'It could be coincidence,' he said.

'No, it's not. I'll tell you another thing. Ion said he saw Max go into the office at the pizzeria. He was probably right. Max goes round all the local businesses getting them to support his latest charity scheme. I know he went to see Jimmie, even though I wasn't there at the time, because he persuaded him to ask Silvio about the San Gennaro sponsoring the programmes for Saturday night. That, of course, was after Ion has seen him there. But just as I missed seeing Freddy there that day, I missed him on the other, previous occasions. I work shift hours. I'm not always there. Ion followed Freddy/Max to the pizzeria, just as he said, and saw him walk in, ignore the restaurant part and go straight to the office. Just as Freddy would do. He'd gone in there to discuss some fund-raising effort.'

'Or,' said Ganesh, 'he had gone there to discuss with Jimmie something to do with this people-trafficking racket and Jimmie is in this after all, up to his neck.'

'Oh, damn,' I said, deflated. 'No, Jimmie isn't, but it will look that way to Morgan when I tell her.'

'You are going to tell her, then?' He raised his eyebrows. 'You want me to come down to the cop shop with you now?'

'Morgan will have gone home. I want to tell her and nobody else. I need to explain, about Jimmie,' I said doubtfully.

Ganesh pulled a face. 'Fran, if you're right, this information is dynamite.' He cleared his throat diffidently. 'There's something else which has occurred to me. I don't know about you . . .'

'What's that?'

'The play,' said Ganesh simply. 'It all depends on Freddy, doesn't it?'

'I haven't forgotten the play,' I told him soberly. 'We've all worked so hard. It means such a lot to Marty. Do you think I shouldn't tell her until after the performance?'

Ganesh signed. 'Actually, I think the right thing is that you should tell her at once. Right for justice, that is. Whether it's right for you, personally, is another matter. I really wish, Fran, you hadn't found out about Freddy being called Max tonight. My worry has nothing to do with the play or with justice for your young friend. It's to do with self-preservation. If you're right, Freddy is a dangerous man and you'll be doing him a very bad turn indeed.'

We stared at one another in the shelter of the doorway, then I said, my voice sounding very small, 'But I can't pretend I haven't found out, Ganesh.'

'Right, the police station it is,' he said.

On the way there, we reached an Indian grocer who did a sideline in takeaway snacks and bought half-a-dozen samosas. Nibbling them, we continued on our way.

'I've been thinking,' I said, breaking the silence which had reigned since we left the doorway.

'So,' said Ganesh, 'have I. But you go first.'

'Right. When Morgan came to see me I thought she was mostly interested in the pizzeria. But she did talk quite a bit about the play and the pub and Freddy's name came up. I thought that was general chat, softening me up, but perhaps she's already on to him. Perhaps she was getting me to talk about Freddy. Morgan's like that, pretty tricky.'

'The whole thing,' said Ganesh, rustling his paper bag to get out the remaining samosa, 'could be linked. This smuggling business could be run by Freddy and, say, Silvio, or someone else at the pizzeria, together.'

'Mario!' I exclaimed.

'Why Mario?'

'Because he lied to me. When Ion came to the back door asking for Max, Mario told me he'd been asking for a job. Why should Mario try and put me off if he isn't involved?'

'Because,' said Ganesh calmly, 'he's a mate of Freddy's, isn't he?'

I gaped at him. 'Who? Mario? How do you know?'

'I've seen them chatting together in our shop. You know, one's been in there already getting a paper or something of a Sunday, and then the other one's walked in and it's all "Hello, mate, how's the wife?" and all the rest of it.'

'Why didn't you tell me this?' I gasped.

'Why should I? You didn't tell me Mario had lied to you. You didn't suspect Freddy of anything before tonight. Where was the connection?' Ganesh shook a finger at me. 'But it doesn't mean Mario is involved in the people-trafficking. If you ask me, if he's a mate of Freddy's, he probably knows about Freddy wrestling under the name of Max the – what was it?'

'Mangler,' I said gloomily.

'Right. He probably also knows that Freddy has a finger in a few dodgy pies, without necessarily knowing just what they are. So when that kid came asking for someone called Max, Mario realised it was probably one of Freddy's business deals going pear-shaped. He bawled him out and lied to you because he was covering for Freddy as any good mate would. He probably went to see Freddy right afterwards and told him about it.'

My heart sank. 'So Freddy knew, right from the first, that Ion was hanging around asking for someone named Max. Poor Ion signed his own death warrant, right there and then. If he'd spoken to anyone but Mario . . . to me or Bronia or Po-Ching, it wouldn't have mattered. But he spoke to Freddy's mate, Mario, and that was that.'

'Be fair to Mario,' said Ganesh. 'He may have tipped Freddy off that someone was asking about him. But he wouldn't necessarily know what Freddy would do about it

– at least, he wouldn't know Freddy planned for Ion to take a dive in front of a Tube train.'

Ganesh contemplated the scrunched-up paper bag as if it held the answer. 'My money's on Freddy running the operation,' he decided. 'He has the contacts. He's a good old local boy. Everyone knows him. He knows all the businessmen, legit and not quite so legit, in the entire area. He'd know, for example, who was sending lorries back and forth to the Continent. He'd know who had a convenient vacant site, like the rear of the cinema, and he could go to the owner and ask to borrow the key. The owner wouldn't ask questions, he'd hand it over, because this is good old Freddy, the man who raises money for charity. Whoever organises this racket is good at it and we know Freddy is an ace organiser.'

'Yeah,' I mumbled. 'Think of our play. Think of all those people he's got to sit in baths of baked beans or jelly over the years, or dress as babies and get themselves pushed in carts down the street.'

'Exactly,' said Ganesh. 'Freddy has organised any number of charitable events and, in addition, he runs a popular pub. Freddy is a very popular man. He has a lot of friends, not only Mario. They range from street level right up to the top in local government. He's on first-name terms with local magistrates, you bet. Forgive me, Fran, but you have comparatively few pals and none of us has the influence that Freddy can bring into play. Come to that, none of us has the muscle that some of Freddy's mates have. Look at that barman of his. The Incredible Hulk. He's only one of many. I personally prefer to have all my limbs attached to my body.'

* * *

As I'd expected, when we got to the cop shop Morgan had gone home for the day. Neither was Parry there.

'I'll see who is here,' offered the guy on the front desk.

'I don't want to talk to someone else,' I said.

'Please yourself,' said the desk man. 'Either it's urgent or it's not. Make your mind up.'

'It's urgent,' said Ganesh, before I could reply.

'Right. I'll go and get someone in CID.' he said. 'Watch the desk for me, will you, Jasmine?'

A figure built like a female shot-putter loomed up and gave us a look of deep distrust. 'Sit over there,' she said in what was nearly a baritone.

We huddled together in a corner.

'I've got a bad feeling about this, Gan,' I whispered. 'Perhaps you shouldn't have said it was urgent.'

'I thought you said it was,' said Ganesh huffily.

As it turned out, I was right to feel uneasy. A man in a scruffy suit who looked, beside Jasmine, positively puny, emerged from the back of the building somewhere and approached us.

'I know you,' he said, looking down at me.

'Yeah,' I mumbled. 'Fran Varady.'

'And Mr Patel,' he said, smiling thinly.

'How are you, Sergeant Cole?' asked Ganesh, rallying well.

Just our rotten luck. I'd met Cole when the police had been investigating Rennie Duke's death. He hadn't liked me then and I doubted he was going to like me any better now. As we followed him to an interview room, I managed to whisper to Ganesh, 'Leave this to me!'

The interview room was the same one Susie and I had talked to Morgan and Parry in. There was a radiator but it didn't seem to be working too well. It wasn't much warmer than Freddy's functions room.

'Right,' said Cole. 'What is it?'

'Inspector Morgan asked me to call by,' I said. 'I told the bloke outside I wanted her. I'm sorry if he misunderstood and you've been bothered.' I made to get up but he waved me back down into my seat.

Cole's acne hadn't improved and he still had the habit of touching the more active spots with his fingertips, in an absent-minded way. He did it now, the fingers of his right hand caressing a red eruption on his cheekbone. 'This is a police station,' he said. 'Not a community centre where you can meet your friends. If you've got something to say, tell me.'

'Nothing,' I said firmly.

Beside me, Ganesh stirred and I was afraid he was going to speak so I pushed my foot against his. Ganesh said nothing.

Cole had noticed, however. He turned his attention to Ganesh. 'Mr Patel? You've got something to tell me?'

'No, he hasn't,' I said. 'He just came with me.'

Cole rubbed his hand over his mouth and fixed me with his mean little eyes. 'You wouldn't be wasting my time, would you?' He leaned his arms on the table and tilted his upper body towards us. 'We had a bit of trouble with you last time, as I recall,' he went on. 'Sitting on evidence. If it'd been left to me, you wouldn't have got away with it.'

I met his gaze and stiffened my own attitude. 'I told

you, I'm sorry you've been troubled. Just tell your boss I called in as requested. Come on, Gan.'

We managed to escape before he could get in another question.

When we got outside Ganesh asked, 'What was all that about? Why didn't you tell him?'

'I don't like Cole and he doesn't like me,' I said. 'I'm not having anything to do with him. He'd only have sneered and told me to get lost, if I had told him. It's up to him to tell Morgan I was there. If he does, she'll be round to see me, you bet. If he doesn't, I'll wait until I can see her.'

'I just wish,' complained Ganesh, 'that whenever the police see you and me together, I didn't always feel like a criminal. I thought he was going to arrest us back there, just for a moment.'

'It's not my fault,' I snapped. 'The police make everyone feel like that. It's the way they treat people.'

'No,' said Ganesh candidly. 'It's something to do with you. You upset them.'

'How?' I demanded.

'I don't know, your manner.'

'Tough. That's the way I am.' I was getting cross now. Cole had already ruffled my feathers. I didn't need Ganesh to start criticising me.

'Oh, I know that,' said Ganesh. 'But I'm used to it and they're not.'

I let it go at that. I had enough on my mind. I didn't have time for introspection.

Instead of getting the good night's sleep I needed, I slept very little at all. I tossed and turned as my newly discovered knowledge buzzed round my brain. Would the police raid the pub, once I'd told them about Freddy? Or was I jumping the gun? Anything I told them, they'd take their time checking it out, especially if the job was given to Cole. But if they did raid the pub? Would the play be cancelled? What would Marty do if it was? Bonnie got off the bed in disgust and curled up on the carpet.

I got up in the morning, drank a large mug of black coffee and set out for work. As I turned the corner into the street where the pizzeria was, I saw a sight which drove everything else from my head. Two police cars were parked outside the San Gennaro, one behind the other.

I ran up to the door and found my way barred by a uniformed man.

'The restaurant's closed,' he said.

'I work here!' I retorted.

'Not today, love.'

I could see past him now and there was Luigi, arguing furiously with, of all people, Sergeant Parry. So that's why they were so cagey down at the nick. They were mounting a raid on the pizzeria this morning. Things had moved faster than I'd anticipated, even without my invaluable input.

'I can see Parry,' I said urgently to the man on the door. 'Tell him I'm here, Fran Varady.'

'Does he want to know that?' asked the doorkeeper, looking me up and down.

'Do you want ever to be promoted above PC?' I retorted.

He gave me a dirty look but called out to one of his

colleagues inside. 'Tell the sarge there's a girl here wants to see him. Name of Verity.'

'Varady!' I shouted.

The other officer went over to Parry and murmured at him. Parry glanced towards the door and said something. The officer came back.

'She can come in.'

Reluctantly, the one on the door allowed me in.

'Sit there,' said the other officer, pointing at the nearest table. 'The sergeant will have a word with you in a minute.'

I sat down. From the sound of the kitchen came a crash of utensils and the sound of Mario swearing vociferously. Other voices were raised. The cops were in there, too. Then, horror of horror, what I'd feared happened. Jimmie emerged from his office accompanied by yet another two officers.

I leapt up. 'Oy! You can't arrest him! Not Jimmie! He hasn't done anything.'

'I keep telling them that, hen,' said Jimmie despondently. 'They'll no' listen to me.'

They marched him out. Then they came back and took away Luigi and Mario, still swearing. This left me and Wally, who'd wandered up from the cellar and stood by us, apparently unmoved, leaning on a broom.

'Right, Fran,' said Parry coming over to me. 'Now I've got time for you.'

'Oh, great,' I said. 'What's going on here?'

My heart was in my boots. They'd traced the smuggling racket to the pizzeria all right. Jimmie was in deep, deep trouble, and my information about the identity of Max, when I told them, would only make things worse.

'Someone,' said Parry with his leaden humour, 'has been a naughty boy.'

'Not Jimmie!' I snapped.

'Yeah, well, we'll sort it out.'

'Get him a lawyer,' I ordered. 'He should have a lawyer.'

'Oh?' Parry's moth-eaten eyebrows twitched. 'Needs one, does he?'

'Of course he does; you know Jimmie. You'll get him all confused. He'll say anything.'

'If he wants a lawyer, he can request one,' said Parry.

'What's the charge?' I shouted.

'Someone,' Parry confided, 'has been running a pretty little racket. This pizzeria is only part of it, part of the distribution network.'

'Distributing the illegal aliens?' I asked.

He blinked. 'What have they got to do with it?'

It was my turn to do a double-take. 'Aren't you investigating a racket smuggling in illegal aliens?'

'Indeed we are. But we do have more than one investigation going on at any one time, you know. This is something else.'

The effect of his words on my brain was like someone slamming on all the brakes of a runaway train. When the sound of grinding metal had subsided in my head, I croaked, 'How, something else?'

'If only a policeman's life was like it is on TV,' said Parry. 'Just one job at a time. Instead of having to be in six places at once following up six different investigations. This has got nothing to do with that lorry you reported. It's something quite different.'

'What?' I almost screamed in frustration.

'Dodgy wine,' said Parry. 'They bring in a tanker of the cheap stuff, take it to a bottling plant they've got hidden out at a farm in Kent, bottle it and label it as expensive stuff and sell it on to restaurants and bars all over the country. They don't just distribute it through their own places. You'd be surprised where some of it ends up.'

Parry indicated the restaurant around us. 'This outfit provides a cover for the paperwork. The wine comes in as if it's coming here, right? Or one of the other pizza places they've opened up. Either that or to some dodgy import company that normally—'

I interrupted him. 'Don't tell me. It normally imports Italian decorated tiles.'

He looked surprised. 'How did you know that?'

'Inspired guess,' I muttered.

'Yeah.' Parry eyed our surroundings. 'Tiles like these. Nice, aren't they? I wouldn't mind some like this in my bathroom. I've just had a new power shower put in.'

This wasn't worthy of comment and I made none. I hoped I wasn't to be invited up to Parry's place to see his new domestic installations. Not that I'd go. But Parry is thick enough to ask me.

Parry, seeing I showed no interest in his private life, returned to the subject of the wine. 'Once it's labelled up, it can go anywhere. You'd be surprised at the posh places that have fallen for it. Some know they're buying duff goods and some don't. People trust a label, don't they? They think they're getting what they pay for. It's a real racket. The Italian police got on to it before we did. International cooperation,' he added self-consciously.

Wally cleared his throat noisily in an expression of

disdain. 'I've heared about these international investigations. They're an excuse for freebies, that's what they are. Free jaunts to Italy, was it?'

'No, it was not!' snarled Parry. 'Leastways I didn't get one.'

'Better luck next time,' I told him.

'Leave it out, Fran,' said Parry wearily. 'I've had enough aggro this morning.' He nodded towards the corridor and the entry to the cellar. 'We found some of it down there, labelled up as the best stuff.'

'I told you,' wheezed Wally from his broom-prop. 'I told you his wine was no good.' He shuffled forwards. 'People think I don't know one wine from another one. That Luigi, he tried to tell me it was all good stuff. I knew better. I'd tried it. He didn't pull the wool over my eyes. I know about wine.'

'Well, I suppose you've drunk enough of it,' said Parry with a look of disgust.

'That's right,' said Wally. 'I'm a connoisseur, I am.' He drew himself up. 'You can't judge a bottle by its label, right? His wine has good labels and it's plonk. Now me, you'd look at me and give me a bad label, right? Think I don't know nothing.'

He pushed his whiskery face into that of Parry, who drew back.

'I used to work in the wine trade,' said Wally. 'Years ago before I got me troubles. I was a buyer for a very reputable company. Everything else has gone wrong for me, but I still know what's a good wine and what isn't! I know about scams, too. I seen 'em worked before. They do the wine trade no good. Here, I got something for you.'

He began to search inside his voluminous shabby raincoat with its booze stains and grease marks. Both Parry and I watched this activity with some alarm.

Eventually Wally located and withdrew a battered exercise book. 'I wrote it all down,' he said. 'I knew you lot would turn up one day, so I kept a record, see? All the deliveries, the dates they come and what was in 'em. And I sampled the wines, too,' he added virtuously. 'Just to make sure they weren't the real stuff. I've drunk some really horrible muck since I've been working here. Still, all in a good cause.'

'My heart bleeds for you,' retorted Parry. 'You didn't think to come to us with this information before?' He took the book gingerly from Wally's outstretched hand.

'Oh, yes, and you'd have believed me, would ya?' scoffed Wally. 'Anyway, we'll all lose our jobs now, won't we? Me, her there –' he pointed a yellowed fingernail at me – 'and Jimmie what is a good mate of mine. He's done nothing. He's got no idea what they was up to. They run rings round him. They treated *me* like dirt. So I thought, right, when the coppers do turn up, I'll be ready with a little bit of information for 'em. Might even get them to give me a few quid.'

'Don't count on it,' said Parry.

Wally glowered. 'It took you long enough to get here, international cooperation or not,' he said in a last thrust.

'You'd better go off home, Fran,' said Parry to me. 'It looks like I've got to take a statement from Deep Throat here.'

I went to the newsagent's and sought out Ganesh.

'Why aren't you at work?' he asked. He lowered his

voice and glanced towards Hari. 'Have you heard from the nick?'

'No – well, in a way, but not what I expected. Ganesh, I need to talk to you. Just as I was thinking I'd got things worked out, it turns out I haven't. Something pretty disastrous has happened.'

In as few words as possible I described what had happened that morning at the pizzeria.

Even Ganesh was silenced for a few moments. Then he whistled. 'You were right about something going on there, after all.'

I took that as an apology for all the doubts he'd expressed and accepted it graciously as such. 'I was right something was going on. It just wasn't what I thought it was.' I sighed. 'What really hurts is that Wally told me, when I chatted to him in the cellar, that the wine was dodgy. Why didn't I listen?'

'Because your mind was fixed on Ion's story of Max. Also because, like everyone else, you thought Wally was just an old soak whose brains were pickled.'

Yes, exactly. I'd searched that cellar and even hunted among the wine racks, handling the evidence, but it had never occurred to me that there was a different sort of racket being run from there. As Ganesh said, my mind had been fixed on Ion and nothing else.

'So what do I do now?' I asked dispiritedly.

'You do what Parry told you to do,' Ganesh said with decision. 'You go home and rest up. We've still got to get through the play. You need to be able to concentrate. Besides, you gave Cole a message for Morgan and she might try and contact you.'

He was making sense. Ganesh usually did. I went home.

My troubles weren't over for the day. When I got to the house, the payphone in the hallway was ringing discordantly, echoing round the hall. Everyone else must be out. I nearly left it to exhaust itself, following Erwin's advice, but it occurred to me it might be Janice Morgan. I grabbed the receiver.

'That you, Fran?' squawked a familiar voice in my ear. 'You all right, love?'

'Susie!' I gasped. 'I've been so worried about you. Did you know that your flat—'

'The cops were here and told me. My sister's kicking up a devil of a fuss. I've moved out of her place and I'm staying in a B and B. At least they don't know me here. I was wondering about you, Fran. Perhaps you ought to move out of town for a while as well.'

'I can't,' I said. 'I've got the play. What I haven't got is a job any more.' I told her about the pizzeria.

'Didn't I tell you?' she asked. 'Didn't I say you'd get there one day and find the place crawling with police?'

'Yeah, you did.' Everyone had been telling me things.

'We were both right, then, after all, Fran. I thought it was a funny outfit, so did you.'

'Only right in principle. Yes, it was dodgy. They were up to something. I just guessed the wrong racket. A scam with wine never entered my head. No wonder Luigi didn't like me criticising the stuff.'

'That Luigi,' said Susie in a sentimental way. 'I suppose they'll put him away for a bit.' She sounded regretful.

I hoped they put him away for a long time. He was the

sort to go looking for revenge and if he ever got to learn that I'd been telling everyone I thought the pizzeria was dodgy, he'd come looking for me.

Susie saw things in a different light. 'So now you can come and work with me at the agency!' she crowed.

Heaven help us. 'Susie!' I yelled into the phone. 'You haven't got an agency. You haven't even got a flat! It's burned out. I was there when it went up. It cost me my eyebrows and the front of my hair.'

'What were you doing there?' she asked.

'Checking on you and I think I saw the guy who torched it—'

I broke off and was silent long enough to make her shout my name repeatedly down the line.

'What's going on? What's up with you, Fran? Are you sure you weren't hurt?'

'I wasn't hurt,' I said slowly. 'But my brain's been on hold. It's just started working again.' Before she could start asking more questions, I added, 'Give me a call when you're coming back to London. I'm really sorry about your flat.' I hung up.

Cole had apparently done as I'd asked. Shortly after my phone conversation with Susie, Morgan turned up.

'Right!' she snapped, marching in and plonking herself down on my sofa. 'What's all this I hear from Sergeant Cole? Why wouldn't you speak to him? If it was about the arson attack at Mrs Duke's flat you could have made a simple statement. You're messing me around, Fran. You ought to know better than that. I'm very busy and I have a lot of things to think about without traipsing out here.'

'So,' I said, 'have I.' What was more, I'd had some time to think about them. She might be in a real old tetchy mood, but I wasn't going to be hassled. 'First of all, I want to ask you something.'

She gave me that blank look the police have to perfection. 'You can ask me anything you like, Fran. I'll answer if I can. But don't count on it.'

'The other night,' I began, 'when you came here and talked about my new job and the play, was that just trying to find out if I knew anything about what was going on at the pizzeria? Or were you also asking about the pub?'

She flicked imaginary fluff from the lapels of her navy-blue jacket. 'General enquiries. We raided the pizzeria this morning, but you know that. You spoke to Sergeant Parry there.'

'And I asked Parry if the raid was to do with the illegal aliens racket you were looking into but it wasn't. So why, when you came to see me here, did you link the pizzeria and the smuggling investigation?'

'I didn't,' she said. 'You did. If you recall, I was also enquiring into a suspicious death.'

'Ion Popescu,' I said. 'He died because he was looking for the fat man called Max and he thought he'd seen him at the pizzeria.'

She nodded. 'Maybe he did. A restaurant is a public place. We have no reason to link the traffic in illegal immigrants with the pizzeria. Nor, in our investigations into the business affairs of the pizzeria and its owners, have we come across anyone called Max.'

'But I have,' I said. 'Only he's not at the pizzeria. Freddy, the landlord of The Rose, used to wrestle under the name of Max the Mangler. I found out last night. That's why I went to the police station. But I wasn't speaking to Cole about it. He makes it clear he thinks I'm trash. But look, seen in poor light, Freddy would appear fat. Freddy is always visiting other local businesses arranging his charity events. Perhaps that's why Ion saw him go in the pizzeria. Incidentally,' I added. 'Jimmie hasn't got anything to do with any of it, not the wine scam, nothing.'

'Stick to the illegal immigrants,' she said shortly. 'I'll check what you say about the wrestling alias, but it could be no more than a coincidence.'

'That pub,' I said firmly, 'is where you should be looking. There's another thing I've realised, and it has to do with Ion's death and the fire at Susie Duke's flat.'

She stiffened and gave me a steely look. 'Go on, Fran.'

'Last night we had a dress rehearsal at the pub. That's when I learned about Freddy also being known as Max. One of the other members of the cast was grumbling about the smell in the dressing room upstairs. The dressing room is just a cubbyhole really and it never gets aired out. All the pub smells that have found their way up there are trapped inside. Do you know the sort of smell I mean? It's like if you go past a pub early in the morning when they've got the doors open and are cleaning the place up after the night before. A real fug seeps out, beer dregs, nicotine, disinfectant, all the dust raised from vacuum-cleaning the carpets and upholstery . . . That's the smell that lingers in the dressing room upstairs, plus all the make-up scents. And that's what I caught on the hooded top the man was wearing at Susie's flat. I told you about him. I passed him as I was going into the block. He was coming out, in a hurry and not wanting to be seen. I told you his clothing had a funny smell. I thought it might be cigarettes. It was, partly. I'd come across it before, but I didn't register what it was. The night Ion died, I followed him into the underground station as you know. A man stepped in front of me as I went to get a ticket, a big chap in a jogger's top. I didn't pay him much attention, I was concentrating on buying a ticket and catching up with Ion. But I got a whiff of the same odour. Pub odour. Whoever the man is, he has to do with a pub, not just as a client but working there. He hangs up his jacket in some back room or other and the smell has got into it.'

'Are you saying the man was Freddy?'

I shook my head. 'I don't think so. I think I'd have recognised Freddy at the Tube station. Even at Susie's flat, when the man had his hood pulled up over his head, I think I might have known it was Freddy, if it was. The fire-setter was the wrong shape. Freddy's broad and barrel-chested but not all that tall. All his muscle has turned to flab. The guy I passed as I went in was tall and mega-fit, so was the man at the Tube station. Anyway, Freddy doesn't do his own dirty work.'

She looked thoughtful but then turned brisk. 'Right, this is what I want you to do, Fran. I want you to carry on as normal. Our investigations are at a critical point. We're not ready to move yet and we don't want to be forced into a move because of a piece of information from you that we'll need to check out very carefully. Don't tell anyone about this. Have you?'

'Only Ganesh,' I said.

'So, don't tell anyone else. Just act natural when you're

at the pub. Tell Mr Patel the same. Concentrate on that play. It's tonight, isn't it?'

'Yes,' I said, surprising myself with the lack of enthusiasm in my voice.

She got up to go. 'I hope everything goes well. I won't wish you luck because theatre people don't like that, do they? So, break a leg, Fran. Remember what I said. Behave naturally. Don't talk to anyone about Freddy being known as Max. It could still turn out to be coincidence, you know.'

'It isn't,' I said. 'It's not going to be easy, behaving normally around Freddy.'

'You're an actor,' she retorted. 'Act.'

I told her thanks and watched her leave. She was right, of course. I needed something else to give her before she could start turning Freddy's place upside down. Right then, I didn't see where I was going to get it.

Chapter Fifteen

Difficult as it was, I had to make a real effort on Saturday afternoon to put everything other than the play out of my mind. I put on my costume and tried speaking my lines and making appropriate gestures – acting, in other words – while wearing it. It was immediately clear I had a problem. Just walking up and down, concentrating on my feet as I'd done for Susie, was fine. It was when I tried to forget my feet that I kept tripping over the hem. Finally I lifted it in both hands to keep it clear of the pink pumps. That made it safer to move around but denied me the use of my arms. I really should have had it with me at the dress rehearsal. That's what dress rehearsals are for, to find out these little problems. To move around the stage in my jeans and trainers had been fine. Moving around in this clobber would be something else. I found needle and thread and settled down to shorten it. I wished I'd let Susie do it when she'd offered. I am not a natural seam-stress. Grandma Varady had been a wizard at this sort of thing. She would measure me up and cut out a beautifully fitting dress or shirt without any paper pattern. If, from heaven, she was able to see me sitting there sticking the needle in my fingertips, twisting the thread into knots and swearing, she'd throw up her hands in despair. That any granddaughter of hers . . .

Erwin knocked on the door around four, just as I'd finished my task and was mopping the blood off my punctured fingers. He wanted to tell me how much he and his mates had enjoyed the rehearsal.

'It was like, really good, you know?' He sat on my sofa, beaming. Along with the gold chains and rings, he also had a couple of gold teeth. 'My mates thought it was great. They'd never seen a play before. Well, only the nativity play at Christmas when they were in infants' school, you know?'

'I remember doing that sort of thing,' I reminisced. 'I played Mary one year. The doll they gave me for the Baby Jesus was so old, when I picked it up from its cradle, the head came away. It was hard to keep the illusion going after that. And then Joseph was sick all over the stage. One of the Angel Gabriel's wings fell off. It was a pretty jinxed production, even by infant school standards. The following year I played the donkey in a papier mâché mask, and fell off the stage because I couldn't see where I was going. I hope our show tonight doesn't turn out like that.'

'No way!' said Erwin confidently.

'What did you think of The Rose?' I asked.

'We liked the look of the place. If the landlord will hire us, we'd like to do some gigs there. We're definitely going to give it a try.'

I made us both coffee and asked him to hear my lines. He entered into the spirit of the thing and fed me the cues with gusto. We got through it at top speed and without any ghastly silences on my part.

'Hey, girl, you're word-perfect!' declared Erwin.

'I've got the collywobbles,' I said. 'Stage fright big-time.'

'Loosen up. It'll be fine. You know your lines. So long as the others know theirs, what can go wrong?'

'I don't know,' I mumbled. 'Everything seems to be going wrong recently. Why should the play be any different? Oh well, at least Silvio and Mario won't be there.'

'Who are they?' enquired Erwin.

I explained they were owner and cook respectively at the pizzeria where I'd been working. 'But I'm not working there any longer, it seems. I suppose the job as manageress Silvio offered me is out, too.'

Erwin asked, why? I told him, because they were all in gaol. He sympathised.

'Maybe they'll get bail,' he said.

'Even if they do, they'll be too busy with their lawyers to give time to come to the play. Funnily enough, I didn't want them to be there. Except for Jimmie, the manager. I wouldn't have minded Jimmie being there. Do you remember him? He used to run the Hot Spud Café.'

Erwin nodded. 'I remember his baked potatoes. They were sort of weird but he was a decent guy. Shit, the cops pick him up too?'

'I'm afraid so. I'm sure he hasn't done anything.'

'The cops arrest people all the time,' opined Erwin. 'But mostly they don't have the evidence to go to court and have to let them go. Don't worry about your mates.'

He jingle-jangled away.

When I got to the pub that evening, I found that everything but the play had been relegated in my mind to 'other business'. Tonight was the show and nothing else mattered. Get through tonight, worry about all the other things tomorrow.

I discovered that Denise had been as good as her word and all the radiators upstairs were belting out raging heat. The cast had gathered and it was clear I wasn't the only one nursing stage fright. Nigel was as white as a sheet. He sat on a chair, shaking his head, and saying he couldn't remember a single word of his part. Mick had swallowed so many antihistamines to stop his nose running that he was in a sort of trance and his throat was too dry to speak properly. Marty, who was playing Sir Henry Baskerville as well as being director, if you recall, kept rubbing his hands together like Lady Macbeth as he prowled up and down the narrow corridor which led to the dressing room.

Inside the dressing room, Ganesh, Owen and Carmel were getting in one another's way. Carmel, in her padded Mrs Hudson costume, took up the most room and kept bumping into things. The padding was also inappropriate now the place was heated like a hothouse. Trickles of perspiration ran down her forehead and smudged her eye make-up. She was grousing non-stop in her usual way.

I got into my costume, making things worse, sticking my elbows into Ganesh and treading on Carmel's foot. Irish Davey then turned up with the hound and slumped down beside his pet in one corner. 'Youse all right there?' he enquired cheerfully.

'Keep that dog away from me!' ordered Carmel.

'And me,' said Ganesh nervously.

'Sure, he's just an owd softie,' said Irish comfortably.

The old softie fixed Ganesh with a baleful eye and growled deep in his throat.

'What's he doing that for?' Ganesh's voice rose hysterically.

'He's in a strange place and you're all running round like maniacs. Just relax and the dog will relax,' said Irish. 'He's picking up on the atmosphere, so he is.'

'He's adding to the atmosphere,' muttered Carmel. There was indeed a distinct doggy odour now blending with the rest.

'I'll go and make up somewhere else,' said Ganesh, grabbing a box of assorted items and fleeing.

He had the right idea. I'd begun to think I was going to be sick, just like poor little Joseph in our school play all those years ago. I left the overpowering fug and found the quietest place, ironically the stage, behind the drawn curtains. The only other person there was Denise, shuffling her prompter's script in a harassed way. I did a few practice walks in my newly shortened skirt.

'Feeling OK, Fran?' asked Denise.

'Butterflies,' I confessed.

'Be all right once you start. Got a good crowd out front.'

Certainly from the other side of the curtain I could hear a loud rumble of voices. I peeped through. The functions room was packed wall to wall. In the front row, left of the aisle, sat Uncle Hari with Ganesh's mum and dad, his sister Usha and her husband, Jay, and Ganesh's friend Dilip with his wife and three children. In the front row right, on the other side of the aisle, sat a set of beefy gents in tight suits, accompanied by bottle-blonde females in frilly blouses and those skirts with uneven hems that look as if they're made out of old net curtains. These, presumably, were friends of Freddy. There was an empty seat among them which I guessed was to be filled by our landlord himself. No sign of Jimmie or anyone from the pizzeria. They were presumably all still in custody. But any seats left empty by their absence had been filled already.

'Full house,' I croaked.

'What's that?' asked Denise behind me. There was a rattle of papers hitting the floor. 'Oh, blast, I've dropped the ruddy thing.'

'I said, full house. You all right there, Denise?' I turned and saw her scrabbling on the floor to recover the script. It hadn't been bound in any way, and the pages were jumbled. I knelt down to help and we managed to sort them into order.

'I'd be all right if I could read this perishing thing,' she grumbled.

'Is Freddy coming up to watch?' It was hard even to say his name and sound natural and relaxed.

'Course he is!' said Denise, wide-eyed. 'Think my Maxie would miss a stage show?'

'Who's minding the bar?' I burbled.

'Oh, Trevor's doing that. You know Trev, our barman, don't you? He can manage. Most of the regulars are up here, anyway.'

Too true. A more critical audience couldn't have been assembled. They'd all come to get their money's worth and gaffes on stage wouldn't be tolerated. For Ganesh's family, our success was a matter of honour.

Denise shook her script at me. 'I hope you all know your cues. It's no use relying on me. I've told you, I can't read the blooming thing.'

It's always a comfort when your prompter says something like that.

With any performance, once it starts, you don't have time to be nervous. You just have to go for it. It all went well, too. It really did. I have to repeat this now because it's easy to forget how smoothly everything clicked together until Irish's hound ran across the stage.

It wasn't the fault of the hound. It did just as it had been trained to do. The build-up to its appearance had been terrific. The audience had heard its howls (tape-recorded) but its actual appearance when it leapt on to the boards was electrifying. The audience gasped. Dilip's wife gave a little scream. The kids all cheered. The ladies in the frilly blouses squeaked, clutched at their décolletés with one hand and at their beefy escorts' arms with the other. Freddy beamed and gave the stage the thumbs-up.

And then it happened.

Someone downstairs had gone out into the backyard and stupidly left the door open. Digger, well aware that something was going on, had slipped in unobserved and made his way upstairs. He plodded in at the back of the functions room just as the hound bounded from one set of wings and hit the stage in a scrabble of claws.

Since originally hearing the tape-recorded howls relayed from earlier rehearsals, Digger's suspicions that another dog had been smuggled on to the premises had festered in his evil little brain. Now he saw the intruder for himself.

Bellowing a challenge in a barrage of furious barks, Digger rocketed down the centre aisle, bounded up on the stage and made straight for the hound. The hound had almost disappeared into the far wings but whirled round and, seeing himself about to be attacked, didn't hesitate. His motto clearly was: get in first. The hound hurled himself at Digger. Digger hurled himself at the hound. The next thing we knew the two dogs were locked in mortal combat with resulting pandemonium on stage and off.

On the stage nothing could be made out but a whirl of fur, blood-curdling snarls and snapping teeth, saliva flying everywhere.

Front of house, Dilip's wife grabbed her children and dragged them down the aisle to the exit. All the kids were crying, not because they wanted to get out but because they wanted to stay. The frilly ladies all stood up and screamed. Some of them, in the hullabaloo, perhaps confusing dogs and mice, climbed on to their chairs. Freddy pounded to the stage, yelling at Digger. Irish appeared from the wings, yelling at the hound. The gents in the tight suits, and nearly every other male customer of The Rose who was in the room, began to lay bets with one another on the outcome.

Denise grabbed my arm. 'Downstairs!' she shouted. 'Soda siphons!'

We got down the stairs somehow, with me stumbling over my skirt, squeezing past the fleeing women and children.

'Dogfight, Trev!' yelled Denise.

Trevor grabbed a soda siphon, Denise grabbed another and I did the same. We all three raced back upstairs, followed by those patrons of the pub who had not been attending the play but now didn't want to miss out on the action.

Our arrival with the soda siphons was greeted with cheers by half the audience and shouts from the other half, the gamblers, not to interrupt, since they had money on it.

We jumped onto the stage and sprayed the dogs with jets from the siphons until they broke apart. In the split second before they re-engaged, Irish dashed in and seized hold of his dog and Freddy tackled Digger. The combatants were dragged apart still barking defiance and dripping blood. The blood had me worried for a moment. But although both dogs had been bitten I was relieved to see, from their heroic struggles to return to the fray, that neither was actually incapacitated.

Freddy began to haul Digger towards the wings. At that moment, the hound slipped his collar and Irish's despairing grasp, and leapt at his opponent. Freddy, seeing the hound coming at him, released Digger and jumped back, and the two animals took up their battle where they'd left off.

'There's no more full siphons!' shouted Trevor.

Something had to be done. I did the only thing I could think of: I yanked at the nearest stage curtain. Old and rotten, it gave way and fell in a heap on the stage.

'Take the other side!' I shouted at Denise.

She understood. She got hold of one side, I grabbed the other and we threw it over the struggling dogs. Freddy and Irish threw themselves on top of the heaving mass in the centre and forced it into two separate writhing shapes. Somehow Freddy extricated Digger and Irish retrieved his

collarless animal, hanging on to him by the simple expedi-
ent of wrapping both arms tightly round the hound's neck.

This time Freddy managed to get Digger off the stage.
He dragged him down the aisle. Digger protested, growling
and trying to sit down. It was a good thing Freddy was so
strong. Eventually, the pair of them disappeared through
the door at the back of the room. We could hear them
going down the staircase. Digger, still refusing to cooperate,
landed on each step of the descent with a thud. Freddy's
language was amazing.

I stood at the side of the stage surrounded by empty
siphons, my costume drenched with soda water. Denise's
red wig had fallen off in the scramble and lay somewhere
out there in the auditorium. Irish was examining his pet
and lamenting. The hound sat with lolling tongue and
heaving flanks. He appeared oblivious of his injuries.
Digger's departure had obviously convinced him he'd won
the scrap. His whole demeanour was of a dog well pleased
with himself.

Ganesh appeared at my elbow.

'I told you,' he said. 'I told you I was worried about that
dog.'

'It wasn't the hound's fault,' I protested. 'Some idiot let
Digger in.'

Ganesh was having none of it. 'Never act with children
and animals. Right?'

'Right,' I said.

After the departure of the two dogs, we attempted to pick
up where we'd been interrupted. We were troupers, after
all. The show must go on. But the audience's attention

had been broken and throughout the closing scenes a soft persistent rumble of chatter from front of house, and distant howls from Digger shut out in the yard, distracted us. We got through it somehow and were enthusiastically applauded. It would have been nice to think the applause had been purely for our acting abilities. But at least we couldn't say the play had been a failure. In its own way it had been a rip-roaring success. The patrons of The Rose who'd formed the bulk of the audience left declaring it was the best show they'd seen in years.

'They're mostly sporting men,' explained Freddy to me afterwards.

The place had cleared and we were trying to tidy up. If he picked up any wariness on my part towards him, it could be put down to what had happened. Freddy was used, in any case, to people being wary around him. Marty sidled up, his round face a picture of misery. He looked near to tears.

'What's the matter with you, then?' asked Freddy. 'Worried about your money? I'll see you and the others get your cut out of the profits. Denise will sort out the financial side of it. She takes care of all that for the pub. You come round tomorrow about ten, before we open. The money will be ready for you.' Freddy added his finest accolade. 'You done well.'

'Thanks,' I said, reflecting that the same sort of sporting audience once attended the Roman circus, cheering on the lions and whooping with delight as one gladiator sliced up another.

'This wouldn't have happened if they'd done one of my plays,' said Marty mournfully, when Freddy had gone.

'It was a pity Digger got in. It was going really well, Marty, up to then, honestly. Anyway, they all enjoyed it.' My poor consolation did little to cheer him up.

'Yes,' he mumbled. 'The dog. I'll – I'll see you around, Fran.'

On Sunday morning I was awoken by the telephone ringing out in the hall. I pulled the duvet over my head and tried to ignore it. Then I heard footsteps running down the stairs as one of the upstairs tenants went to answer it. Moments later, he was hammering on my door.

'Fran, hey, Fran! You awake? Phone for you!'

Wouldn't it just be? Probably Susie again. I crawled out of bed, pulled on my jeans, and stumbled out into the hall. The receiver dangled at the end of the lead. I picked it up.

'Susie?'

'Denise here,' said a woman's voice. 'How are you this morning, Fran?' She sounded remarkably fresh and cheery.

'Just about conscious,' I said.

'That Marty hasn't turned up to collect your money,' she said. 'I worked out what you were owed, divided it up and put it in individual brown envelopes. I tried to ring him. He gave me his mobile number. But he's got it switched off and he isn't picking up on any messages I leave. He hasn't got the phone in his flat. I expect he just switched off his mobile for a bit of peace and quiet, and he's overslept.'

Lucky him. 'What do you want me to do?' I muttered.

'Come over and collect it, if you've got a bit of time free. I don't want it hanging about here. Good night last night, wasn't it? Pity about Digger. I don't know how he got in. Still, nobody seemed to mind, did they?'

She hung up and I realised I hadn't had time to say I was too busy or too tired to go over to the pub.

Once I'd showered, dressed and had a cup of coffee I felt better, almost human. I began to make plans. After I'd collected the money from the pub, I could walk over to the newsagent's. They're open until twelve on a Sunday because of the papers. I could give Ganesh his envelope and even face Hari. Poor Hari, he'd have been so disappointed in the way the play finished up – a dogfight, collapsing curtains and general mayhem. Still, you couldn't say the audience hadn't got its money's worth.

Ganesh and I could decide what to do for the rest of the day. We didn't have to worry about learning lines or rehearsing. Now the play was over, we'd got our free time back again.

I left the house, whistling.

Chapter Sixteen

It was quite a nice, sunny morning and my good mood lasted until I arrived at The Rose. Perhaps it was the memory of the previous evening's disaster, but my heart sank at the sight of its familiar glazed-tiled exterior. It was nearly half past eleven. Though they wouldn't be open for business until twelve, as it was Sunday, the door was ajar. I pushed it wide and went in.

The design of the place didn't admit much daylight. Even now, on a fine day, it was necessary to have a single electric light on, dangling from the ceiling and making a pool of yellow brightness in the centre of the floor. It emphasised the brushmarks left by the vacuum cleaner which had recently been passed over it and made the remnants of the original art nouveau stained-glass glitter. Chairs were still upended on tops of tables. The air had that lingering aroma by now so familiar to me: beer and nicotine, aftershave and body odour, strong commercial disinfectant from the lavatories. It was only slightly dispelled by the fresh air coming in through the front door.

Beyond the light the bar was in shadows and behind it, moving quietly, stood Freddy. He was methodically polishing glasses and setting them back on a shelf. Each was placed the exact same distance from its neighbour, in a dead straight line. There was a mirror behind the shelf and in it the glasses were reflected in crystal ranks. I was again struck by Freddy's bulbous outline, dark in silhouette against the softly gleaming rows of glasses and shining brass of the pumps. A prickle of fear ran up my spine. Was I stupidly walking into the lion's den? I wished my mind hadn't been so fuzzy that morning when Denise rang. Any excuse would have got me out of this visit. I should at least have told someone I was coming here.

It was too late to change my mind and slip out again. He'd seen me. 'Hello, Fran,' he said. 'All right?'

It seemed a harmless enough greeting. I knew he wasn't mad at us because of the play. He'd been pleased with that. He looked happy enough now. Well, as happy as Freddy ever looked.

'Denise rang me,' I said. 'She said to come over and collect our share of the takings.'

'Yeah, we done well.' He shook out the cloth and hung it over a polished brass rail. 'Denise has got it all worked out. Go on in the back room.'

He nodded towards a door beside the bar.

I walked past him and pushed open the door. I found myself in a small crowded room. Here, obviously, was where Denise did the accounts. There was a large old kneehole desk, oak, with a green leather top. It was rather a splendid affair. Freddy must have got it at auction somewhere. The top of it was covered with papers of one kind and another and among them was a neat stack of little brown envelopes. Other things were kept in this back room. There were some spare tubular chairs, stacked in a tower. Beside them stood a wonky pillar of boxes of crisps (cheese and onion). Beyond that was an old-fashioned hat- and coatstand, the sort with a crown of hooks around a central pole, like a kind of indoor tree. Various outdoor garments hung from it. Beyond that a door led out into the backyard where Digger prowled.

Anyone, I thought, coming to work here, would hang his outdoor jacket up there and, over a period of time, it would absorb the odour from the bar seeping through the door.

But apart from all these things, the room was empty. No sign of Denise. I wondered what I was supposed to do. I went to the desk and checked out the brown envelopes. Each was neatly addressed to one of the cast. They were all sealed down so I couldn't tell how much was in them, but they seemed fairly fat.

There was a click from the outside door to the yard. A draught of cold air wafted in. I looked up, expecting to see Denise. But it wasn't Denise, it was Trevor, the barman.

'Hello, darling,' he said. He pulled the tracksuit top he was wearing over his head and, as I'd expected, hung it on the hatstand. He put up a hand and ran it over his shaven head in an automatic smoothing gesture, as if he still had hair up there. He was staring at me. I didn't like the way he looked at me and I hadn't liked the way he'd said hello. I never like being called 'darling'.

I'd never paid really close attention to him before. He'd been just a figure behind the bar. In the small confines of this room, he looked even bigger. His face was broad, flat and scarred with what must have been dreadful youthful acne. His nose and eyes were all too small for the size of his face; they seemed lost in that pockmarked expanse. The eyes, watching me, were dark and somehow feral. Though they studied me, I couldn't engage with them. The surrounding skin was puffed and scarred. At some time or other, he'd been in the fight game. It was like being observed by some large, not very friendly wild animal.

There was another click of a door, the one I'd come through from the bar. I turned, hoping that this time it was Denise. But it was Freddy. He came in and quietly shut the door behind him. I was caught between the two of them. It was payback time.

I was terrified but I did my best not to show it. I tried to keep my head clear. If I was going to talk myself out of this, it would take all my wits.

'Sit down, why don't you?' Freddy suggested. 'Denise will be back later. She just had to go out for a while, see a neighbour. The old lady's not too well. Denise likes to keep an eye on her.'

I didn't know if this was supposed to put me at my ease. It didn't. But I sat down on a chair by the desk.

Trevor had remained by the hatstand. Freddy moved a little nearer and looked down at me.

'I just wanted to have a little word,' he said. 'Nothing to worry about. I'm sure we can sort it out.'

I wanted to say something but I couldn't. I gulped.

'You're a good girl, I know. You and your mates did a nice job on the play and I'm pleased about that. But I'm not pleased about some other things.'

'Yes?' I croaked.

'A little bird's been singing,' said Trevor from his hatstand.

Freddy glanced briefly at him. 'It seems there's been a misunderstanding,' he said to me. 'You told someone you thought you saw me somewhere. But obviously you didn't. It was a mistake.'

A mistake that I had named Freddy – or a mistake to have spoken to the police? Both.

'I didn't tell anyone I saw you.' I said. It was true, I hadn't.

His mouth creased upwards in what would have been a smile if there'd been any humour in it. 'Don't mess me about, darling. You told the cops you saw me behind the old cinema, early on Thursday morning.'

'No,' I said indignantly. 'I didn't say anything of the sort. I told them I saw a fat man.'

It struck me, as I said this, that it wasn't very polite. I hoped Freddy wasn't touchy about his figure.

He patted the swell of his stomach. 'Since I gave up the wrestling game,' he said with regret.

'I didn't say I saw you, how could I?' I hurried on. 'I didn't see the man's face. It wasn't light enough. I was – I was hiding and I couldn't see well from where I was.'

Freddy and Trevor exchanged glances. Trevor said, 'You gave a name to the cops.'

'No, I only said I saw a fat man.'

'You gave them a name later,' growled Trevor.

Though already almost paralysed with fear, I felt my insides tighten even more. There was only one way they could know this. Morgan had put my information into the communal pool and someone on the police side had tipped them off. Susie Duke's voice echoed in my memory. 'An outfit like that has got to have a bent copper or two in its pocket.'

If ever I got out of here in one piece, I'd have to warn Morgan she had a rotten apple to seek out. But this was a big operation, probably involving police forces nationwide. Where did the mole lurk and what else did Freddy know?

I pulled myself together. 'What's your problem, Freddy? All I saw in the cinema yard was a – a shape. Susie Duke's been teaching me to drive. We used the yard. That's why we were there. We didn't dream anyone else used it. It gave us a real shock when we saw a load of blokes getting out of a lorry. We had to report it because Susie's in the investigation business and she has to keep her reputation clean. You know, she gets a lot of work from lawyers and even, sometimes, little jobs from the police.'

He was listening closely, watching my lips form the words, as if he weighed each one.

'So what's your interest in the name Max?' He raised his eyebrows. 'Why did you tell that woman inspector I used to wrestle under that name?'

'She came to see me. She does that,' I added, 'drops in from time to time. I don't invite her. She invites herself. She asked me about the play. It was when I was talking to her about that that I must have let slip what Denise told me, about your wrestling days.'

I was getting my story together now. 'I don't know what she made of it,' I said. 'It's nothing to do with me if it gave her ideas. I'm not party to police business. They don't tell me anything.'

'But you tell them things, don't cha, darling?' said Trevor.

'No!' I snapped at him. 'I'm not a grass!'

Trevor didn't believe me, but Freddy was looking undecided, and it was Freddy who mattered.

I pushed my luck. 'Why shouldn't I tell Morgan you used to wrestle under the name of Max the Mangler?' I asked. 'It's a good name. Why don't you want her to know?'

Clearly Freddy's informant hadn't told him everything. He didn't appear to know of my acquaintance with Ion. If I could just stop them connecting me with Ion, I could yet get out of here, safe and sound. If they discovered I'd known Ion, I'd had it. Fran Varady, the disappearing girl. Just like the magician's cabinet. In this case, the cabinet would be represented by Freddy's back room into which I'd walked, never to be seen again. Where would they dispose of my body? I wondered idly. On a building site probably. In the foundations of a block of luxury flats. Or perhaps they'd just take me down to a lonely spot on the canal one night and hold my head under the water?

There was a noise from the other side of the door, in the bar.

'Freddy!' called Denise's voice. My heart rose. She was back from visiting the sick.

Freddy gave me a warning look. 'What d'you want?' he shouted back.

The door was pushed open and Denise stuck her head into the room. 'I found four blokes outside, come to see you. Oh, hello, Fran. Here for the money? It's on the desk. Freddy, do you want to talk to these fellers? They're a band. They want to know if they can play here a couple of nights.'

'We got references,' said a familiar voice from the bar, behind Denise. 'Other people have hired us to play. They'll tell you, we're good.'

'Erwin!' I shouted, jumping to my feet.

Trevor took a quick step towards me but the door had opened and Erwin, followed by the other three members of the band, crowded into the room.

'Hi, Fran. What are you doing here?' His white teeth gleamed and the gold ones twinkled.

I snatched up the pile of brown envelopes. 'I came to collect our dosh – from the play.'

'Hey,' said Erwin to Freddy. 'That was a pretty good play. We didn't see the real thing. We saw the dress rehearsal. It was really cool.'

I could see Freddy and Trevor eyeing up Erwin and the band. Freddy and Trevor were big men but there were four of the band. None of the quartet was under six-two and hauling all that band equipment around builds up muscles.

'I'll be off, then!' I chirped, making for the way out. 'Thanks for the money.'

'Yeah,' said Freddy. 'Watch out, now. Don't do anything I wouldn't.' His face creased in that mirthless smile again.

There was a look on Trevor's face like that of a tiger, suddenly deprived of the tethered goat. But he worked for Freddy and if Freddy was prepared to let me go, that was it.

I squeezed through the band and scuttled out. I knew I had the play to thank for my escape. My story had been thin, but Freddy was still well disposed towards me because of the show.

I went over to the newsagent's and gave Ganesh his envelope.

'Such a beautiful play,' said Hari. 'A pity about the dog. But the play, it was like Shakespeare.'

Crumbs.

Ganesh and I usually spent Sunday afternoon together and, because it was so pleasant, we went for our walk along the canal again, skirting Regent's Park.

I didn't tell him about my experience that morning. It was better he didn't know. But I felt guilty, not confiding in him, and it made me a poor conversationalist.

Luckily, Ganesh was still full of his grievance about Digger's entrance on the scene the previous evening. I was happy to let him moan on about it uninterrupted.

When he finally ran out of steam, I said, 'Well, we got paid, didn't we?'

'I am not taking part in any more plays,' said Ganesh, still huffy.

'Don't worry, not all plays have dogs in them.'

'With or without dogs,' he insisted, 'my acting career started and ended last night.'

'I hope mine didn't,' I said.

I reflected that, but for the timely arrival of Erwin and his mates, my career might have come to an abrupt end that morning. I looked up at the trees. What did Dr Johnson say about the prospect of being hanged in the morning serving to concentrate the mind wonderfully? I had never thought London so beautiful.

Monday morning saw me with the task of having to contact Morgan and do it in such a way that nobody else on her team knew. What I had to tell her was difficult. She wouldn't like it. She might not want to believe it. But there was no way Freddy could have known what he did, if someone down there at the cop shop hadn't told him.

But first of all, I had another job to do: distribute the remaining envelopes of money. While I was doing that, I might think up a way to get hold of Morgan.

I chose the easiest person to find first. I walked to Carmel's supermarket, collected a pint of milk and went in search of her. I found her on a till marked Baskets Only. She was involved in a heated argument with a fat woman pushing a trolley laden with unhealthy-looking foodstuffs, all high-fat, high-sugar and chemical additives. A surly-looking child stood by her, eating a bar of chocolate. The kid's teeth already looked to be going bad.

'Only one basket!' Carmel was saying, jabbing her finger at the notice above her head. 'That's a trolley.' She pointed at the offending chariot.

'There's queues at the other checkouts,' said the fat woman. 'There's no queue at this one.'

'I can't check your trolley. Someone might come with a basket and they'd have to wait. It wouldn't be fair. This is a basket-only checkout.'

'Well, I'm not moving,' said the woman. 'I'm staying here until you check my trolley.'

Carmel leaned over the shelf and stared hard at the child.

'Where did he get that chocolate bar?'

'None of your business!' snapped the fat woman.

'It is if he got it in here and you haven't paid for it.'

'How can I pay for it if you won't check my trolley?' asked the customer triumphantly.

'He's not supposed to eat it if you haven't paid for it. He's nearly finished it.'

The child crammed the last of the chocolate into his mouth, crumpled up the wrapper and dropped it on the floor. He fixed Carmel with a defiant look.

'Right,' said Carmel grimly. 'We have a policy on grazers in this store. I'm informing the manager.'

'He didn't get it in this friggin' store. He had it when he come in!' shouted the woman. 'Persecuting innocent little children,' she added. 'You oughta be ashamed of yourself.'

Carmel looked past her to me. 'Good morning, madam,' she said with exaggerated politeness. 'Shall I take your pint of milk?' She reached out for it, past the fat woman.

'No, you don't!' snapped the woman, throwing out a beefy arm between me and Carmel. 'I'm in front of her.'

'The lady only has one item,' said Carmel loftily. 'I can take that. I can't take your trolley.'

'I'm in a hurry. I'm double-parked,' I said to the woman in a worried way. 'And I've left my baby in the car seat.'

'See?' said Carmel. 'The lady's double-parked and she's got to get back to her baby. You're holding her up.'

The fat woman hesitated. She recognised she wasn't going to win, but she needed a face-saver. A wailing infant in a car seat would provide it.

'Oh, well then . . .' she muttered ungraciously.

Fortunately a nearby position became free and the woman, still muttering, backed out her trolley and took it there. The child followed. From somewhere he'd now got a tube of fruit pastilles. His pockets must have been stuffed with looted sweets.

'Hello, Fran,' said Carmel. 'Play went all right, didn't it? Except for the end when that dog of Freddy's got in. You want that milk or you just using it for an excuse?'

'An excuse,' I said.

'Leave it there, then.' She pointed at a space by her till. 'I'll get someone to put it back.'

I fished out her brown envelope. 'Here's your share of the money. You haven't seen Marty since Saturday, I suppose?'

'No. Don't much want to. He nearly drove me bonkers with his directing on that play. Honestly, who did he think he was? We weren't putting it on in the perishing West End, were we? I mean, I'm serious about my acting, too. I've been to umpteen auditions.'

'So you haven't got any idea where I can find him?' I interrupted.

She shook her head. 'Only if you try his flat. What do you want him for?'

'To give him his money.'

'He'll turn up,' she said. 'Here, Fran, if you've left a baby in a car, you ought to get back to it. You oughtn't to leave a baby like that, all on its own. People are weird. They might steal it.'

'I haven't got a baby,' I explained.

She thought about this. 'So, whose baby is it?'

Oh, for heaven's sake . . . I wanted to act again but I hoped I wouldn't have to do it with Carmel.

From there I went to the used-car business where Owen worked. Here I was lucky enough to find Nigel as well. They were leaning on a car marked Guaranteed and chatting.

'Hello,' said Owen. 'Looking for a motor, Fran?'

'I haven't passed my test yet.'

'When you have, come and see me,' he offered. 'I'll fix you up with a nice little second-hand number. I'll give you a good deal. You're a mate. I'll see you all right.'

I thanked him and handed them their envelopes. They, too, seemed happy enough with the way the play had gone. I began to think Marty and I must be perfectionists. I asked them if they knew where to find Marty, but they didn't know where he went during the day or if he had any kind of job.

'Try his flat,' said Owen. 'Excuse me, I spot a punter.' He made off towards a man wandering around a nearby vehicle.

Nigel set off with me; it seemed he had nothing else to do. We went over to Marty's place. He had a flat in a converted house, not unlike mine in outward appearance, but a lot less well maintained. At Marty's, the paintwork hadn't been touched for years and had faded and blistered. Weeds grew out of the steps leading up to the front door. The bow window to the left had developed a structural fault and the brickwork was sagging. I rang the bell with Marty's name next to it.

No one came, so I rang all the other bells in turn. Eventually someone came to the door. It creaked open to reveal a cross-looking girl with tangled hair and a real shiner of a black eye.

'Sorry to disturb you,' I said politely. 'But I'm trying to find Marty.'

'You rang my bell,' she said.

'Yes, because he didn't answer his bell.'

'That means he isn't there, then, doesn't it?' she pointed out, reasonably enough.

'I know,' I said. 'But I'm wondering if you've heard him moving around the house, coming or going. I need to contact him.'

'He's been directing a play,' she said.

'I know, we were in it. That was Saturday. Now it's Monday. No one's been able to contact him since we all parted on Saturday.'

'Well, I don't know anything about it, do I?' she snapped, slamming the door in our faces.

'Tell him I've got his money!' I shouted at the panels.

'Is that right?' Nigel asked as we walked away. 'No one's been able to contact Marty?'

'Denise hasn't had any luck. He's got his mobile switched off. I'm a bit worried about him, to tell you the truth. The play meant so much to him and the dogfight just ruined it. He was so disappointed. I honestly thought he was going to cry.'

'Oh, right,' said Nigel. 'Yes, he must be a bit fed up. But he isn't going to go and jump off Waterloo Bridge, is he?'

'Well, I don't know,' I said. 'He was really stressed out at the last couple of rehearsals.'

'I'll look out for him,' said Nigel. 'I'll put the word round that you want him.'

'Thanks. Nigel.' An idea struck me. 'If you not doing anything else now, you wouldn't do me a favour, would you?'

'Like?' Nigel asked.

'There's someone down at the local cop shop I need to speak to. An Inspector Morgan. Only I don't want to go in there myself. Would you go in, ask for her, and when you see her, tell her Fran needs to speak to her urgently? You must speak only to her, not to anyone else, got that?'

'Blimey,' said Nigel. 'I thought we'd left all the mysteries behind with the plot of the play. What's going on?'

'I just need to see her. There's no catch, Nigel. Honestly.'

He took a bit of persuading but, in the end, curiosity got the better of him, and he did it.

'I told her,' he said, when he came back. 'She said she'd meet you at one o'clock at the café in the middle of Regent's Park. It sounds like a perishing James Bond yarn. What on earth are you doing?'

I ignored the question and looked at my watch. 'Crumbs, I'd better get going. Thanks again, Nigel!'

I hurried away before he could quiz me any further.

It was a dry, cool day and it was nice in the park. When I arrived at the little café I saw the silhouette of Morgan against a window. She had decided against sitting outside in the paved area. It was probably just a tad cold for that still, and somebody might conceivably have strolled past and seen us together. I went inside and made for her table.

'What's all this about, Fran?' she asked when I joined her. 'Why did you send that friend of yours to speak for you? Why didn't you come in yourself? This is my lunch hour. It'd better be good.'

She took a bite from a Danish pastry and flakes drifted down on to her plate. Outside, two women had arrived with a mob of dogs. There must have been a dozen of them. No two were remotely alike. There were big dogs, small ones, fluffy ones and smooth ones. Each woman held half-a-dozen leads and was in the centre of a circle of trotting tykes, the leads strung out like the spokes of a wheel. One of the women sat down at a table and unleashed the dogs. They began to potter about without attempting to run off. This was clearly part of their daily routine. The other dog-walker came into the café and bought two coffees which she took back outside.

Morgan and I had been watching the scene. Now we got back to business. 'I had to speak to you on your own,' I said. 'You won't like this, but I have to warn you. Someone on your team has a loose mouth.'

She had been hoovering up flakes of pastry with a damp forefinger. She stopped, hand in mid-air.

'Go on,' she said ominously.

I'll say this for her. She always listens. She never says not to talk nonsense before she hears what you've got to say.

I told her about my run-in with Freddy. 'There is no way he could know Susie and I reported what we saw on Thursday morning, much less that I'd passed on the information that he used to wrestle under the name Max the Mangler, unless someone in your outfit tipped him off.'

'This is a very serious allegation, Fran.' Her voice was quiet and she seemed to have herself well under control, but I'd spotted the split-second flicker of panic in her eyes. It was the one thing no senior officer wanted to hear. 'Do you realise,' she asked, 'just what trouble this is going to cause? Everyone will have to be investigated, from the top down, including me. It will have to be done in a way that won't tip off the guilty party. I'll have to inform

Superintendent Foxley,' she added in a voice which betrayed her emotion. Poor Morgan, all those male colleagues waiting for her to mess it up and now . . .

'I know,' I told her grimly. 'It's already got me into one tight corner and the next time I mightn't be lucky enough to get out of it in one piece.'

She had pulled herself together. 'You're right, you should stay away from the station. The same goes for Mrs Duke. I'll get in touch with her and tell her to stay in Margate for the time being.'

'By the way,' I said. 'I don't think the blabbermouth is Wayne Parry.'

She raised an eyebrow. 'Neither do I. But it's not like you to defend Sergeant Parry.'

'I don't think he's crooked just because he's a pain,' I said.

I also didn't think Parry would drop me in it with Freddy because I knew he fancied me. But I didn't tell her that.

'Will you be investigating Freddy now?' I demanded. 'If he's on the level, why would he be getting tipped off by a dodgy copper?'

She gave me that steely look. 'I'll sort it out, thank you, Fran.' She then relaxed her attitude a degree and added, 'I'm sorry I couldn't warn you about the restaurant you worked at. I suppose that's left you without a job.'

'I was going to pack it in anyway.' I eyed the dogs outside. 'I'll think of something else I can do.'

She left the café first. I gave her five minutes to get clear and then left myself. The women had gathered up the dogs and gone. Faintly, from across the park, I could hear a shrill whistle.

I set off back down the Broad Walk, heading towards the Gloucester Gate by which I'd entered the park. At this time of year there were fewer tourists and people spending their lunch hours in the open. It was too damp and chilly for sunbathers on the lawns and even the seats along the Walk beneath the trees were empty except for one or two huddled forms with heads sunk into their chests.

I was about to turn right, towards the exit, when I heard the soft regular thud of running feet behind me. I whirled round. A figure in a tracksuit was jogging down the path towards me, but as I turned he veered off and ran away across the grass. I didn't need to see his face to know who he was.

I hadn't spotted him hanging round the café and, with luck, he'd not seen Morgan. All the same, I couldn't be sure and I didn't like his being there. It seemed unlikely to be a coincidence. I suspected that, either on Freddy's orders or on his own account, Trevor was keeping an eye on me.

Chapter Seventeen

Nothing happened for a couple of days after that. This didn't make the period restful. I was on tenterhooks, wondering what was going on, whether Morgan had found out who had tipped off Freddy that his name had been mentioned and if Trevor had seen me with her in the park, asking myself where Marty was and if he was all right, and fielding daily phone calls from Susie in Margate, wanting to know if it was in order for her to come home.

'You haven't got a home to come to, Susie,' I said brutally.

'I know, I've been on to the council about that. I've written to the insurance company about the flat's contents, too.'

'How did they take it?'

'The council or the insurance company?'

'The insurers,' I said. I had a shrewd idea what the council had told her.

She was frank. 'They just about accused me of setting fire to my own place. Imagine! Luckily I was out of town at the time. I think they'll pay up. They paid up when Rennie died. The only thing is, they might be a bit funny about insuring me again. They say I'm high-risk.'

Ganesh would agree with that. To be honest, I wasn't that keen to see her back in town too soon. She'd be round, wanting me to join her detective agency, even if it didn't have a base from which to operate. She'd probably suggest it operate out of my flat! I certainly wasn't having that. Not only because I'd found out it was difficult enough keeping my privacy even with my own place, but because I'd seen what had happened to Susie's flat. Unfortunately, I hadn't the excuse of a job at the San Gennaro now.

We'd moved into March and, true to folklore, a gusting wind was rattling my window-panes. I was cooking my supper – frying up bacon and eggs – when my doorbell rang. I knew it couldn't be Ganesh because earlier I'd left him at the shop, where I'd been doing two hours a day helping out, and he hadn't said he meant to come over. I peered out, hoping Susie hadn't, after all, taken it into her head to return. Whoever it was huddled inside the shelter of the porch, mostly out of sight. I could just make out that the visitor appeared to be male. He didn't look large enough to be either Freddy or Trevor, so that was all right. That left Wayne Parry. I went to open the front door, fingers crossed against this possibility.

It was Marty. He stood on the doorstep shuffling his feet and looking utterly miserable. The wind drove drizzling rain into the porch and tossed the rubbish on the pavement behind him into the air where it became trapped in the skeletal privet hedge. It was bitterly cold. Marty was wearing a big polo-neck sweater which made him look even more like a large knitted toy. His small pale blue eyes blinked nervously at me behind his rain-speckled spectacles.

'I've been away,' he said without preamble. 'I got a message last night, when I got back to London, from someone in one of the other flats. She said you'd been at the front door with some bloke, and you wanted to see me.'

'That's right. I've got your money,' I told him.

He looked warily at me. 'Who was the bloke with you, then?'

'Only Nigel, why? Are you going to stand out here while we both get pneumonia, or are you coming in?'

He trailed in after me, looking as suspiciously about him as Ion had done on his first visit. It prompted me to ask him, 'What's the matter with you? You've been in my flat before.'

He just hunched into his woolly pully and sat down on the sofa in a heap of cable-stitch despondency. I made him coffee which he took with mumbled thanks and then sat, nursing the mug in his hands, without drinking it.

'Do you mind if I eat my supper?' I asked, growing impatient. 'It's getting cold. Do you want any bacon?'

'Thanks, I'll have it in a sandwich,' he said. 'If you've got enough to spare.'

'You'll have to cook it yourself.'

He took his mug to the kitchenette whence the sound of sizzling rashers could soon be heard. I finished mine and took the plate out there. He was cutting his sandwich into two precise halves.

'Where have you been?' I asked curiously. 'Since you weren't in London. You didn't say you were going away.'

'I went down to Wiltshire to see my parents.' He contemplated the sandwich. 'They farm. Pigs.'

'Oh, right. So you've been eating a lot of bacon. Pig-farmers? That's, um, interesting.'

'No, it isn't,' said Marty.

We had progressed back to my sitting room and he sat by the gas fire, munching his sandwich. The awful thing was, now that I knew his people kept pigs, I couldn't help but see Marty himself, with his round pink face, as a large porker in a sweater.

'Cheer up,' I said, quelling a giggle. 'Is it the play you're depressed about? Is that why you went off to Wiltshire? Most of the audience was delighted.'

'Philistines,' said Marty indistinctly through a mouthful of bread and bacon.

'Look, what kind of audience did you expect at The Rose? It went really well until Digger got in on the act. Freddy paid up.' (The circumstances in which I'd collected the money were none of Marty's business.) 'I've got your envelope here. Hang on, I'll get it. Yours is the only one I haven't delivered.'

I got to my feet, intending to fetch the envelope.

Marty looked up and behind his spectacles his eyes sparkled with unexpected anger.

'That bloody Trevor,' he said. 'He let that dog in on purpose, I'll swear he did!'

'Let in Digger?' I was taken aback. 'I shouldn't think so. He works for Freddy and the play was Freddy's idea. Trevor wouldn't deliberately mess things up.'

'You don't understand.' Marty was despondent again. 'Trevor did it on purpose because of me.'

I sat down again, trying to work that one out. I'd not been aware that Trevor and Marty had been acquainted –

other than Trevor pulling the odd pint for Marty to drink. I said as much.

He had finished his coffee and sandwich. He took off his spectacles and began polishing the lenses with the sleeve of his sweater.

'Fran, I've got things to tell you. Things I should have told you before.'

He broke off and I urged him to go on. Whatever it was, his mind clearly wouldn't be at rest until he'd told someone. If it had to do with Trevor and The Rose, I wanted him to tell me. Perhaps, after all, he was more involved than I'd realised.

'You'll understand, won't you?' he pleaded.

'I'll do my best. But I don't yet know what it is,' I pointed out.

'That play meant so much to me.' His little blue eyes blinked pathetically.

I joined him on the sofa, put an arm round his woolly shoulders and attempted comfort along the lines I'd already put forward. The play hadn't been a failure. The audience had been happy. Freddy was happy, etc. We'd been paid.

'Yes, yes!' he interrupted. My words, far from consoling him, seemed to have irritated him. But I lack the womanly gifts, the gentle touch, the hand on the brow, that sort of thing. It isn't my style.

I took my arm away. 'Go on, then. Tell me about it. Get on with it, Marty.'

'That's it!' he shouted. 'I wanted to get on and stage the play. It mattered more than anything else to me. I thought, if we did well and word got round, I'd be asked to do some more work in some other venue. Not a flippin' pub! Freddy's got influence. He'd spread the word. I was absolutely determined that nothing, nothing at all, would interfere with the play, do you see?'

'Yes, I do see,' I assured him, although I was beginning to feel that I didn't.

'And now,' he said, 'I feel as though I got it wrong. I was so set on the play and its importance to me that I refused to see anything else might be as important.'

'You're not the only one who's been getting things wrong lately, Marty,' I told him.

He turned his head to look full at me. I was reminded of those 'happy' or 'sad' faces people draw, just a circle with two dots for eyes and a curve upwards for a smiling mouth or downwards for a sad one. Marty's face with its drooping mouth and screwed-up little eyes could have made a Greek mask of tragedy.

'You remember that evening I met you by the Round-house?' he asked unexpectedly.

'I remember.' How could I forget? It was the night Ion died.

'You were looking for someone. I walked with you down the High Street to the Tube station. Then you saw the person you were looking for and took off.'

'That's right.' I was beginning to get a crawling feeling in my stomach.

'I followed you into the Tube because I decided I might as well go home. You didn't have a ticket. I had my Travelcard with me, so when you went to buy a ticket I went on. There was a man in front of me, a big bloke—'

'With a hooded top?' I broke in.

He nodded. 'That's right. I followed him all the way down to the platform. It was pretty crowded there. He was pushing his way through, so I tacked on behind him, taking advantage of the space he opened up. Perhaps he sensed someone was following him, because he glanced back at me – and I saw his face. It was Trevor, the barman at The Rose.'

Trevor, who else? I should have known. Trevor, with his clothes smelling of the pub. Trevor, Freddy's loyal employee. Trevor, surely the man who'd passed me in the entry to Susie's block of flats.

'I didn't see you,' I said dully. But I had been intent on searching only for Ion. As a result, I'd missed seeing other things I should have noticed.

'The thing is,' Marty was saying, 'he saw me and obviously recognised me. He gave me a dirty look. I was a bit taken aback. I mean, I didn't expect him to act delighted to see me. But he knew I was in the play at the pub and I'd have thought he'd at least say hi! But what he did say was, "You want something?" He said it very nastily, too, I can tell you. I didn't want trouble. I never do. Trevor's built like a brick barn and there's something about him always did remind me of Digger, that dog of Freddy's. A mean look, you know what I'm describing?'

I nodded. Too well.

'So I dropped back,' Marty went on. 'But I kept an eye open for him because I didn't want to go bumping into him again. I watched him make his way down the platform. He's tall, taller than most of the people down there. He was looking around him. I thought at first it might be me he was after, and it worried me. But then I decided he was looking for someone else. I got curious and I sneaked a bit further down, towards him.'

Marty pushed his spectacles back on to his snub nose. 'Then I saw this young kid.'

I couldn't speak. Marty had paused as if he expected me to say something but all I could do was nod again.

Perhaps Marty thought I hadn't got the message because he began to describe the youngster he'd seen. 'Dark hair, very thin, small build. His clothes looked too big for him. Then he, the kid, saw Trevor. I've never seen anyone look so scared. The kid would have run if he'd been able to, but with so many people on the platform he couldn't. Trevor had spotted him. He went after him. The train was coming in. Everyone was moving forward. No one was looking at Trevor or the kid except me.'

Marty stopped.

I whispered, 'Go on.'

'The kid was trying to wriggle his way through the crowd and looking back over his shoulder to see Trevor closing in on him. He reached the end of the platform and couldn't go any further. He turned to face Trevor. He was saying something, or, at least, his mouth was moving. Trevor reached out and put a hand on his shoulder, like you do if you're trying to reassure someone. Then – the crowd shifted. The train came. The kid fell.' Marty made a snuffling noise. 'I can't swear that Trevor pushed him. Maybe he was just trying to get out from Trevor's grip on his shoulder and he stumbled.'

I said slowly, 'Whether Trevor pushed him or not, Trevor is responsible. Ion fell because he was trying to get away from Trevor.'

Marty swallowed, his Adam's apple bobbing in his throat. 'What did Trevor want with him, Fran?'

'It's a long story,' I said.

Marty licked his lips. 'Well, I didn't then know the kid was a friend of yours. All I knew was, I didn't want any trouble with the pub because of the play. So I didn't tell anyone what I'd seen. Then, coming to rehearsal one night, I was handed a leaflet at the Tube exit. The police were looking for witnesses. That's the leaflet which fell out of my pocket and you picked up. You said you'd known the kid. I felt dreadful.'

Marty hiccuped. I realised he was very near tears. 'I should have told you what I saw. I should have told the police. But I didn't, because of the play. The play just seemed to matter more than anything.' He looked at me sorrowfully. 'But it wasn't more important, was it?'

'You need to tell the cops, Marty,' I said. 'The person to speak to is Inspector Janice Morgan. But things are a bit tricky down at the station just now. If I fix up a meeting with Morgan here, you'll come along and tell her about it?'

He hesitated. 'All right. If I can meet her here. I don't fancy going to the police station. Someone might see me going in and, you know, want to know why.' He leaned forward. 'That business with Digger. I'm sure it was Trevor sending me a message. He knows I saw him on that platform. He may suspect I saw him with the kid. He was letting me know. Don't mess with him.'

'Marty,' I said. 'This is something much bigger than you know.'

I told him all of it. Ion's search for his brother, the people-smuggling organisation the police were after,

Susie's flat being firebombed, everything. I didn't tell him about the pizzeria and the dodgy wine racket, because frankly I was embarrassed by the way I'd misread the signs on that. Anyway, in the end, it hadn't had to do with the people-trafficking. Ion had got it wrong and so had I.

Marty didn't say a word as I spoke. His face got whiter and more frightened but when I'd finished he croaked, 'I understand.'

'They're bad people, Marty,' I said. 'If you and I keep quiet and do nothing there will be more Ion Popescus falling under Tube trains or off bridges, whatever suits the bad guys best.' He didn't look entirely convinced, so I went on, 'You remember talking to me about my role of Miss Stapleton in the play? Our conversation wasn't really about her, was it? It was about this. About keeping quiet when you see evil at work. The cops are investigating Ion's death and they're investigating the smuggling racket so, in a sense, if we go to them with this, we're not telling them something they're not already on the track of. You can't swear to seeing Trevor push Ion, but what you saw matters all the same. It's a little piece of the jigsaw and without it the picture can't be completed. Do you see?'

He nodded. 'I see.'

At the end of our lunch in Regent's Park, Morgan had given me a contact number, should I need her. I rang it and she came over to the flat straight away, where Marty told his story.

She said, 'Thanks very much. We'll be in touch.'

The police are always annoyingly casual about any help

they get. Still, Marty said he felt better after she left. It wasn't on his mind any more. He knew he'd done the right thing.

'But I think I'll pop back to Wiltshire,' he added. 'My mother said she wished I'd stayed longer. It might be a good time.' His round face turned pinker. 'I'm not running away. I'll be back for the inquest if I'm needed.'

'Strategic withdrawal,' I said.

'Yes, that's it. How about you, Fran?'

'Nowhere to go,' I said.

He shuffled his feet. 'I just don't want to get a threatening phone call in the middle of the night, you know.'

'Marty, just go to Wiltshire and chill out,' I begged him. 'Stop agonising over it. Don't forget to tell Morgan where you are.'

That night I couldn't sleep. I couldn't put it all out of my mind. I was glad Marty was going back to Wiltshire for a while. It was the safest thing for him to do and his absence had probably kept him safe until now. The police have a witness protection programme but, even if they'd applied it to Marty, with a leak somewhere in the system it might not be enough.

Around two in the morning I heard the front door close and then a door inside the house. Bonnie sat up and whined. I told her to be quiet, it was only Erwin coming home from a gig. But Bonnie wouldn't settle again. She jumped off the bed and ran to the door, still whining, and, when I didn't get out of bed, she began to scratch at it. To save my paintwork I had to crawl out from my snug nest beneath the duvet.

'Honestly, Bonnie,' I said as I picked her up. 'It's too cold for fooling around.'

But she wriggled in my arms and, when I put her down again, back she went to the door where this time she gave a little bark.

I sighed. She didn't normally need to go out during the night but now it seemed that she did. I looked out into the street. The rain had stopped and the cloud cover blown away. It left a fine if breezy moonlit night. Everything was bathed in silver and I could see almost as clearly as by daylight out there. I pulled on my jeans and a sweater.

I intended to let her into the garden but as soon as I opened my door she ran to the front door and gave another sharp little bark.

I shushed her. 'You'll wake everyone up. Just round the block once, right?' I couldn't let her out into the garden if she was going to bark and if she chose to disappear into the jungle darkness out there I might have a job getting her back. I fetched my jacket and we set off.

In fact, being out of doors in the cold night air wasn't unpleasant. The quiet of the surrounding streets was soothing. I felt the stress seep from my tense muscles and battered brain as I drew in deep lungfuls of oxygen.

Bonnie hurried along in an agitated way. She kept stopping and listening. I felt more relaxed but she was uneasy although I couldn't see why.

We had nearly completed our tour of the block, and had just turned the corner back into my road, when I saw him.

In the clear moonlight he was unmistakable. He stood on the pavement before the house where I lived, wearing his jogging outfit with the hood pulled up over his head as he'd worn it in the park, and when I'd seen him at Susie's, and before that at Camden Tube station. The moonlight threw his inky-black shadow across the forecourt in a second grotesque figure. It was as if the Grim Reaper accompanied him, as in fact it so often had. I grabbed Bonnie and stepped back, with her in my arms, into the alley where I'd found the glue-sniffer the night Ion died.

With my hand clamped over Bonnie's muzzle to stop her barking, I peered out of the alley. Trevor was contemplating the house front. He moved to stand directly before the window of my flat. The hair prickled on my head and Bonnie wriggled in my arms like a creature possessed.

Trevor was holding something in one hand. I couldn't see what it was but then, with his other hand, he pulled what must have been a cigarette lighter from his pocket. There was a tiny flicker of flame which suddenly grew bigger as he held it to the object. The black shadow mimicked every movement and now raised its arm, which became elongated and splashed across my window, reaching out to claim a new victim. With horror, I realised what Trevor was about to do.

I leapt from my hiding place and yelled, 'Trevor, don't! I'm not there! I'm not in the house!'

Startled, he whipped round towards me and, fatally for him, he hesitated. Bonnie hurled herself from my arms and raced down the street towards him, barking her head off. She seized his pants leg in her strong little teeth. He kicked out, sending her flying. The bottle which I could now see he was holding slipped from his grasp. There was a crash of breaking glass, a whoosh, and an explosion. The flame escaped its prison and grew in an instant to a dancing monster. A high-pitched scream issued from Trevor as it reached him and turned him in a split second into a pillar of fire. He came stumbling towards me, still screaming, and holding out his burning arms in useless supplication.

Chapter Eighteen

'Molotov cocktail,' said Parry. 'He was going to chuck it through your window, burn your place out like he burned out Susie Duke's. Nasty type, our Trevor.'

He sat on my sofa. Bonnie crouched nearby, keeping an eye on him. Bonnie can tell a police officer at once, even in plain clothes. She'd met Parry before and she knew he was allowed to be there, on the sofa, but she also knew the permission was a temporary one. He still wasn't a friend.

'How is he?' I asked dully.

Parry hissed. 'Not so good. Touch and go. They got him in a specialist burns unit. You should see him. He ain't half a mess.'

'I don't want to see him again,' I said. 'I saw him then.'

'Right, you've seen enough nasty sights to be going on with,' Parry agreed.

'I tried to help him,' I said.

My actions had been panicky, probably muddled, and, as I recalled them now, seemed to be part of a nightmarish whirl of events spinning increasingly out of my control. I'd run indoors and dragged the duvet from my bed. On my way out again, passing Erwin's door, I'd hammered on it and yelled for him to come and help. I knew he hadn't long arrived home and there was a good chance he was still awake. He came charging out and together we smothered the flames with the duvet as Trevor squirmed and squealed like a tormented animal. Then Erwin called an ambulance on his mobile.

I shivered as I relived the scene in my mind. Everyone had come running into the street, out of our house, out of the neighbours' houses, all in their nightwear. They stood round asking what was happening, staring down at the scorched form of Trevor like he was a freak show. His clothes had burned away and his skin had split and peeled, but he wasn't unconscious. He kept moaning, moving his blistered lips, and closing and unclosing his fingers which looked like so many grilled sausages.

I told the police, when they came, that he'd been about to torch the house and everyone in it. That's why I had yelled out to him. It was me he was after, not anyone else. I couldn't stand there and let him throw the bottle into the building.

Now Parry said in a thoughtful voice, 'I particularly don't like fire-raisers. An ordinary common-or-garden murderer, he goes after one victim. An arsonist doesn't care how many he kills. You've got guts, Fran. He might just have chucked his home-made incendiary straight at you, you know. It wouldn't have been him went up in flames, it'd have been you.'

'Yes, I realise that now,' I said testily. 'I didn't have time to think about it then.'

'We won't be able to question him,' said Parry. 'Not for a long time.'

As it turned out they didn't question him, ever. That

night Trevor died from his burns. I supposed that, for him, it was the best thing. I didn't like to think what he might have looked like had he survived.

Doing the right thing isn't easy and it isn't always simple. People don't divide up into the sheep and the goats. There's always someone on the fringes who gets hurt more than seems justified. That's life, I guess.

The person in this case was Denise. I always liked her. I don't know how much she knew about Freddy's illegal activities. She must have had some idea something was going on. She was the one who kept the business accounts, after all. But other than keeping the books, I don't think she knew about the dirtier side of it.

The police raided the pub and arrested Freddy in connection with the smuggling racket. They objected to bail because of the possibility that witnesses might be intimidated, even though Freddy had lost his hitman in Trevor. Funny thing, Freddy's influential friends who'd been happy to be pictured with him in the local press, accepting cheques for charity, suddenly couldn't remember who he was. Denise ran the pub on her own for a while and then the brewery put in temporary managers. Denise left the district. I never saw her again.

They held the inquest on Ion, and I went along but I wasn't asked to give any evidence. I hadn't seen Trevor, not to recognise him, on the platform. Marty came back from the country and gave his evidence, but it was weak, what one man thought he'd seen and no one to back it up.

It was obvious the coroner had his doubts. But in the end he said there wasn't enough evidence to return a verdict of unlawful killing, especially as it was not now possible to question the person whose actions at the time had been suspicious, meaning Trevor. Ion's death was put down as an accident.

As I walked away from the inquest I heard a voice call, 'Hang on, Fran!' and Wayne Parry caught up with me. He fell into step beside me.

'I know how you felt about that kid, Fran. But accidental death was all we could hope for. Your mate didn't see Popescu pushed. He only saw him appear to be frightened of Trevor and Trevor take his shoulder. He couldn't swear to the cause of the fear being Trevor. Some people get panicky in crowds and some people don't like being underground. Popescu's scared appearance could have been due to any number of things.'

'I know what he was scared of,' I muttered.

'Well,' said Parry, 'Trevor paid a high price, whether he did it or not.'

'I know,' I said. 'It wasn't a nice thing to happen, even to a lowlife like Trevor.'

I stopped and turned towards Parry so that he had to stop, too, and face me.

'What's up?' he asked.

'Ion's brother,' I said. 'What are you doing about him?'

'Fran,' he said gently in a remonstrating tone. 'What do you want us to do?'

'Look for him! The Romanian police can ask Ion's family for details,' I shouted. 'They'll back Ion's story!'

'That's been tried. At first the family didn't want to admit either of the sons had left the country. They insisted they'd gone to Bucharest to look for work. The family lives out in the sticks somewhere in a tiny village. Informed of Ion's death, they were frightened enough to come clean and admit both boys had set out for England. The elder, Alexander, left home first over a year ago. The younger, Ion, six months later. But there's no record of their journey. A year is a long time if you're trying to find someone who went out of his way to leave no trace of himself. It's over six months since the family had word from him, a single printed or type-written letter, the only one they ever got, and it gave precious few details, just that he was here and to send the other boy, he'd meet him. There was no return address. We don't know where he lived or where he worked. We don't know the names of any associates or what plans he might have had. There's no record of his entering the country, just as there's no record of Ion coming here. From the point of view of the authorities it's as if both boys didn't exist and that's just the way they wanted it. We only know Ion was here because he fell in front of that Tube train. It's chasing shadows, Fran. For all we know, Alexander might have left the country again, moved on to pastures new. There again, he might never have got here. The family burned the letter they had from him, afraid it might fall into official hands and lead to his being traced. So we can't even check it was genuine. Perhaps Alexander never reached England. Perhaps he came to grief en route and the traffickers sent the letter, making it look as if he'd got here. After all, they didn't want news like that getting back home. It would be bad for future business. If you want to know what I think, I think Alexander Popescu was never here. That's what the traffickers didn't want young Ion to find out. When he wouldn't give up the hunt, he had to be taken out.'

'So,' I snapped. 'You're going to do nothing at all.'

'Oh, we've opened a file on him and a pretty slim one it is. Now the trafficking organisation, we'll get that. Police forces across Europe are on to it.'

'But you're not taking any more action to look for Alexander? That's as good as doing nothing at all, as far as I'm concerned.'

I stomped off. Parry followed me.

'You know what, Fran?' he said after a few minutes, when he reckoned I'd calmed down enough to listen to him. 'You want to get over this habit you've got of playing Good Samaritan. Leave things to the police, eh?'

'You don't get the results I want!' I snapped.

'We don't always get the results we want. To be honest, we rarely do. Still, we do our best.' He waited for me to say something, but there was nothing I wanted to add. He went on, 'You remember a sergeant called Cole?'

I looked up in surprise. 'Yes, I remember him.'

'He got chucked out of CID, sent back to uniform, traffic division. He got busted back down to constable, too.'

Parry didn't explain why, but I could guess.

'Why didn't he get chucked out of the force altogether? Blabbing information around,' I asked.

'Investigation still in progress. I didn't tell you that,' said Parry craftily. 'You deduced it.'

'Yeah, well, I like to play detective, don't I?' I returned sourly.

Parry hesitated. 'You keep stum about that, right, Fran? Or they'll have me for passing on inside information to you.'

'Sure. So long as Cole isn't still chatting to the wrong people. I don't want a visit from a couple of guys wearing ski-masks and carrying baseball bats. I've had enough trouble.'

'It won't happen. Too risky for anyone to try it with all the arrests we've made recently. You've got a sort of protection, Fran.'

'Great.'

He smiled. 'For the time being, anyway. Just don't get into any more scrapes. See you around.'

He strode off down the street, his hands in the pockets of his old waxed jacket.

I do think of Ion quite often. People will continue to traffic in human misery, offering hope where there is little to be had, a better future where only exploitation lies. Sometimes I think of Ion's family, back home, wondering what really happened to both their sons, and destined never to know.

There was an inquest on Trevor. I went along and this time was the main witness. That returned a verdict of accidental death too. As far as the law is concerned, it seems to me that 'accident' covers a lot of things.

As regards the other business, at the pizzeria, Silvio and Luigi were charged in connection with the dodgy wine scam and sent down. Neither had previous form, so they got negligible stretches. The police found lots of helpful information on the computer which had sat in the corner of Jimmie's office. I can see now why Silvio wanted some techno-ignoramus like Jimmie as manager. Anyone else would've played around on the computer and found some very interesting stuff about Silvio's business deals. But they'd known Jimmie wouldn't touch it.

Mario wasn't charged, and went off to be a cook somewhere else. Ganesh sticks to his opinion that Mario did no more than tip off Freddy that Ion had been asking for 'Max'. Ganesh says, as Mario wasn't even charged over the wine scam which *was* being run from the pizzeria, it's unfair to accuse him of being involved in Freddy's trafficking business, which wasn't. Look, says Ganesh, when the police finally busted the trafficking ring, they'd have found Mario, if he were part of it. Me, I'm not so sure. I tell myself, better the police catch the big fish, even if they have to let the smaller ones slip the net. There are always unanswered questions in anything to do with people and their motives.

Jimmie was eventually released without charge for lack of evidence, but with a warning. Theoretically he still owns half the pizzeria. The last time I saw him, he was talking of turning it back into a baked spud café – if Silvio will agree from his gaol cell. I told him I still thought he should get Silvio to buy him out. Silvio was the sort of entrepreneur who, released from prison, would soon be on the up again. He wasn't short of cash, that was for sure. He'd have some other fantastic business project up his sleeve and, very likely, some other scam. The biggest danger to him comes from the taxmen. I heard they were taking the accounts of that tile import company apart. I doubt they'll find anything. There are company books – and there are company books. I don't know how many sets Silvio kept.

'You don't need him as a partner, Jimmie,' I urged. 'If

you ask him to dissolve the partnership now, he can hardly refuse. Don't let the opportunity slip.'

Jimmie said he'd think about it.

I'm sorry Freddy won't be putting on any more shows at The Rose. Resting actors like me need every chance they can get. So do musicians, and Erwin also lost a possible gig. But his band has been signed up for others, so he isn't worried. Carmel landed on her feet too. She went along to another audition and got a tiny part in a TV soap opera. Now, that does hurt.

Susie came back. The council declared itself unable to rehouse her for the time being. She was a single woman without children and had low priority. I could have told her that. They offered her a room in a bed-and-breakfast place. She took one look at it and turned it down. I couldn't blame her. She was renting privately, living in a bedsit in a shared house. The insurance company, though surly, paid up for the lost flat contents.

'My Rennie always believed in insurance,' she said.

It struck me that the late Rennie Duke had been a walking example that insurance is good for you. I don't have any myself, mind you, but who'd insure me?

She came to my flat and perched on my sofa, looking quite happy and confident. She'd changed her hairstyle again and this time gone for a smooth bob, aiming for the professional look. I thought I'd liked her better with the curls but I admired the bob politely.

'You're looking good,' I said truthfully. She'd also acquired a black business suit and a red shirt, black tights and high heels. She was one of those people to whom life isn't always kind but who, no matter the circumstances, pops up again undaunted. I had to admire her.

'Yeah, well,' she said, smoothing her short black skirt over her knees, 'I reckon if the bad guys were going to do anything more to me, they'd have done it by now. Inspector Morgan says I won't have to testify in court about what we saw. You know, the people getting out of that lorry, because we couldn't identify either the driver or the other man for certain and we didn't get the licence plate.' She frowned. 'We should've got the licence plate. That's basic detective practice, that is.'

'The light was too poor, Susie. Besides, how could we have read the licence plate of the lorry from forty feet up in the air, on top of a roof?' I added that Morgan had told me the same thing, I wouldn't have to testify. 'She did say we were right to report it, though. It all added to the knowledge they already had about the way the racket worked.'

Susie was looking thoughtful. 'You know, if it was that Trevor who firebombed my flat, he did it because he was a mean bastard and not just because he thought I might have been able to stand up in court and tell everyone about the lorry.'

'Marty thinks Trevor let the dog loose.' I had told Susie about the play and the interruption of the dogfight. 'Just as a warning.'

'He might have done,' she agreed. 'It's the sort of thing Trevor would do. When I think how he used to pester me to go out with him, but I never would.'

This was news. I wondered if, despite his attempt to torch my place, there hadn't been a personal reason why

Trevor had fired Susie's flat. He was the sort of macho type who wouldn't take kindly to a woman turning down his advances, especially if he'd heard that she'd started dating Luigi. I remembered how Morgan had pointed out to me that private detectives made enemies. Pretty women did too. Perhaps Susie had just made an enemy of Trevor. In that case, she was lucky only the flat had suffered damage.

'Listen, Fran,' she said to me now. 'Have you thought any more about coming into partnership with me in the agency? I'm still running it from my new address. I've had some new cards printed. Here . . .' She delved in her bag and handed me a small white rectangle.

I drew a deep breath. 'Yes, I have, and Susie, I can't do it.'

Her face fell. 'Why not? We can work together.'

'Yes, but . . .' It was hard to explain. Partly, Jimmie's experience with Silvio had warned me that having business partners can turn tricky. Partly it was because I'd realised that I worked best on my own with Ganesh to back me up if necessary.

'I need my independence, Susie,' I told her.

'And I need you to work with me,' she said sadly.

I noticed for the first time how small she was. I'm short but stocky. Sitting on my sofa with her black-stockinged legs dangling, Susie Duke looked like a child. I also noticed how, beneath the make-up, her fine skin was crumpling like tissue paper, crow's-feet about the eyes and lines engraved either side of her mouth. She was right about time not being on her side.

I felt rotten but there was nothing I could do about it. It

had struck me that Susie's life tended to run to complications and so did mine. Put us together and the complications would be likely to get completely out of hand.

'I've been on my own since I was sixteen,' I said, twisting her card in my hands. 'I've got used to it. I like waking up in the morning and knowing that whatever I do, it will be something I've decided on and not anyone else. I appreciate the offer, I really do. It means you've got confidence in me and that's very nice to know. But I just can't join you.'

Perhaps unwisely, because she looked so despondent, I added, 'If you find yourself really short-handed in a case and need someone, I might help out, just as a one-off thing, you know. Depending on what sort of case it is,' I added hastily.

She brightened. 'I'll remember that.'

I was afraid she would.

That night I went to see Ganesh. We sat on the old faded red velvet sofa in front of the TV while Hari, in the background, fretted over the paperwork as usual.

'By the way, Gan,' I said casually. 'I'm not going to join Susie in the detective business. I've told her.'

He turned his head and I saw the relief on his face. He'd been seriously worried I'd do it. 'Good,' he said simply.

'I'm not giving up on being a detective. I mean, a freelance, non-professional one. I might still look into things for people, if they ask me.'

He groaned. 'I suppose you will and I can't stop you.'

'The thing is,' I went on, 'I prefer to act independently and have you to back me, if you can or want to. I know you don't approve of my investigating things. But you've helped me before, haven't you? So really, I couldn't go into partnership with Susie. I sort of like working with you.'

'Just don't call on me too often!' said Ganesh firmly.

And then he did something he'd never done before. He reached out and patted my hand.

We sat in silence for a while, watching the screen. It was one of those programmes where experts move into some poor soul's house and transform it into something you wouldn't want to live in if you valued your sanity.

'You're not going to ask me to be in another play, though, are you?' Ganesh said suddenly. 'Because I'm not interested. I'm never setting foot on stage again.'

So now I'm back at square one, having to think up a way to make some money. Silvio was an organised man and a fair one. The accountancy system still functioned, even though the Pizzeria San Gennaro remained closed. Po-Ching and I, and Pietro the accordionist, each received a week's wages in the post, together with our P45 forms. The squat accountant sent them. We were officially on the labour market again, only as far as I'm concerned the labour market doesn't seem very interested.

But seeing the dog-walkers in the park has planted an idea in my mind. I have to walk Bonnie anyway. I could walk other people's dogs. I'll ask Hari if I can put up a small ad in the shop. But I'll have to choose my moment carefully, because I don't know how Ganesh will take it. Well, I do know. That's the trouble.

With the inquest on Ion over, Marty was another one who now returned to the area. I bumped into him in the street. This time he looked his old self with his smiling round face.

'I'm glad I've seen you, Fran,' he said. 'I know things got a bit out of hand when we did the last play. But you were good. If I get the chance to direct another play, would you consider being in it?'

I thought of the quarrels at rehearsals. I thought of how cold it had been in the functions room and how grubby the costumes had looked as they came out of the wicker basket. I remembered the cramped dressing room and the smell in there. I pictured the disaster of the dogfight and reflected on the uncertainty as to whether we'd be paid. I thought of Ganesh's horror at the idea of being on stage again and I knew that this was one thing Ganesh would never understand about me.

'Of course I would!' I said to Marty. 'As soon as you've got a role for me, get in touch.'

Risking it All

Ann Granger

When Fran Varady, aspiring actress and part-time sleuth, is approached by Private Investigator Clarence Duke, she mistrusts him on instinct. But she can't ignore what he has to tell her. Her mother, Eva, who walked out on Fran when she was only seven years old, has hired Clarence to find her daughter. And for good reason. Eva is dying.

Within days, Fran is reunited with the mother she hasn't seen for fifteen years, and is soon to lose again. But the biggest bombshell of all is still to come. Eva has another child – a daughter she gave up soon after her birth – and she wants Fran to find her.

Matters aren't helped by the fact that slippery Clarence Duke seems intent on discovering what she's up to. But it's when he's found dead in his car outside Fran's home that the trouble really begins . . .

Praise for Ann Granger:

'Ann Granger's skill with character together with her sprightly writing make the most of the story . . . she is on to another winner' *Birmingham Post*

'A good feel for understated humour, a nice ear for dialogue' *The Times*

'A delight. Darkly humorous but humane . . . fluent, supple and a pleasure to read' *Ham and High*

0 7472 6801 0

headline

Now you can buy any of these other bestselling books by **Ann Granger** from your bookshop or *direct from her publisher*.

FREE P&P AND UK DELIVERY
(Overseas and Ireland £3.50 per book)

Mitchell and Markby crime novels

A Restless Evil	£6.99
Shades of Murder	£6.99
Beneath these Stones	£6.99
Call the Dead Again	£6.99
A Word After Dying	£6.99
A Touch of Mortality	£6.99
Candle for a Corpse	£6.99
Flowers for his Funeral	£6.99

Fran Varady crime novels

Risking it All	£5.99
Running Scared	£6.99
Keeping Bad Company	£6.99
Asking for Trouble	£6.99

TO ORDER SIMPLY CALL THIS NUMBER

01235 400 414

or visit our website: www.madaboutbooks.com

Prices and availability subject to change without notice.